THE
AWAKENING

LAURIE HARRISON

ISBN-13: 978-1-7332859-5-7

Library of Congress Control Number: 2021925748

Emerald Rain Publishing LLC
7643 Gate Parkway, Ste. 104-156
Jacksonville, FL 32256

For Brian and Pam

ONE

NATALIE

I twisted my body to the right, and his fist whipped past my ear. As I spun around to face him, I prepared to strike.

He narrowed his eyes on me, anticipating my reprisal. And all I could think about was Chad Henley. My body tensed, yearning to make contact.

I pivoted on the ball of my left foot, and in one fluid motion, I rotated my hips as I brought my fist forward, making contact with his jawline. I didn't use all my strength though. My opponent wasn't Henley, and I didn't want to hurt him.

He smiled in response, surprised that I'd gotten him. I expected him to retaliate despite being proud of me. He wouldn't want me to get too confident.

My instructor, Steven, wasn't aware of my special talents. Although hired by Alexander, he wasn't privy to the fact that I could predict his next move by allowing my intuition to guide me through the fight. He had no clue that I could read his mind or throw him across the room by simply thinking about it, if I wanted to.

He didn't need to worry about me using my powers on him though. Allowing myself the unfair advantage would defeat the entire purpose of our training. The point was for me to learn how to fight in case I lost my powers again. Michael and Raina could protect themselves regardless, but I'd never learned hand-to-hand combat.

Steven slid his foot out, sweeping my leg from under me. My back hit the mat as he approached, gaining top position. I kicked my leg up, hitting him in the stomach and dropping him to his knees.

I scooted backward to get away, but he was quick and already crawling for me again.

"What do you do?" He was testing me.

We'd been over this scenario several times. The key was for me to think and not freeze. Mind over instinct.

I grabbed his wrists, holding them downward as I brought my foot up to kick him in the face. I stopped when the sole of my sneaker tapped his cheek.

He nodded, and I released his wrists. We stood up, both working to catch our breath.

"You did well today." He walked across the garage that we'd converted into a home gym, picked up his towel, and wiped the sweat from his face.

I grabbed my water bottle off the weight bench and took a swig. "I still have a long way to go."

"You'll get there. It just takes time and practice."

I set my water bottle back down. "Speaking of practice, remember I won't see you again until next week."

We normally met at least three times a week, but tomorrow, I'd be leaving for St. Augustine, Florida, where my best friends, Seth and Jen, were getting married.

He put on his jacket and pulled his keys out of the pocket. "That's right. I'll see you when you get back."

I hit the button to open the garage door and waited until he was in his car before closing it again.

With my hands still wrapped, I walked over to the seventy-pound bag hanging from the ceiling and jabbed it. With each strike, I imagined the bag was Henley.

A jab for hunting Michael and Raina their entire lives.

A cross jab for all the torture he'd inflicted on them and me.

Another jab for killing Lorena.

And finally, a hook for using Becca to do it.

I stopped. The air drained from my lungs, as it always did when I thought about Becca killing Lorena eight months ago. She'd almost killed Jen as well.

"Keep your hands up," Michael said from behind me.

I hadn't heard him enter the garage.

I didn't turn around as I brought my gloves up higher, protecting my face. Once I regained my composure, I repeated the combination again.

"Good." He walked over and stood beside me. "You're getting stronger."

"I still can't tap into my adrenaline."

It was frustrating because Michael and Raina could, and I'd inherited all their other abilities. Alexander believed I had the ability, but I just hadn't found the right trigger to release it yet.

"We need to get going soon," he said, changing the subject. "You don't want to be late. Jen's stressed out enough as it is."

He walked around, standing between me and the bag. Then, he took my left hand and started unwrapping it.

"She's scared that Henley or Becca will show up at the wedding," I said. "I wish I could reassure her, but I'm not convinced they won't try something."

He pinched his eyebrows together as he switched out my hands to unwrap the right one. He said nothing, but I sensed his concern. Becca had already tried to kill Jen once, and she'd kill all of us if given the chance.

Jen and Seth had considered eloping and having a quiet ceremony with just the two of them. But Jen had always dreamed of having a big wedding, and Seth didn't want to deny her that experience. So, they decided on St. Augustine. Michael and I had offered to bow out to minimize the chance of Henley showing up, but they wouldn't hear of it.

"There's no way I'm getting hitched without you being there," Seth had insisted. "You'd be my best man—er, woman—if Jen hadn't already claimed you as her maid of honor."

Seth had ended up asking Michael to be his best man. After everything we'd been through, they were like brothers now.

Michael finished unwrapping my hand and placed a reassuring kiss on my forehead. His stubble scratched the surface, but I was used to it. At first, I'd missed his clean-shaven face, but I'd come around to his new rugged look.

He followed me into the house and stopped at the fridge to pull out a soda.

"I'll just be a sec," I said over my shoulder as I trotted up the stairs, dodging a pair of Raina's boots on the way up.

She was incapable of picking up after herself. Ever.

Within ten minutes, I showered and redressed. Although I was positive Jen would sport a cute outfit for the occasion, she wouldn't mind if I just threw on a pair of jeans and a sweater. Not wanting to be late, I only put on mascara and lip gloss, and then I piled my long auburn hair into a messy bun on top of my head.

As I descended the stairs, I heard Michael's voice in the kitchen.

"He wants us to come in and talk, but I haven't called him back yet." He was on the phone but tensed when he heard my footsteps. "I've got to go." He hung up and turned to look at me. "Ready?"

I nodded, waiting for him to say something about his conversation but he didn't. Instead, he grabbed his keys off the counter.

I envisioned the wheels turning in his head as we walked outside.

"Were you talking about Detective Thompson?" I asked once we were in the car and halfway there.

Michael drew in a deep breath and let it out before responding. "He left me a voice mail earlier, saying he wants to meet with you and me. It's likely nothing though, just a scare tactic."

The way he tightly gripped the steering wheel told me it wasn't nothing. I could see the whites of his knuckles.

"What did Alexander say?" I already knew that was who had been on the phone.

"Not much. Just that we'll sit down and talk about it tonight."

We were in a tough predicament. Our normal response would've been to leave town a long time ago, putting as much distance between us and Henley as possible. That was our standard protocol. But now, things were more complicated.

When Michael and I'd returned home from the warehouse, we'd found both Lorena and Jen unconscious, barely clinging to life. We couldn't heal them because we didn't have our abilities. Henley's people had hit us with darts, laced with a serum that temporarily disabled our powers.

Despite our best efforts, we were on the verge of losing them both, so Michael called 911 for help—something we never did.

The paramedics couldn't save Lorena. She was already dead by the time they arrived. But Michael's split-second decision saved Jen's life. The doctors told us if help hadn't gotten there when they did, she would've died. Her internal injuries were extensive, and she needed emergency surgery. Luckily, after months of recovery, Jen's health was almost back to normal.

The aftereffects of that 911 call continued to linger because the police had become involved. The investigators deemed the situation a criminal attack and ruled Lorena's death a homicide. Although we figured out that Becca was to blame, we couldn't tell the police because Alexander suspected Henley already had some of them in his back pocket.

Instead of telling the truth, we stuck to a story of finding them like that with no clue who could've done it. With the house ransacked, we suggested it must have been a robbery gone bad.

As the investigators had collected evidence, they'd realized that two small-scale explosions had occurred within the house—one upstairs and one downstairs. The idea of it being a robbery didn't add up for Detective Ray Thompson, and he wouldn't let it go.

With an open investigation, a story full of holes, and a suspicious detective, we couldn't pick up and leave town. It would send a red flag to the detective, and we'd likely end up running from both Henley and the police.

"Did you tell Raina yet?" I asked, knowing that she got especially upset whenever Detective Thompson's name or Lorena's death came up.

He shook his head. "No. It's probably better to wait until we're all together tonight."

Raina had been pushing us to leave town for months now. In her defense, it was a miracle that Henley hadn't attempted to kill or recapture us already. Alexander believed Detective Thompson's frequent presence and persistence with the case was the only reason. If that was true, then Henley would surely make his move the moment he assumed the detective wasn't keeping tabs on us.

Michael pulled up to the bridal boutique, which was in a freestanding brick building with several other stores and restaurants nearby.

"Do you want Seth and me to stay?" he asked as I unbuckled my seat belt. "We can wait outside to make sure you and Jen are safe."

"No, we'll be okay. I'll stay on guard, and if I notice anything suspicious, I'll call you." I wanted to keep this experience as normal as possible for Jen.

He was silent for a second, and I expected him to protest. Then, his face relaxed, as if he'd talked himself out of it. "What time do you think you'll be home?"

"Jen wants to grab dinner at McCarthy's after we're done." I pointed to the pub, which was within walking distance. "We'll come home right after."

Michael looked at the restaurant, scoping it out.

I didn't have the best track record of making the right decisions when faced with danger. On multiple occasions, I'd almost gotten myself killed. My past recklessness made Michael anxious, but I was determined to earn his trust.

"Jen's craving shepherd's pie, and what the bride wants, she gets." I tried to sound lighthearted, not wanting him to worry about us.

He attempted a smile. "They won't make it the right way though."

I playfully rolled my eyes at him. "I've told you before, if you go in there and ask them to make it with sweet potatoes, they're going to think you're a psycho. Nobody eats it like that."

He laughed as Seth came out of the boutique and walked over to us.

"I'd better go," I said to Michael, giving him a quick kiss good-bye.

Seth opened my door. "You're late, nerd. Jen's already in the fitting room. Madame Adaline kicked me out, so I wouldn't see Jen's dress."

"Shoot." I jumped out of the car.

Seth slid into the passenger seat as I sprinted toward the store.

I flung the door open, and the owner, Madame Adaline, pursed her bright red lips. She peered up at me from behind gold-rimmed glasses that barely clung to her pert nose. Her chin-length silver hair was always styled to perfection, and her outfit today was all black, except for an oversize leopard-print silk scarf. The massive accessory wrapped around her neck into a long bow that swallowed the right side of her petite frame.

"Sorry." I had nothing to apologize for, but I always got the impression that my presence displeased her.

The fitting room door opened, and Jen emerged, wearing her wedding dress, which suited her perfectly. It was a simple fitted gown with a modest train. Thank goodness because I wouldn't be able to help her bustle a long one. The fabric draped slightly in the front into a soft V-neck.

She smiled with excitement as she turned to face the full-length trifold mirror. Her dress was completely backless from the waist up, except for the straps holding it in place. Seth's eyes were going to pop out of his head when he saw her.

Jen gathered her shoulder-length blonde hair into a low bun, and Madame Adaline handed her a hair tie to secure it in place. She'd be wearing it up for the wedding.

Madame Adaline gasped. "You look like a princess."

I had to agree.

Jen looked at me for my approval.

"Stunning."

She visibly relaxed. "I love it."

"Splendid." Madame Adaline turned to me and frowned. "Are you ready to try on yours?"

"Ready as ever."

Jen returned to her room to change while Madame Adaline handed me a garment bag with my dress in it.

I took it into the room next to Jen's and hung it on the hook inside. Once undressed, I pulled the full-length lavender dress out of the bag and put it on. The A-line shape worked well on my body, and I loved how light the chiffon fabric was.

"Does it fit okay?" Jen asked.

"Yes." I adjusted the spaghetti straps on my shoulders and then came out, so she could see for herself.

She clapped her hands together in excitement. "You look beautiful!"

Madame Adaline looked down at my feet, which were still in my boot socks, and scowled.

Jen smiled cheerfully. "Okay, now, go get changed back. I'm starving."

I gave her a salute and retreated to the dressing room.

A few minutes later, I checked out while Jen waited by the door.

Madame Adaline looked at me expectantly. "Three hundred seventy-four dollars."

For a dress?

My chin dropped, but I recovered before she—or Jen—noticed.

I handed her the cash. Luckily, I always carried extra in case of emergency.

With our dresses in tow, Jen and I stepped outside. She nodded toward her SUV. "I'm parked over there. Want to put our dresses in the car and then walk over to McCarthy's?"

"Sure." I didn't care what we did. I was just happy to be out of Madame Adaline's boutique of scrutiny and judgment.

Jen sighed with relief. "The wedding is finally coming together. Maybe I've been anxious over nothing."

"I think it's normal to be nervous."

I'd heard how stressed out brides were under the best of circumstances. Jen had all of that, plus the added danger of my brainwashed sister wanting to kill her.

Jen opened the back door and hung her dress up on the garment hook. I did the same on the other side.

"That'll keep them from getting wrinkled," she said. "And I've already checked with the airline. We can just carry them onto the plane instead of packing them in suitcases."

With the dresses put up, we started walking toward the pub. We hadn't made it six feet when Jen patted her coat pocket and stopped.

She reached into one pocket and then the other. "I think I left my phone in the fitting room. It must've fallen out when I changed."

We turned and walked back.

"I'll just wait for you out here," I said, wanting to avoid another encounter with Madame Adaline.

I lingered outside the front door and remembered my promise to Michael about being vigilant, so I used it as an opportunity to check our surroundings. I observed shoppers walking to and from their cars, but nothing seemed out of place or suspicious.

A couple of minutes later, Jen emerged with the phone in her hand, and we resumed our walk toward the pub. "Got it. Sorry that took longer than expected. Madame Adaline started talking my ear off about Pierre."

"Who's Pierre?" I wondered if he was her husband and envisioned her giving him that same disapproving look when he left the toilet seat up.

"Her dog. He's a papillon. She showed me a picture of him wearing a tiny beret."

"Pierre the papillon." *Poor dog.*

Jen giggled and turned her head to say something to me when a blast consumed the air around us. It knocked us off our feet, tossing us backward.

I tried to catch myself but ended up landing awkwardly on my side.

My ears rang as I raised my head to look over at Jen. She was lying on the ground next to me. It brought back the memory of finding her unconscious after Becca had attacked her.

"Jen?" I reached over and gently pressed my hand to her arm.

She rolled over with a groan.

"Are you okay?" I asked, barely able to hear myself even though I was practically shouting.

She nodded, still in shock.

I scrambled to my feet and into my fighting stance. I expected to see the woman who'd almost killed me and Michael at the warehouse, but she wasn't there.

That was when I realized the blast had come from McCarthy's, which was now up in flames. The explosion had taken out the front window and door. Smoke poured from the space where they once had been.

Jen picked herself up off the ground and stood next to me, watching it in awe.

People ran out of the pub, gagging from the smoke.

Are people still inside?

Without thinking, I stumbled forward, ready to heal the injured.

Jen reached out and grabbed me by the arm, yanking me back.

"What are you doing?" Her voice sounded muffled.

"They need my help."

"I understand you want to, but you can't." Her eyes pleaded with me.

I stood there, dumbfounded.

"Stop and think." She tightened her grip. "We need to get out of here."

I looked back at McCarthy's. *Can I just leave these people hurting and suffering?*

Jen tugged my arm. "Come on. Let the professionals take care of this."

A fire station must've been nearby because a fire truck pulled into the parking lot.

I followed Jen to her SUV. It didn't seem right, leaving without helping those people, but Jen was right. It wasn't just my life I'd put at risk if I used my abilities to save them. I'd be risking us all. Henley could track when any of us used our outward abilities, like healing or telekinesis. We didn't need another target on our backs.

Jen hopped into the driver's seat, and I was opening my door when something—or rather, someone—caught my attention. Amid the chaos of people, I noticed a slender figure wearing black pants, a hoodie, and sunglasses. Their physique was similar to Becca's.

Is it her?

She stopped walking, as if staring in my direction, but I couldn't see her face.

Does Henley allow Becca to go out on her own?

If it was her, then she was either watching us or her psychic abilities had told her we'd be here. Not that we would be hard to find. Thanks to Detective Thompson, we'd only relocated ten miles outside of McHenry, Illinois, to Crystal Lake.

"Get in." Jen begged me to listen to her.

I didn't know if Jen had noticed the mysterious woman, but I knew one thing for sure—she had seen *us*.

TWO

MICHAEL

Detective Thompson walked to the front window and pulled back the curtain to look outside.

He doesn't believe me.

"Have you heard of Tyler Twins Paper Company?" He glanced over his shoulder.

"I have."

"Did you know they had a warehouse just outside McHenry?"

I didn't like where he was going, but I kept my expression stoic. "Yes."

Stay as close to the truth as possible.

But if he asked me if I had ever visited it, I would have to lie and pray there weren't any cameras on the property.

Detective Thompson released the fabric from his thick fingers. "Looks like your ladies are home."

I'd hoped he wouldn't be here when Natalie and Jen arrived. The more people he questioned, the more likely he'd be to find discrepancies in our stories.

Detective Thompson looked expectantly at the front door, calmly crossing his arms across his broad chest.

The door opened, and Jen smiled robotically when she noticed the detective. Natalie, however, seemed completely freaked out. She was probably wondering why he'd visited instead of waiting for us to call him back.

Just stay calm.

For the first time, I wished Natalie could read my mind. I wanted to tell her not to panic. I didn't understand why he'd just shown up, but I doubted he had any actual evidence to prove that we knew more about Lorena's death than we'd said.

Although Natalie couldn't hear my thoughts, she could read Detective Thompson's. Her ability worked on everyone, except me, Raina, and our half-brother, Luke.

"What brings you by?" Jen asked the detective. "Are there developments in the case?"

"It's good to see you up and about, Miss Walsh. I'm here because there was an explosion at the old Tyler Twins Paper Company last night."

Natalie paled.

Detective Thompson narrowed his russet-brown eyes. "There've been several explosions throughout the state these past two months—mostly abandoned buildings."

Jen feigned confusion. "I'm sorry, Detective, but what does that have to do with my case?"

"Well, the explosions have similarities to the one in your previous residence. And no one can figure out the source of them."

My pulse quickened.

Is Becca behind this?

"What can we do to help?" I asked, wanting to seem cooperative and open, as if we had nothing to hide.

He ignored me and set his sights on Natalie.

"Do you have something you want to tell me?" he asked, towering over her.

"No." She swallowed and shook her head.

He stared her down, waiting for her to crack under the pressure. When she didn't, he pulled a piece of paper out of his trench coat pocket and unfolded it.

I expected him to hand her the paper, but he didn't. Instead, he stood in front of her with his back to the rest of us. She timidly looked up at him as he peered down at the paper in his hands. I wanted to intervene, but I forced my feet to stay planted where they were. If I jumped in, it would only make him more suspicious.

"The first explosion occurred at a vacant bowling alley on North Chester Street." He gave her a knowing look, as if she should already understand what he was talking about. "The second was an hour away at a car wash on Anthony Court. Do you see a pattern here?"

Natalie shook her head, clearly confused. To be honest, I didn't understand it either. Natalie had never been to any of the explosion locations other than the abandoned Tyler Twins Paper Company warehouse.

I wished she would calm down enough to read his mind and get ahead of him.

"The others were on Tyson Boulevard, Arden Way, Lenox Street, and Ingram Road." He paused with a smirk.

Jen looked at me, her expression showing she'd put the pieces together already. I gave a subtle shake of my head, telling her not to interfere. Not yet anyway.

"Okay ..." Natalie pinched her brows together, unsure of what to say to him.

"See for yourself." He offered her the paper. She hesitated before taking it.

As she looked it over, any trace of color left in her cheeks vanished. "Looks like a strange coincidence to me."

Natalie wasn't a good liar, and it was showing.

"Coincidence?" He coughed before clearing his throat. "Yes, indeed. That's an understatement."

"What is?" I asked, unable to remain silent any longer.

Natalie stepped around the detective and handed me the paper. Seth peered over my shoulder to see what it said.

It was a list of street names that Detective Thompson had jotted down, but he'd underlined the first letter of each and traced over it a few times with his pen to make sure it stood out loud and clear.

North Chester St.

Anthony Ct.

Tyson Blvd.

Arden Way

Lenox St.

Ingram Rd.

They were spelling Natalie's freaking name.

I couldn't fathom what it meant. *Is it a threat? A warning? An attempt to frame her?* My mind raced with possibilities.

Detective Thompson's phone chimed in his pocket. He pulled it out and checked the message. When he looked up, his glare hardened on Natalie again, like she was a puzzle he was trying to solve. "It seems we just got our *E*. There was an explosion at McCarthy's on East Sage Street."

Natalie straightened her back. "I just hope you find out what's causing them."

"Believe me, I will." He looked over at Jen. "Your wedding is coming up, isn't it?"

"Yes," Seth replied on her behalf. "We leave for St. Augustine tomorrow."

"Congratulations." There wasn't a trace of sincerity in Detective Thompson's response. He turned back to Natalie. "I can't stop you from leaving the state, but we'll talk again *when* you return."

Without another word, Detective Thompson walked out of the house. When his car left the driveway, Jen walked over to the couch and practically collapsed on it. Seth hurried to her side.

I turned to Natalie. "What happened?"

She shuddered. "We were on our way to McCarthy's when it exploded."

"We would've been inside if I hadn't forgotten my phone at the boutique," Jen said, burying her face in her hands.

Seth rubbed her shoulder. "You're safe now."

"Am I though?" she asked, looking up. "Are any of us?"

We weren't, and we all knew it.

Natalie looked at me. "What do we do?"

Everyone's attention shifted to me, but I didn't have a clue. Not only had Becca attempted to kill again, but our situation with Detective Thompson had gone from bad to worse as well. It was clear that Natalie was his number one suspect.

The front door opened, and I expected it to be Detective Thompson, coming back for round two. Thankfully, it was just Alexander and Raina.

Earlier in the day, Raina had convinced Alexander to go to dinner with her. Before that, he hadn't left the house in over a week. With Lorena gone, he preferred to spend most of his time alone. At first, I'd thought it was just his way of moving through the grief. But as time carried on, I worried that the change was permanent.

"What?" Raina asked, sensing the tension in the room.

"There was an explosion at McCarthy's. Natalie and Jen were on their way there when it happened," I said. "You just missed Detective

Thompson. He left this." I handed Alexander the paper with the street names listed on it.

Alexander rubbed his chin. "Becca?"

I gave him a nod of confirmation, unable to come up with another explanation. "I think so."

Raina took the paper from Alexander and read it.

When she finished, she tossed it onto the coffee table. "We have to do something. I mean, we can't just stay here, waiting for her to come blow us up next."

"Well, we're leaving town tomorrow," Alexander said.

"But then what?" Raina raised her eyebrows.

"After your honeymoon, you need to move somewhere safe," Natalie said, looking at Seth and Jen.

Seth shook his head. "No. I'm not leaving you here to deal with this without me."

Raina threw her arms in the air. "You're missing my point. We should *all* be leaving."

Alexander turned to Raina, trying to calm her down. "We have to keep a level head. We might have been able to run from Henley before, but it's a completely different story now. Even with Stan's help, I'm not confident we could evade both Henley and the police."

"We haven't committed a crime," Raina said. "They can't just arrest us for moving away."

Alexander rubbed his forehead and sat down in the armchair. It was too much for him.

I jumped in, trying to reason with my sister. "If we move, we have to change our names to throw Henley off. That means, we need to assume new identities and disappear, which will make us look guilty to Detective Thompson." I tried to keep my voice down, but I was on the verge of losing my patience. I'd already explained this to her several times before.

"Then, let's end this." Her tone was pleading. "Let's kill Henley and Becca before they come for us."

Everyone remained silent. Natalie's eyes dropped to the floor, and she looked like she was going to be sick.

"What's wrong with you?" Raina pointedly looked at each person in the room. "They deserve it!" She turned to me. "For Mom."

She was in pain. Hell, I was too. But despite everything Becca had done, I wasn't certain that I could bring myself to kill her. Regardless of how much she deserved it, she was still Natalie's sister, and Natalie loved her.

"We can't do that." I tried to say it as gently as I could. "And I'm not convinced we'd win a battle against Henley right now."

Raina's face fell, but deep down, she realized I was right. Natalie and I had barely escaped Henley's two assassins at the warehouse. Who knew how many others he had?

"We just need some more time to figure out the right solution," Alexander said.

Raina refused to back down. "So, in the meantime, we just wait for them to come for us?"

I wished I could tell her no, but I didn't see any other way. We needed to tread carefully with the police, especially now that Detective Thompson believed the street names connected Natalie to the explosions.

Alexander rubbed his forehead again, appearing defeated.

I needed to take charge. "We act normal but stay vigilant," I said. "We go to St. Augustine tomorrow, but then everyone, except Seth and Jen, will return after the wedding. It'll be too suspicious if we don't."

Raina huffed as she tossed her freshly dyed black hair over her shoulder and pivoted back to the front door.

"Where are you going?" I asked. I didn't want to fight, but it wasn't safe out there.

She shot me a spiteful look. "Don't worry. I'm not skipping town." She walked out, slamming the door behind her.

Alexander stopped me as I moved to chase after her. "Let her go. She needs to cool off."

Raina had always been temperamental, but it was ten times worse now with Lorena gone. Her mood swings were unpredictable, and I couldn't seem to get through to her like I used to.

"I saw someone leaving McCarthy's ..." Natalie said. "The figure was feminine. I couldn't see her face, but she stopped and looked at us."

Seth tensed. "Becca."

Alexander glanced at me, concerned. Neither of us had any idea how to dig ourselves out of this mess.

"Let's leave tomorrow, as planned," I said, talking it through. "And we'll take the next couple of days to figure out our game plan. Staying might not be an option, but perhaps there's something we can do to lead Detective Thompson in another direction, so he'll leave us alone."

"If it helps, I read his mind, and he's confused about the situation," Natalie said. "He thinks I'm involved with the explosions somehow, but he doesn't think I'm foolish enough to implicate myself by spelling out my name."

It wasn't much, but it was something. Could we justify leaving town to Detective Thompson if we told him we were afraid for Natalie's life? I mean, it was the truth. Perhaps then it would seem a little less strange when we disappeared. Or would it backfire and draw more attention if he thought we were the targets of the explosions?

I don't know.

Jen stood up, wringing her hands. "I'm going to finish packing and then go to bed."

Seth saw her distress and hopped up. "I'll come with you."

Jen had been through a lot in the past eight months, and Seth had really stepped up to be there for her. Between helping her recover from surgery and taking her to physical therapy, Seth had been by her side every step of the way. Without a doubt, he was a good guy.

After almost losing Jen, Seth understood why I was so overprotective of Natalie. He now fought the same battle of wanting to give Jen space to be independent while also not wanting to let her out of his sight. He expressed the struggle to me occasionally, but unfortunately, I didn't have any impressive words of advice for him. It was an internal fight I dealt with every single day. And sometimes, I lost.

"I'm going to contact Stan tomorrow and give him a heads-up about our situation," Alexander said once Jen and Seth left the room.

Stan was Alexander's best friend. They'd grown up together, and when Alexander and Lorena had rescued me and Raina from Henley, Stan had agreed to help them live a life on the run. I wasn't sure what exactly Stan did for a living, but he had access to a lot of things a normal person didn't. Alexander had mentioned that Stan owned a car dealership, but I had a feeling that was just a front for whatever his actual profession was.

On countless occasions, Stan had helped us assume new identities—names, driver's licenses, birth certificates, the whole nine yards. Stan provided us with anything we needed to restart our lives in a new place or to survive where we were. We never would've made it this far without him.

"I need to finish packing too," Alexander said. "This will be the first time I've packed a suitcase myself in over twenty years." He zoned out for a moment before standing up and wandering to his bedroom.

I sat down on the couch, and Natalie joined me. I pulled her into my arms and rested my chin on top of her head. Physically, she seemed unharmed. But now that we were alone, I wanted to see how she was dealing with the fact that her sister had tried to kill her. Again.

"Talk to me," I said.

She let out a sigh. "I'm scared."

Her words tore at my heart, and I squeezed her tighter, wishing I could make all her problems go away.

"I would do anything to protect you," I said, hoping it would comfort her. And I meant it. I'd give my life to spare hers without even thinking twice about it.

"What if Becca is coming for me?" she asked.

"Then, we'll deal with it." I pulled back slightly and kissed her temple.

She lifted her face to look up at me. "We won't have to kill her, right?" Her voice was barely above a whisper.

"I don't know ..." I brushed back a strand of hair from her face. "But not if we can help it."

Natalie hoped we could save Becca. She wanted to undo the damage Luke and Henley had done, but I didn't think Becca's condition was reversible.

Becca had outsmarted me once and murdered someone I loved. As much as I didn't want to hurt Natalie, I would kill Becca if I had to in order to stop her from doing it again.

THREE

RAINA

Sitting ducks. That was exactly what we were.

I picked up the tiny glass and took another shot of whatever awful whiskey the bartender had poured for me. It didn't taste good, but it was getting the job done.

Well, sort of.

I gagged and flinched as the burn hit my nose.

Even if drinking wasn't normally my thing, sitting here at the bar seemed more productive than hanging out at home. It was better than waiting for Henley or Becca to just stroll into the house and kill us all. At least here, I could numb the fear a little.

The bartender, a man who reminded me of a twenty-pound-heavier version of my dad, looked over at me.

I gave him a small nod, which was apparently my signal for another drink. *So cliché.*

He walked over, bottle in hand, and was just about to make the pour.

"It doesn't have to burn like that," a voice said.

I turned my chair, ready to rip into whoever had offered their unsolicited opinion but stopped the second I laid eyes on him.

I know him.

"May I?" he asked, gesturing toward the barstool next to me.

I shrugged as the bartender finished pouring my shot.

"What can I get you?" the bartender asked the guy who'd joined me.

"A glass of water." My unwelcomed companion glanced at me. "Make that two."

I stiffened my back. "A drinking expert who orders water. I'm not sure I should follow your advice."

He smiled wide, his dimples piercing the sides of his cheeks. "Trust me, I did my fair share in college."

He appeared to be around my age, so that couldn't have been long ago.

"We haven't been formally introduced. I'm J.T." He extended his hand.

I looked down at it for a second and then took it.

Great, I'm turning into a touchy-feely drinker ...

J.T.'s hand was warm but rough. His calluses pressed into my palm.

He raised his eyebrows, and I realized he was waiting for me to introduce myself. Normally, when guys asked for my name, I made up a fake one. I mean, my last name was always phony anyway, so what difference did it make?

"Raina." I withdrew my hand and then gestured to my full shot glass. "So, what exactly am I supposed to be doing here? It seems pretty self-explanatory, but apparently, I'm doing it wrong."

I flashed him a deliberate smirk.

He'll be out of here any second now.

I expected him to check his phone and pretend he had an emergency or make up an excuse about having to be somewhere else, but he didn't. Instead, he continued to smile at me, as if I amused him or something.

"What?" I asked. The way he looked at me made me suddenly self-conscious. "Don't tell me that was just a really lame pick-up line. Do you know what you're doing or not?"

He laughed. "Okay. Pick up your glass."

I complied.

"Now, what you're going to do is take in a small breath before you shoot it. Then, as soon as you swallow, exhale through your mouth. Don't breathe through your nose, or you'll get that burn."

There's no way this is going to work.

"Just try it," he said, as if he could read my mind.

I picked up the glass, drew in a breath, and then tipped the whiskey into my mouth. It went down easily, and the second I felt the warm sensation go past my throat, I blew out my breath.

20

Only minor burning. No gagging. And I could actually taste the smoothness of the whiskey itself.

"A whole new world, right?" J.T. raised his eyebrows, impressed with himself.

"Not bad."

Where do I know him from?

The bartender walked over and dropped off our waters. As tempted as I was to order another shot and try J.T.'s trick again, I opted to cool it for a bit.

I shifted my body, so I was facing J.T. Even sitting down, I could tell he was tall—at least six foot three. He wore a blue flannel button-up shirt and a pair of perfectly fitted jeans. His dark brown eyes caught mine, and I looked away.

I cleared my throat. "So, tell me, what are you doing in a bar if you aren't drinking?"

"I just got off work." He nodded to a table of six guys on the other side of the bar, reading menus. Only one guy had a beer in front of him. They were there to eat, not to get drunk, like me. "I'm working at the fire station down the street now."

"You're a firefighter?"

"A paramedic." His eyebrows pinched together.

Then, it hit me. I knew exactly who he was.

Mom was sprawled out on the floor. Lifeless. Dead.

I sat next to her with my back against what remained of the living room wall. With my knees pulled up to my chest, I wanted to bury my face in my arms, but I couldn't take my eyes off her.

We wouldn't have a funeral because it would draw too much attention. I didn't have any pictures of her either.

"Are you hurt?" someone asked, but I didn't respond. "Miss?"

A man in a uniform knelt down in front of me, blocking my view. My eyes settled on him even though they didn't want to.

I didn't know it at the time, but it was J.T.

I looked around and realized that other people had arrived as well. Another man and a woman approached Mom as two additional men hovered over Jen.

Then, I remembered Michael calling 911.

I shook my head.

"Would you mind coming with me? So I can look you over?" J.T. asked.

My mind told me to make him back off, that I was fine, but I stood up instead. I allowed him to guide me out of the living room, outside, and to one of the two ambulances parked in the street.

I vaguely noticed Michael's car in the driveway, the engine still running.

J.T. brought me to the back of an ambulance, which was open and likely waiting for the others to load up Mom or Jen.

"I'm not going anywhere," I said, thinking of Mom inside the house.

"You don't have to get in. Just sit on the back."

I sat on the edge, letting my feet dangle.

J.T. climbed in as well but disappeared inside. I heard him rattling around behind me.

A moment later, he set down a red duffel bag and then hopped down to stand in front of me. He pulled a blanket out of the bag and wrapped it around my arms. I gladly accepted its comfort as I pulled it tightly around my shoulders.

He reached out and took one of my hands, examining my fingernails. There were still traces of Mom's blood on my hand.

With no indication of whether or not he found what he was looking for, he placed a pulse oximeter on my index finger. He lowered my hand, so it rested on top of my thigh. Next, he grabbed a stethoscope from his bag and listened to my heart and lungs.

He put the stethoscope away, removed the pulse oximeter, and then pulled out a light that resembled a pen. Dad had one, and I recognized it.

"Look straight ahead," he said before shining it into my right eye and then my left. He turned it off. "Any weakness, dizziness, or nausea?"

I shook my head.

She's dead. I can't believe she is dead.

We heard a noise, and the front door to the house opened. Two paramedics brought a gurney through the doorway. They were using an Ambu bag to deliver oxygen to whoever it was. I jumped off the back of the ambulance in anticipation.

Seth came out behind them, and I realized they had Jen on the gurney. I watched in silence as they loaded her into the back of the other ambulance. Seth climbed in and reached for her hand just before they closed the doors and sped off.

I looked back to the front door, which was now empty.

"We can't move her yet. We have to wait for the police to get here," J.T. said. "I'm sorry."

I wanted to reply, but I didn't know what to say.

"You don't have to go back inside if you don't want to. I don't mind waiting out here with you if you prefer."

Why is he being so nice to me?

I wanted to tell him to go away and leave me alone, but I didn't. Something about him was soothing, and I really didn't want to be alone.

J.T. and I sat in silence. A few times, I got the impression that he wanted to talk to me, but he didn't. He just gave me space to process everything in peace. It was exactly what I needed.

A few minutes later, the front door opened again, and Dad stepped out of the house. He looked around until he found me.

Without even thinking about it, I jumped up and took off toward him. I threw myself into his arms, like I used to when I was a little girl. He always made me feel so safe, and I desperately needed to feel that way again.

It was just an illusion though. No one could protect me, and it would never be safe. Not as long as Henley was alive anyway.

My head wobbled as I came back to the present, the memory making me dizzy. Or maybe it was the whiskey. Or perhaps it was J.T. All three seemed to make my head spin.

I need to leave.

"Are you okay?" J.T. asked, seeming sincerely worried about me. For the life of me, I couldn't figure out why.

"What are you doing here?" The question came out harsher than I'd intended.

"I told you. I just finished my shift, and I came here with the guys to—"

"No, I mean, in town. When I met you before, we were in McHenry."

"I live here." His reply was slow and deliberate.

"Then, what were you doing in McHenry that day?"

"I was living with my brother there, volunteering as a paramedic. Then, about four months ago, a full-time position opened up here, so I moved."

I need him to go.

"And what made you come over here and talk to me?" I asked.

"I saw you sitting alone." He seemed taken aback by my question, and I could hear the hesitancy in his voice.

"So, you remember me?" Obviously, he did, but I felt the need to call him out on it.

He frowned. "You were hard to forget."

"Why do you say that?"

He didn't answer.

"Why?"

He frowned. "Because you seemed so lost and what happened to your mother was tragic."

A lump formed in my throat, and I forced it down by taking a sip of water.

"How's your friend doing?" he asked. "I asked around the hospital, and they told me she pulled through surgery." He followed my lead and took a sip of his own water. "Did she make a full recovery?"

"Yeah, she's great. She's getting married in two days." I instantly regretted the words the second they left my mouth.

What am I doing? We didn't give people, especially strangers, details about our personal lives.

"I need to go," I said, standing up and immediately wobbling.

J.T. jumped up to catch me as I swayed.

I rested my hands on his muscular chest for balance and looked up at him.

To my surprise, he didn't move or try to push me away.

"How are you getting home?"

I took a step back and moved my hands to the safety of the bar top.

"I drove here, so …" I stopped talking, realizing I had no plan to get home.

He shook his head. "There's no way I'm letting you drive like this. I've seen too many accidents from people who thought they were okay to drive when they weren't."

Right on cue, I rocked again on my feet. *He's right. I'm in no condition to drive.*

I groaned. That left me one choice—to call Michael and ask him to pick me up. He'd do it, of course, but I'd never hear the end of it.

"I'll take you," J.T. said.

I shook my head. "No, that's okay. I can call my brother."

He shrugged nonchalantly. "But I'm already here. It's no problem. I'll drive you home, and my buddy Hector over there can drive your car back to the station. You can pick it up tomorrow."

I shouldn't accept a ride from someone I barely knew. But then again, if he tried anything, I could take care of myself. Even in my inebriated state, I was confident I could channel my abilities if I needed to.

"Fine," I said, pulling my keys out of my jacket pocket.

J.T. smiled as he took them from me. "I think what you mean to say is, thank you."

I smirked at him. "Thank you."

He dipped his head. "You're welcome."

I settled the tab with the bartender while J.T. passed my keys off to Hector. Then, I made my way to the door, trying not to trip over my own two feet.

J.T. came up behind me, pushing the door open and holding it for me.

"I'm just over there." He pointed to a silver pickup truck as he led the way.

When we reached his truck, he opened the passenger door and waited for me to climb in before shutting it.

Great, he's a gentleman. I watched as he walked around the truck and climbed into the driver's seat.

He started the car. "Where to?"

"Walden Road." It wasn't my exact street, but it was close enough.

He nodded. "I know where that is." He pulled out of the parking lot and glanced over at me. "How do you enjoy living here? As opposed to McHenry?"

"It's okay, I guess." I'd lived in so many places that they all ran together at this point.

"I stopped by your old house to check on you, but you'd already moved."

"You did?" I didn't hide my shock. "Why?"

He shifted in his seat. "I wanted to make sure you were doing all right."

"Well, that was ..." *Nice. Caring. Thoughtful.* "Unnecessary. I'm doing just fine."

"Clearly," he replied, and I shot him a dirty look.

"I don't drink very often." I felt compelled to say it, but I wasn't sure why.

"No offense, but that's obvious."

I leaned my head back against the headrest and looked out the window. For the first time in a long time, I felt relaxed, and it had nothing to do with the whiskey.

"You can just let me out here," I said as Walden Road came into view.

J.T. obliged but turned to me. "I can drop you off at your house to make sure you get in safely."

"I'll be okay," I insisted as I unbuckled my seat belt.

He raised his eyebrow with skepticism.

"I *promise*."

He eyed me for a second and then chuckled, picking up on the fact that he wouldn't be able to change my mind. "Stop by the station sometime."

"I will because I have to get my car, remember?" I smiled sarcastically, refusing to admit that I wanted to see him again. Although I did, and I was pretty sure he knew it.

"Have a good night, Raina."

The sound of him saying my name made my heart flutter.

Great. One guy gives me a ride home, and I'm turning to goo.

"Later," I replied as I shut the door, cutting myself off from him.

I didn't turn around, but I could hear J.T.'s car still running until I disappeared around the corner.

The house was quiet when I got home. Everyone had likely gone to bed. Everyone, except Michael, of course. He was sitting in the living room, waiting for me.

He glared at me. "Where have you been?"

"Out." I wasn't in the mood to argue, but something told me he wouldn't let it go.

He stood up, eyeing me closely. "Are you drunk?"

I didn't respond, but my feet betrayed me, and I stumbled.

"You drove home like this? What if you'd wrecked, or gotten arrested, or killed someone?"

His accusation made my blood boil.

"I didn't drink and drive, thank you very much. J.T. drove me home."

"Who the hell is J.T.?"

Yeah, I should've known that response wouldn't go over much better.

He took a breath and ran his hands through his hair. I knew him well enough to recognize he was trying to have patience with me but was really struggling.

"He was the paramedic who took care of me after ..." I didn't want to finish the sentence. "After Mom died."

He stared at me. I could see the questions swirling in his head. He hadn't expected that answer.

"I get that you're upset," he said, his voice deliberately softer. "But you can't be out, drunk in public, accepting rides from people you barely know."

I frowned. "I can take care of myself."

He tilted his head. "I'm not worried about him physically hurting you. Trust me, I'm aware you could take him."

Then, I realized what he'd meant. His concern was about what I might say, that I might slip up and reveal something to compromise us all.

I crossed my arms over my chest. "So, it's only okay when you tell strangers our secrets?"

"The situation with Natalie was different, and you know it."

I rolled my eyes. "Whatever." It wasn't the most clever or mature response, but I was too tired to argue. "I need a ride to pick up my car in the morning before we leave for the airport."

I shoved past him and toward the stairs without looking back.

The next morning, I awoke to the sound of someone knocking on my bedroom door.

"Be ready to go in five if you want to get your car," Michael said from the other side.

My head pounded as I struggled to sit up.

Ugh. Whiskey.

I forced myself to climb out of bed and grabbed a long-sleeved shirt and a pair of jeans out of the dresser. Then, I stumbled to the bathroom to wash my face, get the knots out of my hair, and brush my teeth. In my drunken stupor last night, I'd taken a shower. So, luckily, I didn't have to deal with that right now.

A few minutes later, I walked downstairs and put my sunglasses on as I entered the kitchen.

Why is everything so bright?

Seth was leaning against the counter, eating a giant bowl of cereal. He looked up at me when I walked in.

"Good morning, sunshine." His tone was cheerful despite him knowing that I hated perkiness in the morning. "I heard you had a rough night, so I put on a pot of coffee for you."

"Thanks," I mumbled. That was exactly what I needed—coffee and lots and lots of sugar.

I grabbed my travel mug out of the cabinet, and just as I finished assembling my hot beverage, Jen and Natalie walked into the kitchen. Natalie had dressed casually, like me, but Jen was all dolled up. She had on so much makeup that you'd think today was her wedding day.

"The custom favors I ordered online got delivered to the hotel yesterday," she said to Natalie. "And the lepidopterist confirmed she'll have the butterflies delivered right after the ceremony."

This girl has lost her mind.

I planned to ask her why the heck she would intentionally bring insects to her wedding when I noticed Seth shaking his head. It was as if he already knew what I wanted to say and was advising against it.

I sipped my coffee instead.

"What am I forgetting?" Jen asked, spinning on her heels to face Natalie.

"Nothing," Natalie replied. "I'm positive that you've covered everything."

"What if we forget something?" Jen sounded borderline frantic. "We only get one shot at our wedding day. It has to be perfect."

"Your wedding day will be perfect," Natalie said. "Everything is going to be just fine."

Just as I was sure that Natalie was going to pull Seth into the conversation to comfort his crazy bride, she stopped me mid-sip to drag me into it.

"Right, Raina?"

Jen turned to look at me, hope in her eyes.

I glanced at Natalie, who mouthed, *Say something.*

"Natalie's right ..." I replied, unsure of how to respond. "Stop being stupid."

The expression on both Jen's and Natalie's faces told me that wasn't the right thing to say.

"Very motivating," Seth whispered, stifling a chuckle.

"I've got to go." I quickly slipped past Seth and out of the kitchen, taking my coffee with me.

Michael was waiting for me in the living room with his car keys in his hand. He didn't speak to me. Instead, he just turned around and walked to the front door.

I guess he's still pissed.

I followed him out to the car and felt the tension as he drove us to the fire station.

I hated fighting with him. Sure, we bickered every day and constantly got on each other's nerves, but we'd only had a handful of real arguments over the course of our entire lives. Besides being my brother, he was also my best friend. No one understood me like he did.

"What time does our flight leave again?" I asked. I knew the answer already, but I wanted to break the painful silence.

"Two fifteen, but it'll take us almost an hour to get to the airport, so we need to leave around eleven. That should give us enough time to check in and get through security."

He pulled up to the fire station, which was a freshly painted building with a large brick sign on top that read, *Fire Station 3*. The station had four large garage-style doors. One was open, revealing a shiny red fire truck parked inside.

To the right of the building, I saw my car. My stomach flip-flopped when I noticed J.T.'s truck parked next to it.

"I need to go find out who has my keys," I said.

"Want me to wait?"

I shook my head. "No, that's okay." The last thing I wanted was my brother scrutinizing my interaction with J.T.—assuming I got to see him.

I hopped out of the car with my coffee in hand and watched Michael leave. Then, I turned toward the station, wondering if I should go inside and look for J.T.

Before I could overthink it, J.T. appeared in the entryway to the garage. He smiled and walked over when he spotted me.

"How are those shots treating you this morning?" he asked, handing me the keys to my car.

"Ugh," I replied. "Pretty rough."

"Coconut water."

"Excuse me?"

"It'll help you recover from the hangover faster. You need to rehydrate."

"Your extensive knowledge of alcohol-related activities is a little concerning," I teased.

He smiled widely. "What are you doing tonight?"

I groaned. "I'll be in bachelorette party hell." Why I'd agreed to go, I would never understand.

"I don't know. It might be fun. You seemed to get a good start last night."

"Yeah, it won't be that kind of party, unfortunately. We're taking a cooking class."

It wouldn't have been my first choice for a bachelorette party, but then again, Natalie wouldn't have been my first choice for maid of honor either. This was Jen's thing, and I was just along for the ride.

"Perhaps there will be some cooking wine. You know, to get your fix."

"I'm not an alcoholic," I said, my voice an octave higher. "I told you, I rarely ever drink."

He raised an eyebrow, giving me a doubtful look.

"I don't!"

He held up his hands in defeat, his face serious. "You don't have to be such a mean drunk."

I swatted, hitting him in the arm and making him laugh.

I need to go.

"Tell your friend thanks for taking care of my car," I said.

"Sure thing."

I turned to walk away. My legs were eager to get out of there, but my heart was … conflicted.

"If you ever want to hang out—when you're done with all the wedding festivities—you know where to find me," he said.

I spun around, surprised. Most people outside of my family didn't want to spend more time with me than they absolutely had to. That was the way I wanted it after all.

"I'll see you around, J.T.," I replied, fighting a smile.

FOUR

MICHAEL

Natalie stirred in the seat next to me. She lifted her head, which had been resting on my shoulder while she slept.

I reached forward and stuffed my book in the seat's pocket in front of me. I didn't know what it was about anyway. For the past thirty minutes, I'd just stared at the same page, reading it over and over but never comprehending it. Between everything going on with Detective Thomas, the explosions, and Raina, I'd lost my ability to focus.

"How long was I out?" Natalie asked.

"About an hour and a half," I replied. "We're almost there."

She frowned. "I missed the end of the movie."

"Trust me, be glad you did."

Natalie glanced across the aisle at Jen and Seth. Jen was talking a mile a minute, her words muffled because of the altitude. But I'd bet every dollar I had that she was talking to Seth about the wedding. Seth, being the excellent sport that he was, just sat there, occasionally giving her a patient nod.

"She's nervous," Natalie said.

"That's the understatement of the year."

"I can't blame her though. I mean, we have a handful of psychopaths out there, wanting to kill us." She cringed, and I was positive she was thinking about how Becca fell into that category.

I gently nudged her with my shoulder. "It'll be okay." I didn't know it for sure, but I hated seeing her so worried.

"I just don't get it though. What's the point of the explosions?"

I wished I had the answer. I'd run through it in my head a million times, trying to make sense of it.

"No one has died, right?" she asked.

"Right."

The whole situation was strange. After reading up on the blasts, I'd found that most had occurred in the middle of the night, when the buildings were empty. The only exception was McCarthy's.

What if Natalie had been inside?

She rested her hand on my knee to stop it from bouncing. "I don't think they were trying to kill me."

I remained unconvinced. "They are literally spelling out your name."

"It seems like more of a warning." She paused and thought for a second. "Like maybe they just want me to think they're coming for me."

It was the same debate I'd been having with myself since Detective Thompson's visit.

"If they really wanted to take me out, they would've made sure I was inside the pub when they blew it up," she said.

As much as I wanted to believe that, I also knew for a fact that Becca wanted Natalie dead. I'd pried Becca's hands from Natalie's throat once. It was impossible to forget the look of hatred in Becca's eyes. She'd do it again in a heartbeat if given the chance.

The *fasten seat belt* sign flashed, and the pilot came over the speaker to prepare us for landing in Jacksonville, Florida.

Natalie looked out the window and smiled. She missed Florida, and I hated the fact that she'd moved away because of me.

She and I sat quietly as we landed and waited to disembark the plane.

Jen gasped. "No!"

Natalie and I looked at her, expecting the worst. Jen stared at her phone, horrified.

Has there been another explosion?

"My grandparents are stuck in an airport in Pennsylvania," Jen whined. "There were issues with their plane, so the airline diverted them."

Natalie jumped in her seat, grasping my arm. "That's it!"

"What is?" I wasn't following.

"The explosions," she said, lowering her voice. "They are a *diversion*."

She watched me intently, digging her fingers into my forearm as I considered her theory. I had to admit, it made sense.

"I know I'm right." She gave my arm another squeeze before removing her hand. "But what are they trying to distract us from?"

I leaned in closer to her. "Do you think it's because of Project Josie?"

She tensed. Project Josie was a sore subject.

"You heard someone mention Project Josie before we had Becca in captivity," I said.

"I was dreaming."

"What if you weren't? Maybe it wasn't just part of Becca's escape plan, and it's really something Henley is plotting?"

She glanced around to ensure no one was eavesdropping.

I raised my eyebrows at her. This theory was, without a doubt, the best one so far. Henley was creating a diversion for us, so he could move forward with Project Josie under the radar.

The only problem was, we had no clue what Project Josie actually was.

After we got off the plane, Seth went with Jen to baggage claim to retrieve her checked luggage. The rest of us had just carried on our bags, so we headed to the rental car counter. Natalie and I stood off to the side while Alexander got the keys to the rental. Raina, who was still keeping her distance from me, waited by the airport exit.

I looked down at Natalie, who was deep in thought.

"What's on your mind?"

She blinked and tentatively looked up at me. "I think I should use the wedding as an opportunity to get Mr. Weber alone."

I shook my head. "No. I want you to stay away from him."

I had known William Weber was going to be at the wedding when I agreed to come. Despite Seth's rocky relationship with him, he was still Seth's dad, and I understood that. But I couldn't forget how William had been secretly working with Henley, how he'd turned us in when we visited Natalie's parents in Richmond, and how he'd stood by and done absolutely nothing to help Natalie after Henley shot her. He was a greedy, deceiving coward.

"Hear me out," Natalie said. "We need to know if Project Josie is real, right?"

I pressed my lips firmly together, not wanting to admit she was right.

"What if Mr. Weber knows what it is?" she asked. "If I can get him alone, I can ask him about it and read his mind. Maybe he'll give us some insight into what Henley is plotting."

I didn't like her plan, but I didn't have a better one to offer. "Okay, fine. Just do it at the wedding, when other people are around. I don't trust him, and I don't want you to be alone with him."

"It's going to be tricky," she replied. "My and Seth's parents are joined at the hip, but I need to speak to him when they aren't around. My parents still don't know about Becca or Mr. Weber's involvement in her kidnapping. I doubt Seth's mom does either. It would absolutely crush them."

Alexander waved to us from the airport exit, keys in hand.

"Come on," I said, putting my arm around her shoulders. "Let's go focus on celebrating Seth and Jen."

Two hours later, we were all checked into our hotel. I'd showered and dressed, and I stood in the lobby, waiting for Seth. We planned to meet the rest of his wedding party at a nearby bar for a low-key bachelor party.

The hotel, Casa de la Belleza, was the same one Jen's dad managed and was going to be where the wedding would take place. The last time I had been inside, it was the night of the masquerade ball, when I broke Lance's nose after he and his friend Ben tried to drug Natalie and Jen. That piece of crap had deserved worse, and if security hadn't intervened, I probably would've put him in the hospital.

"Where's Natalie?" Raina asked, coming to stand next to me.

I raised an eyebrow at her. It was rare that she ever asked me about Natalie. Then, I realized it was her way of extending a peace offering.

"She's upstairs with Jen, getting ready."

Raina let out a nervous laugh. "I'm sure Jen's getting all glammed up for this cooking class."

"I know this isn't your thing, but I appreciate you agreeing to go. I'm sure it means a lot to Jen."

Raina rolled her eyes. "I didn't want to hear her whine about it for the next hundred years."

It was best not to make a big deal about it, but I knew that when Raina made her mind up about not doing something, there was no changing it. She could be irrationally stubborn. So, for her to agree to go meant a small part of her actually wanted to be included.

I noticed Natalie the minute she entered the lobby. She'd dressed up from her normal attire, and she was effortlessly beautiful. She wore a pair of jeans that hugged her in all the right places and a green blouse that matched her eyes. Her hair hung loose and cascaded down her back in soft, large curls.

I peeled my eyes away from Natalie long enough to notice Jen was with her. Jen, of course, was all dolled up in probably the worst outfit to pick for a cooking class. She had on a short white dress that clung to one shoulder and a pair of gold stilettos.

"Good grief," Raina mumbled under her breath. Then, she looked around, confused. "Where's Dad?"

I frowned. "He's not coming. Said he wasn't feeling up to it."

"I'm worried about him. I keep thinking he'll snap out of it and go back to the way he was before."

"I'm concerned, too, but Alexander is tough. He'll pull through." I hoped it was true.

An ear-piercing scream radiated throughout the lobby, making Raina and me jump. We had a heightened sense of hearing, so loud noises could be borderline painful. My heart pounded as I anticipated conflict, and I turned in the direction it had come from. I fully expected to land eyes on Becca or one of Henley's assassins.

Instead, I found three twenty-something women, all dressed up in short dresses and shoes so tall that they could barely walk. They squealed in unison, clapping their hands together as Jen approached them. When she finally reached them, they took turns excitedly kissing her cheeks and talking all at once.

The girls quickly accepted Natalie into their circle, each greeting her with a warm hug. One of them looped her arm in hers and immediately started talking her ear off.

Raina stepped back, ready to bolt, but I caught her elbow.

"You're committed now. There's no turning back," I said, stifling a laugh.

She moaned and then walked away to join them.

"Don't worry. My friends won't react that way when they see me," Seth said as he walked up. He waved to Jen and the group of girls, which sent Jen's party-going friends into another round of high-pitched wails.

Raina turned and rolled her eyes.

Seth and I watched as Raina reluctantly joined the other girls. She was rigid as they surrounded her, hugging her and introducing themselves. I was proud of her for not pushing them away.

When they finished their introductions, they shuffled out of the lobby and into a limo waiting outside. Natalie had rented it to take the girls to their class, knowing Jen would love it. I'd offered to rent one for Seth's party, but he'd said the bar he wanted to go to was walking distance, just around the block.

He turned to me. "My dad is coming tonight. I wasn't planning on inviting him, but he asked me what we were doing …"

"He's your dad. I get it." And I did.

Seeing William wasn't ideal, but this wasn't about me. It was Seth's night, and he had a right to invite anyone he wanted.

Seth's phone buzzed in his pocket, and he took it out to look at it. "The guys are waiting for us at the bar, so we should head out."

Seth and I left the hotel and walked the short distance toward a dingy hole-in-the-wall bar. The neon sign over the door simply read, *Beer*. Direct and straight to the point.

"It's the only bar in town with pool tables," Seth said, as if he sensed that I was wondering why anyone would choose to have their bachelor party there.

We walked inside, and I followed Seth over to the bar, where a group of guys were gathered around. They greeted Seth with a row of shots they'd preordered and laid out for him.

"No," Seth said, lifting his hands up in defeat. "Just a couple of beers for me. If I show up hungover at our wedding tomorrow, Jen will kill me."

I ordered a beer for Seth and water for myself while the guys razzed him about already being whipped.

Seth ignored them and introduced me. First, there was his cousin Isaac, who looked like a shorter, stockier version of Seth. Then, there were two of his roommates from college, Mateo and Aaron. They looked like stereotypical frat boys in pastel-colored shirts and baseball caps, and if I had to guess, they'd started drinking about two hours before the party actually started. The last was Seth's friend Austin from high school. He seemed to be a lot like Seth—laid-back, likeable, and still sober.

It didn't take long for us to migrate to the pool table. Austin and I sat out for the first round and just watched. I discreetly assessed the bar as I pretended to watch them play.

At the pool table, it was Seth and Isaac versus Mateo and Aaron. If I were betting, I'd put my money on Seth and Isaac. Aaron swayed as he waited for his turn.

"How do you know Seth?" Austin asked me.

I was sure it seemed strange to him that Seth would ask me to be his best man, someone none of them had likely ever heard of.

I glanced at Seth, who was lining up to take his shot. I should've asked him what he'd told his friends.

"Through Natalie." It was a watered-down version of the truth, and if Austin had been Seth's friend in high school, then I assumed he knew her.

"Ah, yes. Natalie Clark." Austin's expression turned serious. "It was a shame about Becca. I can't believe they never found her. I didn't think Seth would recover from it, but I'm glad to see that he's found someone else who makes him happy."

"Jen's good for him."

"How is Natalie? I didn't see her much after Becca disappeared."

"She's good." *Although Becca is alive and wants to kill her.*

"I'm glad to hear that. I had such a thing for her back in the day. The only reason I didn't ask her out was because I knew Seth would kick the crap out of me for thinking of her like that."

I didn't respond, and Austin's eyes widened with realization.

"Wait, you said you met Seth through Natalie ..."

"Yeah. She's my girlfriend."

Austin winced. "Sorry, man. Putting my foot in my mouth has always been one of my top ten skills."

"Don't worry about it."

It wasn't exactly a surprise to me that boys had been interested in Natalie in high school. She was beautiful, and no one realized that more than me.

Austin held up his beer bottle. "Cheers to landing yourself an awesome girl."

No argument from me as I tapped my water glass on his bottle. I knew how lucky I was.

"Austin, you've gotta step in," Mateo said. "I'm taking this lightweight back to the hotel." He motioned to Aaron, who was sitting on a barstool, propped up against the wall, looking like he might topple over at any moment.

Austin left to join the others at the pool table, and after a quick protest from Aaron that he was "fine," Aaron allowed Mateo to call a cab, so they could get back to their hotel in one piece.

"I'm going to take a break," Seth said, leaving Isaac and Austin at the pool table.

He sat down on the stool across the table from me and pointed to my water. "Always on guard, huh?"

"You never know." I shrugged, trying to seem more relaxed than I actually was. If Henley or Becca made an appearance, I'd be ready and clearheaded.

"Do you think the girls are okay?"

I nodded. "Yeah. Natalie said she'd stay vigilant; plus, Raina is with them. Jen is double covered."

"If given the choice, I'm not sure which one of us would be at the top of Becca's hit list."

Without a doubt, Natalie was her primary target. But I recalled how jealous Becca had been when she found out that Jen and Seth were engaged. If she knew this was their wedding weekend, I wouldn't put it past her to move them up on her priority list.

"No one is getting past me to hurt any of you," I assured him.

He took a swig of his beer. "This must be exhausting for you."

"What is?"

"Always trying to keep everyone safe. Especially now. With Alexander being, you know, not himself, that responsibility has shifted to you."

He was right. The duty now rested on my shoulders, and I'd do anything to protect my family, which now included Natalie, Seth, and Jen. As overwhelming as it was, someone had to do it.

"Where does all of this end?"

I looked at him, puzzled.

"I mean, we're not spending the rest of our lives like this, right?" His eyes were hopeful.

I didn't want to break it to him, but I'd likely be dealing with this for the rest of my life, however long that was.

"No, not you and Jen," I replied. "After the wedding, it's time for you two to put all of this behind you."

"What about you and Natalie?"

It was something I tried not to think about. The present was hard to enjoy when you knew it wouldn't last forever.

"I want Natalie to figure out what will be best for her in the long run. And I'm not convinced that's me." I hated saying it aloud, but it was the truth, and Seth was one of the few people in my life I could be brutally honest with.

"You know she'll choose you."

"What kind of life can I give her though?" I asked. "Sure, we could get married, but there is no living happily ever after. We can't settle down anywhere and have a family. If I can just find a way to keep her safe—"

The door to the bar opened, cutting my train of thought short. The hair on the back of my neck prickled.

Lance and Ben.

Every muscle in my body tensed as I fought with myself to remain seated on the barstool.

Ben came to a screeching halt when he noticed me staring at him. He reached over to stop Lance from coming any closer. Lance seemed confused but then narrowed his eyes when he spotted me.

Give me a reason. Please.

Ben leaned closer to Lance and said something to him. Normally, I would've been able to hear it, but with the loud '90s alternative rock music blaring in the bar, I couldn't make it out. Lance took a step back and averted his eyes.

They turned around and headed for the exit. Ben gave one quick, wary glance my way before they left.

Seth looked at me and then back at the exit. "What was that about?"

I guessed Jen never mentioned the incident to him, which made sense because it'd happened before they met. I wouldn't be the one to get him all riled up. Seth would likely go after them, and they weren't worth his trouble.

"Just a couple of local troublemakers." It gave me satisfaction to know that at least two of our enemies had enough sense to stay away. I picked up Seth's empty beer bottle. "I'll go grab you another."

FIVE

NATALIE

I contemplated removing my shoes as I made my way down the hall to Seth's suite. My feet already hurt, and I didn't know how I was going to make it through the wedding in them, let alone the reception.

I knocked on the door, and a second later, Michael opened it. A smile hit his lips when he realized it was me. He stepped out into the hall and closed the door behind him before kissing me hello. I had been so busy this morning, getting ready for the wedding, that I hadn't seen him yet.

"You look beautiful," he said. "Everything going okay?"

"Yeah, I just wanted to see Seth before the ceremony. Also, I was hoping Mr. Weber would be here."

"Seth is inside, but his dad hasn't shown up yet. We don't know where he is."

"You haven't seen him at all today?" I found that shocking since his only child was about to get married.

"Nope. Seth invited him to the bachelor party last night, but he didn't come. He called Seth around midnight, claiming to be tired or something. Then, this morning, he allegedly overslept and missed breakfast with us."

"He's avoiding you." If Mr. Weber was avoiding Michael, he'd avoid me as well. Getting him alone was going to be tougher than I'd originally thought. "But I'm sure he'll at least come to the wedding. The second I see him alone, I'll talk to him."

The door opened, and a guy wearing a tux stepped into the hall. As he passed, he reeked of sweat and booze.

"That's Aaron," Michael said when the hungover groomsman was out of earshot. "Aaron had *a lot* of fun last night and isn't feeling well today."

Michael opened the door to Seth's suite and held it for me. I stepped inside to find two familiar faces—Isaac and Austin. There was another guy in the room that I didn't know, but he seemed almost as miserable as Aaron. Seth's suite was like Jen's and had a living room area. The guys were all sitting around, watching a basketball game.

"Hey, Nat," Isaac said while Austin gave me a friendly wave from the couch.

"Hi," I replied.

"Seth's in here," Michael told me as he knocked on the bedroom door.

"Got a minute?" I asked when Seth answered.

"For you? Of course."

Michael stayed behind with the other guys to give us privacy even though I knew he wasn't watching the game. He hadn't grown up, playing or watching sports, so he had very little interest in them.

Once in Seth's room, I realized I'd never seen him in a tux before. "You clean up nice."

"Thanks." He smiled and then looked at me expectantly. "So, what's up?"

"Well, I wanted to stop by and wish you luck or whatever a sister does on her brother's wedding day." We weren't actually brother and sister, but we'd pretty much been raised that way, and I considered him to be family. I was closer to him than I was to my own parents.

"Thanks. It's kind of surreal, you know?"

I nodded with understanding. It seemed like just yesterday, we had been little kids, building blanket forts in the living room and climbing trees in the backyard. And now, here we were, minutes away from him getting married.

"How are you holding up?" he asked.

"Me?" It took me a second to realize he was referring to the explosions. "Oh yeah, I'm good."

"I find that hard to believe."

I looked away, unable to lie.

"What is it?" he asked, realizing I was holding out on him. "Tell me what's going on."

I didn't want anything to take away from his wedding, but I realized the unknown would be worse.

"Fine," I replied. "I think the explosions are just a diversion."

"For?"

I shrugged, trying to avoid answering.

"Project Josie?" Nothing got by Seth.

"Maybe ..."

I was still having a hard time, admitting that Project Josie was real. The last time I had gone on a wild goose chase, trying to save a little girl who claimed to be Josie, it'd turned out to be an elaborate setup.

He furrowed his brows, deep in thought.

"Hey," I said, snapping my fingers. "None of that. Today is the happiest day of your life."

He smiled as his attention turned back to his wedding day. "It's an amazing feeling, knowing that I'm going to spend the rest of my life with her. I can't believe it."

His words warmed my heart. If anyone deserved to be happy, it was Seth.

"Do you see you and Michael here someday?" he asked, catching me completely off guard.

I looked up at him, dumbfounded. "I ... I don't know. Maybe, but I haven't had time to think about it with everything else going on. Our relationship hasn't exactly been typical."

Seth nodded but didn't reply. I sensed he was holding back.

I'd never been good about planning for the future, but I probably needed to. It wasn't like I was a kid anymore. The future was coming whether or not I prepared for it.

For me, that future included Michael. He was the love of my life. That I was sure about.

As I struggled to pull it together to express my thoughts to Seth, the wedding coordinator opened the door and popped her head inside.

"Time to go," she said to Seth. Then, she looked at me. "You need to get back to the bride, missy. It's almost showtime."

I turned to Seth, fighting back a wave of emotion as it suddenly encroached.

"Don't do it." He shot me a warning look.

I nodded before wrapping my arms tightly around his waist.

"I love you," I said.

"I love you too," he replied, his arms still around me. "But you are such a nerd."

Everything about Seth and Jen's wedding ceremony was perfect. From the flawless display of ombré purple roses that framed the arch at the altar to the antique candelabras that lined the hotel's famous Amada room. It was a place where people from all over the world came to get married.

And of course, there was my favorite part—the look of wonderment on Seth's face when Jen made her grand entrance. They'd waited until the ceremony to see each other the day of the wedding, and even though it took longer to take photos after, I was glad that I got to see Seth's initial reaction to his bride. It was priceless.

Throughout the ceremony, Michael was behind Seth and in my line of sight. We'd catch each other's eyes periodically, and each time, my mind wandered back to my earlier conversation with Seth.

Does Michael envision us standing up here at the altar together someday?

The thought made me excited about the future. I wouldn't rush things, but it was definitely something to look forward to.

As I finished my last bite of filet mignon at the reception, I looked up and made sure Mr. Weber hadn't moved from his table. He'd expertly avoided Michael and me all day.

Seth and Jen had decided against assigned seating, so Michael and I'd strategically sat with my parents and Aunt Gael at a table for eight, hoping that Seth's parents would join us.

I wouldn't have grilled Mr. Weber in front of everyone, but I planned to listen in on his thoughts to see if he gave anything away about Henley. Having him at our table would also make it easier to keep tabs on him, so I could find the right moment to get him alone.

But as my parents chose their seats, the Webers opted not to sit with them. After sitting down, my mother kept an eye out for Mrs. Weber. She waved to her, assuming they'd join them, but Mr. Weber caught Mrs. Weber's arm before she could approach my parents' table. He guided her to a different table and sat with Isaac and his parents.

Mrs. Weber seemed confused by his choice but not enough to challenge him on it.

Alexander and Raina had joined us instead. Raina sat quietly on the other side of Michael while my dad talked Alexander's ear off about golf. I didn't know if Alexander golfed, but he graciously engaged in the conversation.

After I handed the waiter my empty plate, Aunt Gael leaned closer to me.

"Why don't we stretch our legs for a minute and catch up?" She stood up, smoothing out her silk dress.

I smiled at her. "Sure."

I anxiously followed her onto the patio that led out into a beautiful garden courtyard. As much as I was happy to see her, I knew she wanted so many answers that I wouldn't be able to provide.

She sat down on a bench and patted the spot next to her. "I see that you and Michael got back together."

"We did." I tried to seem casual and nonchalant as I joined her, but I could tell she was testing the waters.

"Is that the reason you left in the middle of the night?"

She was referring to the night I'd left her house to rescue Michael. I was staying with her when I had a dream that Henley captured Michael. My intuition told me it was true, and I knew I needed to leave to save him. I'd written Aunt Gael a vague note, hoping she wouldn't freak out when she realized I'd left.

"It was. He needed my help, and then we got back together after that." *Stay close to the truth.* "I'm sorry I left without saying a proper good-bye."

She sighed. "I'm not mad at you, but I am concerned."

She reached into her purse and pulled out an envelope. It was *my* envelope, one that I'd sent her. She opened it and pulled out my rose-gold lotus necklace.

I'd mailed it to her on my way to surrender myself to Henley. I knew that Henley wouldn't allow me to keep it, and I worried it would get left behind when Michael and his family moved locations. Aunt Gael had seemed like the best choice to hold on to it, but now, I had some explaining to do.

"Your note didn't tell me why you'd sent it, but you asked that I keep it safe," she said. "May I ask from what?"

I didn't have an answer for her.

She put her hand on my shoulder. "Honey, are you in some kind of trouble?"

I shook my head, and she narrowed her eyes.

She has intuitive abilities of her own and probably knows I'm lying.

She waited patiently to see if I'd say more, and when I didn't, she sighed and removed her hand. "I can't force you to tell me what's going on, but you can always come to me with anything if you change your mind. No judgment, I promise. Okay?"

"I know. Thank you."

There was nothing else to say. She wanted an explanation—and rightfully so—but I couldn't give it to her. Not only would I betray Michael's trust by telling her the truth, but it would put her in danger as well.

She dropped the necklace into my hand. I looked down at it, turning it over and tracing the outline of the flower with my finger. It was my most valued possession because it had been a gift from Becca when she was still *her*.

"This is hard on your parents too," Aunt Gael said.

I looked up, startled. At first, I worried she was talking about Becca—that, somehow, she'd figured out the truth about her being alive. But then I realized it was probably just my guilty conscience making me feel that way.

She noticed my blank stare. "The wedding. We all expected this to be your sister's wedding day. Jen seems like a sweet girl, but it's difficult to see anyone up there with Seth besides Becca."

The remorse crept back in. Keeping the truth from my parents and Aunt Gael denied them the closure they deserved. But I rationalized that telling them she was a completely different person now—a *murderer*—would be so much worse.

"I'm just glad he found someone who makes him happy," I said.

She tilted her head toward the hotel. "We should probably get back in there."

As I followed her back inside, I fastened the necklace around my neck to make sure I didn't lose it.

"I'll be right there," I told her.

I needed a moment to make sure I was composed before going back to the table with my parents. We were finally on good terms, and I didn't want them to worry about me.

She rubbed the side of my arm, understanding that my sudden emotion stemmed from the loss of my sister. "Take your time."

I turned and walked into the restroom. Inside was a lounge with cream velvet couches and antique oak vanities. Gold-rimmed mirrors hung above the porcelain sinks. Beyond the lounge was another room, where all the stalls were located.

I plopped down on a couch, and my feet felt instantly relieved. The shoes were absolutely killing me.

"He left?" my mother asked. "But they are just about to cut the cake."

I sat up straight, listening to her from the other side of the wall.

"He's been acting so strange. It's been going on for a while, but this whole wedding has really put him over the edge," Mrs. Weber replied.

"What did he say?" Mother asked right before I heard the faucet turn on.

"Nothing," Mrs. Weber replied. "Just that he was going to leave a few minutes early and he'd meet us at the bar. This is *our son's wedding*. I know things have been rough lately between the two of them, but he should be here, not planning the after-party."

I stood up and hurried out before they spotted me. If Mr. Weber left the reception, he was likely alone. Mother had said nothing about Dad leaving with him, but I also knew that she wouldn't allow him to anyway.

As I flew through the door, I almost ran straight into Raina, who was on her way to the restroom.

"What the—"

"Tell Michael I got my opportunity and I needed to go," I said, cutting off whatever snarky comment she had planned for me.

She watched me, dumbfounded, as I darted around her. "Where are you going?"

I heard her, but I didn't slow down. In fact, I practically ran out of the hotel.

As soon as I made my way outside, I glanced all around for Mr. Weber, but there was no sign of him. I headed left, in the direction where the nearest bar was located.

Ignoring the throbbing in my feet, I forced myself to pick up the pace, knowing it might be my only chance. If I had to guess, Mr. Weber planned to hop on a plane and go home as early as possible tomorrow to avoid interacting with Michael and me.

I rounded the corner and noticed him three blocks ahead. I took off after him, treading as lightly as I could so he didn't hear the clanking of my heels as I approached. If he heard me coming, he'd likely try to get away.

When I got within a block's distance of him, I tuned out all the noise on the street and zeroed in on his thoughts.

The first attempt was a bust. A group of sorority girls walked past, and all I heard was a jumbled mess, mixed with their actual conversation.

They crossed the street, and as soon as they were on the other side, it got quiet, so I tried again.

"What if she blows up the hotel? She wouldn't do that, would she?" he thought.

His thoughts shook me.

Is Becca here?

If Becca was there, I needed to know, so I could go back and get everyone out of the hotel.

I stepped onto the street, dashed past Mr. Weber, and stopped in front of him, blocking him from being able to continue down the sidewalk.

He jumped, startled, and then cowered back when he realized it was me. Then, his thoughts told me he didn't think Becca would blow up the hotel. He worried *I* would do it.

Although I was aware of the fact that Mr. Weber had seen me blast a hole through the wall of Henley's office, I couldn't help but feel offended by his reaction.

"I wouldn't do that," I said. "Unlike you, I don't betray the people who trust me."

His eyes widened and then darted around, looking for an out. "Please don't hurt me."

Good grief.

Instead of telling him how ridiculous he was being, I used it to my advantage. "Answer my questions honestly, and I won't." The words sounded foreign, coming out of my mouth. I'd never bullied anyone before, but the situation called for extreme measures. We had to get to the bottom of what was going on. "What is Project Josie?"

"I—I don't know what you're talking about," he replied.

On the exterior, he seemed confused by my question, so I forced myself to focus on his thoughts.

"Is she going to kill me? Should I just make something up?"

"Think," I said. "Maybe you overheard a conversation in passing at Henley? Or witnessed something out of the ordinary?"

Mr. Weber insistently shook his head, starting to panic. I needed to tread carefully. We were in public, and it would draw a lot of unwanted attention if he had a full-on meltdown.

"I wonder if it could have something to do with Dr. Rees …" he mumbled more to himself than to me.

"Who?"

"This doctor, a lady who visited Henley. On more than one occasion when I went to his office to meet with him, he got pulled away to speak with her."

"What did she want?"

Beads of sweat formed on his forehead. "I don't know. I wasn't a part of those conversations. They were private."

"What type of doctor is she?"

"He never told me."

I zeroed in on his thoughts and confirmed it was true.

A couple stepped off the sidewalk and onto the street to get around us. The man gave me a dirty look from over his shoulder.

I needed to wrap this up. There were too many people around.

My intuition told me that Mr. Weber knew nothing else, so I moved to the side and gave him a nod to continue walking to the bar.

He eyed me for a moment, worried that if he did, I would strike him from behind. As much as I wanted to assure him I wouldn't—that he was too weak-minded and pathetic to make it worth my effort—I turned around instead and started back toward the hotel.

I was a couple of feet away when I heard Mr. Weber call my name.

"I'm sorry," he said. "For what it's worth, I wish I could go back and change what I did."

I turned back around, surprised by his penitence.

He took one step closer and then stopped. "About Becca. I never planned for things to happen the way they did."

I felt the sting of his genuineness.

"Why did you do it?" I asked, although nothing he said would ever make it right.

"Seth doesn't know, but we were in *a lot* of debt," he replied. "It was to the point that I'd even drained his college fund. So, I started the side deal with Henley to help him get the pharmaceuticals he needed for his business, and he compensated me well for my services and my discretion."

I'd never suspected that he and Mrs. Weber suffered from financial problems.

"How did Becca come into it?"

"I was in a meeting with Henley, and he stepped outside the conference room to take another call. I overheard him saying he was exhausting all of his options to locate two of his test subjects. He offered whoever he was on the phone with five hundred thousand dollars if they could locate them." He looked down at his feet.

"So, you sold my sister for five hundred thousand dollars?" My voice was flat and bitter.

He lifted his eyes, pleading for understanding. "The agreement was for her to stay at the facility for two weeks. She'd help locate Michael and Raina, and then Henley would wipe away her memory of it all and return her home. But as you're already aware, he isn't a man who holds his word. I just didn't realize that until it was too late."

I balled my hands at my sides, willing myself to stay in control of my emotions. If they overwhelmed me, it could easily trigger my abilities, and I didn't want to do something I'd regret.

"I don't care if it was two weeks or two minutes," I said through gritted teeth. "You had no right to do that to her, to us. Think about what you did to Seth."

His eyes returned to the ground, and I slowly pivoted back around. There was nothing left to say. He had taken advantage of the trust my family had in him and peddled my sister to a madman.

I turned down a random side street, eager to get as far away from him as possible. If I'd continued talking to him, I couldn't guarantee that I'd be able to keep my powers in check. It would only take one burst of energy to hurt him or trigger a signal to Henley.

As I made my way back toward the hotel, I thought about all of the things I could've and probably should've said to Mr. Weber when I had the chance. I should've told him that because of his greed, he'd permanently ruined my sister's life. The domino effect he'd created meant that he had Lorena's blood on his hands, and I wasn't even sure if he knew. Because of him, his daughter-in-law had almost died. He'd come so close to completely devastating his son *again*.

I turned down a side road, away from the tourists, to be alone with my thoughts. The street appeared to be empty, but I came to a halt when I felt the muscles in my stomach contract. The scenario reminded me of the time Henley's men had tried to grab me, and I'd ended up jumping off a bridge to get away from them.

I stood still and listened, not only with my ears, but also with my mind. If someone were nearby and planning something, I should be able to hear their thoughts.

Everything was silent.

I continued walking back to the hotel but more briskly than before. As I crossed a vacant street, I glanced to my left, down the dark alley. I saw the shadow of a dumpster in the dim lighting but nothing else.

The sound of glass breaking somewhere in the distance made me jump. Instinctively, I stopped again and turned around. There was no one behind me, and I rationalized that the noise had come from the next street over. It was likely someone carelessly dropping a beer bottle on the ground.

I let out a breath, and just as I was sure I was alone, I felt the warmth of a body standing behind me. My stomach clenched as the hairs on my arms stood on end.

Before I could react, a hand clamped down over my mouth, and a muscular arm wrapped around my waist, forcing me into the alley.

SIX

NATALIE

My first instinct was to panic, and I struggled against the arms that had me trapped. Then, thankfully, muscle memory kicked in. Steven had prepared me for this, and I knew what to do.

I let my body lead, going through the motions Steven and I'd practiced repeatedly. With my knees bent, I dropped my weight toward the ground, shifting my elbows outward. My attacker's grip loosened as his body curved into the back of mine, trying to get me upright. I seized the moment to step one leg back and pivot my body into his, driving my elbow into his groin. The strap on my dress snapped.

My attacker cried out as I latched on to his leg, flipping him off his feet and onto his back.

I was about to strike him again when he held out his hands.

"Natalie! Stop!"

I froze in place, recognizing his face. *It can't be …*

"It's me," he said, as if reading my mind. Fortunately, mine was one of the few he couldn't.

"Luke?" My mouth went dry.

He scrambled to his feet with his hands still up, as if worried I would attack again now that I realized it *was* him.

"I'm not here to hurt you," he said.

"That's why you grabbed me and dragged me into an alley?" I watched him closely to see if he'd lunge at me again. If he did, I'd be ready to fight.

"I didn't think you'd talk to me otherwise."

His eyes met mine as he swallowed a lump in his throat. "It's Becca."

Please don't tell me she's dead.

"She's ..." he said, and I held my breath, bracing for it.

The news wouldn't be a shock, considering she was with Henley, but regardless of what she'd done, her death would devastate me.

He cleared his throat. "Well, she's ... pregnant."

My breath came out in one fell swoop, and I just stood there, unsure of what to think or feel. It relieved me to hear she was alive ... but *pregnant?*

"There's more." He paused, checking to make sure I was okay.

I forced myself to breathe again and responded with a swift nod, readying myself for the possibility of pain.

"I need your help," he said, "because the baby is mine."

For a moment, I feared I might explode. The energy, composed of anger and anxiety, consumed me. I paced back and forth, resisting the urge to lunge at him. He watched me in silence, knowing better than to say anything further to provoke me.

After I got my emotions under control, I stopped in front of him, inches from his face. "What is wrong with you? Becca isn't in her right mind because of you. And yet you took advantage of her?"

He stared me down, refusing to be intimidated by my accusation. "I wouldn't, and I *didn't*. If you want someone to blame, it's her. And Henley. They did this."

I closed my eyes, took a deep breath, and talked myself out of punching Luke in the face. A soft vibration coursed through my veins, and I wondered if I'd finally tapped into my adrenaline.

I flexed my hands as I slowly reopened my eyes. "What are you saying?"

"*She* took advantage of *me*."

I waited for him to laugh and tell me it was all just a sick joke, that he'd made it all up to get back at me for kicking him out of the house. That was the story I wanted to believe, but my intuition told me he was telling the truth.

"She seduced me."

My stomach twisted. "That's not an excuse."

Becca was mentally unwell, and he knew better.

Luke reached out, firmly placing his hands on the sides of my arms. He looked me in the eyes, and I could see a hint of sorrow in them. "I thought she was you."

I pulled out of his grasp and stumbled a few steps before sitting down on the curb to rest my shaking legs. He sat with me but kept about a foot between us.

For all I know, my intuition is wrong, and he's making it all up.

If it was a trick to get me to let my guard down, it was working. My defenses were gone.

"Say something," he said, shifting his body to face me.

I had so many questions and none that I really wanted answers to. But I needed to understand the situation better, so we could deal with it.

"How? I mean, *why* would you think she was me?" That part of his story made little sense.

He leaned to the side, dropping his hand to the concrete to prop himself up. "Becca manipulated my thoughts. I didn't know she had powers outside of her intuition, so it never even crossed my mind that it wasn't you until after."

I recalled how Luke had fooled me into thinking he was Michael when I was a prisoner at Henley. He'd done it to stop me from trying to escape because he believed the attempt would get me killed. The only way I figured out it was him and not Michael was because he didn't have the same scars on his arms. Luke had had me so convinced that he was Michael that I actually kissed him before seeing the truth.

The fact that Becca now possessed this ability was troubling. It was bad enough that Luke could manipulate people's thoughts, but he didn't want to harm us. At least, I didn't think he did.

I looked at Luke, recalling the painful events that had led to Becca inheriting these dangerous abilities. "Becca tried to kill herself, but Michael saved her," I said. "He healed her, and it unlocked powers within her, similar to when he'd healed me."

He stared at me in disbelief.

"She killed Lorena when she escaped." I forced myself to remember how to breathe.

Luke's face softened. "I'm sorry. I didn't know. Lorena was … nice, kinder to me than I deserved."

Of course she had been. Lorena hadn't been the type of person to be mean to anyone. Not even Luke.

"If Becca can use mind control, then I guess you can too," he said.

Unable to wrap my head around that theory at the moment, I changed the subject. "How did Becca find you?"

He lifted himself, so he was sitting upright again. "After you told me to leave, I went back to Henley." His tone wasn't bitter or accusatory, but I felt a twinge of remorse.

I'd kicked him out of the house after learning he turned Becca against me, and I had done it, knowing he had nowhere to go. Luke had grown up at Henley and didn't have any experience in the outside world. He might have gone back because he didn't have any other option.

"Luke …"

"No, don't," he said, stopping me. "The only reason I returned to Henley was because I wanted to get information on Project Josie. I thought if I figured out what it was, you'd consider forgiving me."

"Weren't you afraid Henley would kill you?"

Henley wouldn't pardon Luke for helping me escape. He wouldn't just welcome him back with open arms.

Luke flashed a mischievous smile. "I told Henley that you and Michael kidnapped me."

"There's no way he believed that."

Henley was a lot of things, but stupid wasn't one of them.

He frowned. "You're right; he didn't, but I needed to try. He played along at first, but when I realized he wasn't really buying it, I had my escape plan all ready to go, but then Tonya told me they'd captured you."

The sound of Tonya's name made my stomach turn. She was Henley's head nurse and had taken great pleasure in making my life a living hell when I was a prisoner.

"I went to check on you that night, and that's when it, you know, happened," he said.

I stood up. It was a lot to take in.

He rose to his feet as I tugged at the top of my dress again, wanting to make sure it covered me up. With a sigh, I turned to walk back toward the hotel. Although I wasn't sure if it was a good idea to bring Luke with me, I didn't have my phone to call Michael to meet us. I'd left it in my hotel room.

"Where are you going?" Luke asked, catching my arm.

I stared at him, confused. "We're going back to tell the others what happened."

"We can't do that. They won't understand, especially Michael. We should just take care of this and then tell them after."

I jerked my arm from his grip. *Maybe this is a trick to turn me in to Henley.*

There was no way I was going to break Michael's confidence by running off on a random, dangerous mission, especially with Luke. "I'm not going anywhere with you. If you want my help, we're telling Michael."

As much as I believed Luke was telling the truth about the baby, I prepared myself for a fight if he tried to force me to go with him.

He eyed me, as if waiting to see if I'd change my mind. When he realized I wouldn't, he lowered his head in defeat and let go of my arm. "This is a bad idea, but let's go."

Luke quietly followed me onto the hotel property, and I didn't start a conversation with him. I had nothing to say. His presence and Becca's pregnancy added a whole new level of complexity to our situation. Michael was already under a lot of stress, and this additional problem wouldn't help. He didn't get along with Luke, and the fact that he'd shown up out of the blue wouldn't go over well.

As the hotel came into view, I headed toward the courtyard. It was the easiest way to get back to the reception area, and even though the celebration was over by now, I predicted Michael would linger, waiting for me to return.

The second we stepped into the courtyard, I spotted Michael pacing back and forth in front of Raina as she sat on the same bench Aunt Gael and I had occupied earlier.

Michael's enhanced sense of hearing picked up on the faint sound of my shoes as they tapped the concrete, and he swung around in my direction. He flashed me a momentary smile of relief before his gaze landed on my torn strap and then migrated over to Luke's face.

Rage stormed in his eyes as he charged toward us, heading straight for Luke. "What the hell did you do to her?" Before I could intervene, he shoved Luke backward, knocking him to the ground.

"No! Stop!" I pleaded.

Raina jumped up, as if trying to decide if she should pull Michael back.

Michael turned to me, grasping my shoulders as he looked me over. "Did he hurt you?"

I shook my head. "No, I'm fine."

"Yeah, man. You should ask me that," Luke said, standing up and brushing himself off. "She beat me up worse than you did."

Michael gave me a quick squeeze before releasing me and turning back to Luke. "Good. Now, tell me what you're doing here."

I glanced around the courtyard, confirming we were alone.

Luke looked at me, his expression saying, *I told you so.* I didn't care though. Michael needed to know what was going on. I refused to keep any more secrets from him.

"He came to talk to me about Becca," I said.

"What about her?" Raina asked, stepping beside Michael. She peeked over her shoulder, as if Becca might be lurking behind.

"She's not here. At least, I don't think so. He told me she's pregnant." I proactively placed my hand on Michael's chest to stop him from attacking Luke again. "And he's the father."

Michael's expression turned to pure revulsion at the sight of Luke. "There's no end to how low you'll stoop, is there? Was that your sick way of getting back at Natalie for kicking you out?" He shook his head. "Unbelievable."

As much as I didn't want to tell Michael the rest of it, I had to. He needed to know that Becca had mind control powers, making her even more dangerous than we'd assumed. Luke cringed, waiting for me to deliver the final blow that would send Michael over the edge.

"Becca fooled him into believing she was me," I said. "She can manipulate people's thoughts, the way Luke does." I lowered my hand as I avoided everyone's eyes. The situation was beyond awkward.

When I gathered the courage to lift my gaze, I found Michael staring at Luke in disbelief. The storm in his eyes had evolved into a hurricane.

"You son of a—" Michael didn't even finish the sentence as he maneuvered around me and lunged at Luke again.

Raina intervened, trying to peel Michael off him.

"Stop," I said again. "The last thing we need is a scene, to draw attention."

Michael gritted his teeth but allowed Raina to pull him back.

Luke regained his footing and smiled at Michael. "I hear you're to thank for turning Becca into a monster, hero boy."

Before Michael went back into a fury, I jumped in between them. I looked pointedly at Luke. *"Stop."*

Luke, always determined to have the last word, wanted to get under Michael's skin. I understood they had unresolved issues, but if they kept this up, someone would hear us, see them fighting, and call the cops. Not exactly ideal when we were trying to lay low.

I turned my attention to Michael and Raina. "Luke came here to ask for our help. Regardless of how it happened or how you feel about him, the reality is, we have a nephew or a niece who is going to need us."

"A niece," Luke said. "She—*we* are having a girl."

A girl.

"She's due any day now," Luke continued. "I get that you hate me, and that's fine, but I don't want my kid growing up there."

"Why didn't you wait until she was born and escape with her?" Raina asked.

"Are you kidding?" Luke raised his eyebrows. "They were going to kill me the second they cut the cord and confirmed she was healthy. They wouldn't need me anymore. The only chance I have of rescuing her is to go back and catch them off guard."

Michael took a breath, trying to calm himself down. "Where are you staying?"

"A hotel about two blocks away." Luke smiled. "I made the clerk think I was some guy on the cover of the magazine she was reading. She was so excited; she just gave me the room for free."

I grimaced.

"Meet me here at ten in the morning, and we'll go from there," Michael told him.

We needed to be at the airport at nine a.m. to go home. I wasn't sure if Michael planned on us staying longer or if he'd forgotten what time we needed to leave. I decided to just go with it and figure out the details later.

Luke looked at me for confirmation, but the second his eyes landed on me, Michael stepped forward, blocking his view.

"Don't look at her." He pointed to the courtyard exit. "Turn around and go back to your hotel."

Luke opened his mouth to say something but then wisely thought better of it and did as he had been told. Michael sharply watched him until he disappeared around the corner.

"Let's get inside. Just in case," Michael said.

"Where's Alexander?" I asked as Raina and I followed him back into the hotel.

"He said he was tired and went to his room after Seth and Jen left," he replied. "I didn't tell him about you following William though. I didn't want to worry him."

We stepped onto the elevator, and Michael hit the button for the fifth floor, where Raina's room was. His room was on the eighth, and the deluxe suite I'd been sharing with Jen until tonight was on the tenth. He didn't press the button for either of our floors, so I knew he wanted us to go to Raina's and strategize for a bit.

A young couple dressed in shorts and T-shirts got on the elevator with us. The girl looked at my torn dress and disheveled hair, and she gave her boyfriend a concerned look. He turned and glanced at me and then at Michael.

"Things got a little wild on the dance floor," I blurted out, feeling the need to explain my unkempt appearance.

Raina choked out a laugh, and I smiled in response. That was the first time I'd ever made her laugh. I hadn't even known she *could* laugh.

The elevator stopped at the fifth floor, and we got off, leaving the confused couple behind. Raina's room was only two down from the elevator, and I was glad. I didn't know how much more walking I could do in my shoes. It was a miracle I'd chased down Mr. Weber in them. As soon as she opened the door to the room, I peeled them off and tossed them on the floor.

Raina plopped down on the bed while Michael went to the window to pull the curtains tightly closed. I moved a pile of Raina's clothes off the end of her bed and sat down.

"So, if Becca can manipulate thoughts like Luke can, does that mean you can too?" Raina asked me.

"I don't know," I replied. "I've never tried. It never crossed my mind before tonight." The thought of being able to control someone's perception of reality scared me a little. Like mind reading, it just seemed wrong.

Michael crossed his arms over his chest as he leaned back against the wall. "Luke could be lying about the baby."

"But what if he's not?" Raina asked. "We can't just leave our niece with Henley."

I nodded, agreeing with her. "We need to confirm Luke's story."

"I'm going to stay behind and question him for a day or two to see if his narrative changes," Michael said.

I didn't like the idea of him remaining behind by himself. What if this was all a setup and Henley was in St. Augustine, just waiting to recapture him?

As if reading my mind, he said, "I'll be okay."

"We could all stay." My offer was hopeful even though I knew Michael wouldn't take me up on it.

"You can't," he replied, right on cue. "Detective Thompson is already suspicious, and I guarantee he's watching to make sure you come back tomorrow, as planned. It won't look as bad if I'm the only one delayed."

"I wish there were something I could do to help." I dreaded the thought of going back home to twiddle my thumbs and worry about Michael.

He thought for a moment and then said, "If Becca is pregnant, her baby will be invaluable to Henley. He probably doesn't have her drugged up, like he did before."

I sat up a little straighter. "Do you want me to try connecting with her again?" I hadn't attempted since she'd killed Lorena.

"Yes, but be cautious," he replied. "Don't let on that you've spoken to Luke. See what she offers up on her own. Hopefully, you'll be able to tell if she's pregnant just by looking at her."

Raina picked at a pull on the hem of her black dress. "This might be some elaborate story the two of them cooked up together."

Michael looked at me, his expression earnest. "Use your intuition. If something doesn't seem right, bail out. I trust you."

I nodded, recognizing that those last three words meant we'd overcome a big hurdle in our relationship. "I promise I'll be careful."

"Did you speak with Seth's dad?" Raina asked.

With everything that'd happened with Luke, I'd almost forgotten. "Yes. He didn't know what Project Josie was. However, he mentioned someone named Dr. Rees. Does that name sound familiar to either of you?"

They both shook their heads.

"I'll do some digging when I get home," I said. "Mr. Weber said Dr. Rees visited Henley regularly, so it's possible she's near Chicago. It's a long shot, but maybe she has something to do with whatever Henley's planning."

"Be extremely vigilant about going home tomorrow and especially once you get there," Michael warned, looking at me and then Raina.

We had known that already, but he wouldn't be the Michael I loved if he didn't say it anyway.

It was all settled. Michael would stay behind to grill Luke on his story while Raina, Alexander, and I went home. I'd try to contact Becca and research Dr. Rees. I preferred having a plan, especially one where I had a part to play. One that Michael *trusted* me to play.

Michael pushed off the wall. "Want me to carry you?" He reached out a hand to help me up.

"No, thanks. I'll just go barefoot and carry my shoes."

We said good night to Raina and then headed back to the elevator. Michael hit the button for the tenth floor and walked me to my suite.

I opened the door and flipped on the light. All of Jen's stuff was gone. Her dad had sent a bellhop earlier in the day to retrieve her bags and take them to the honeymoon suite, where she and Seth were staying the night before heading to St. Croix in the morning.

"I hope Jen and Seth weren't mad that I'd left early. I'm disappointed that I didn't get to say good-bye," I said.

Michael took off his tuxedo jacket and placed it neatly on top of the couch. "They were so overwhelmed by the number of guests; I honestly don't think they ever put two and two together."

"Okay, good. Hopefully, that means Seth didn't realize his dad had slipped out early too."

"I don't think Seth noticed, but Mrs. Weber did. She complained to your mom about it nonstop after you left."

"Mr. Weber was worried about me blowing up the hotel," I said. "I can't believe he thought I'd do that."

Michael wrapped his arm around my waist and used his free hand to tilt my chin up. "Who cares what a guy like that thinks about you? He thought an explosion was possible, and he left his wife, son, and best friends inside. What does that say about him?"

I understood what he was saying, but it still stung.

"If I contact Becca tonight, will you come home with us tomorrow?" I asked.

He wrapped his other arm around me, folding his hands around the small of my back. "Probably not. Even if Luke's telling the truth, I have a lot of questions for him. Like how did he get to Florida and find us without Henley's help?"

"What if you determine he's lying and it's all a ploy?"

"Then, it's just another day with Luke." He attempted to put me at ease.

As much as I appreciated his effort, I was still a bundle of nerves.

He released me and undid his tie. "I can't wait to get out of this thing. I hate it about as much as you hate those shoes."

I stepped in to help him take it off. "Are you staying here tonight?" I asked even though I already knew he would now that I had the room to myself and had finished my maid-of-honor duties.

He pulled the tie completely off and tossed it on top of the jacket. "Of course I am. There's no way I'm letting you stay here by yourself with Luke in the same zip code. Especially after …" He shook his head in disgust. "I mean, why would he *ever* think you'd sleep with him?"

I bit my lip. "There's something I never told you. The evening before I kicked Luke out of the house, he came to my room."

He tensed. "Did he try something?"

"No," I replied. "He found me upset and tried to comfort me. But then I got the impression that he … I don't know … wanted more. I told him to leave, and he did."

He grimaced. "Why didn't you tell me? I would've saved you the trouble and thrown him out that night."

"You and I weren't on the best of terms, and I was afraid of making things worse," I admitted. "After we made up, it didn't seem worth mentioning. Luke had already left, and I honestly thought we'd never see him again."

"All the more reason for you to head home while I stay here to monitor him." He took off his shirt, revealing the deep scars that ran across his arms, chest, and abs.

I reached out and ran my finger just above the largest one on his stomach, making his breath hitch.

Early in our relationship, he'd worried that they'd repulse me, but that was never the case. Every time I looked at them, I thought about how he was the bravest and most resilient person I'd ever met. They were a part of him and his past, and they were a permanent reminder of all he'd overcome. Despite all the evil done to him as a child, he was still kind and honorable.

His scars were the reason I'd figured out Luke had been pretending to be Michael. Luke's impersonation of him had been flawless, except he'd forgotten the scars on Michael's arms. I cringed, thinking again of how I'd kissed Luke, believing he was Michael.

"I think we need a code," I said.

Michael tilted his head, confused.

"We each need a word that we can use to identify each other. Not all the time, but just if there's ever any doubt. And also, when, you know, we want to make out and stuff ..."

"And stuff ..." His first reaction was to smile, but it faded when he realized I wasn't joking. The reality that Becca or Luke could easily manipulate either of us was unsettling. "Yeah, I agree. Luke fooled you once, and I wouldn't put it past him to try it again."

"What should our words be?" I walked over to my suitcase and pulled out a clean pair of pajamas.

He thought for a moment. "Mine will be *masquerade*."

I wrinkled my nose, thinking back to everything that had happened that night with Lance and Ben. "Why that one?"

"Because Luke would never guess it," he replied. "And that night, after we left the masquerade ball, was the first time I realized you weren't just a girl who'd appeared in my dreams. I discovered, standing out there on the balcony of the hotel with you, that you were really the person I'd fantasized you were. And I knew I had already fallen in love with you."

"Oh." My cheeks grew warm. I knew Michael loved me, but I hadn't realized it had been for that long. I contemplated my word, wanting it to complement his and also have a deeper meaning from my perspective. "Okay, then I want my word to be *fireworks* because our conversation on that balcony, right before the fireworks started, was the first time I opened up to anyone about Becca after she disappeared. You made me feel safe in a way that no one ever had before. And you still do."

He smiled thoughtfully and then touched the dangling strap on my dress. "Did you really knock Luke on his ass?"

I couldn't help but chuckle. "I did."

"I would've paid to see that." A proud grin spread across his face.

He pulled me closer, and I rested my hands against his bare chest.

"You'd better be careful." I arched my eyebrow. "I'm tough, and I could have you on your back in two seconds flat."

"Is that right?" His smile faded as his eyes smoldered. He spun me around so that my back was to him. "That doesn't sound so bad.

Should I be worried?" He unzipped the back of my dress, letting his fingers linger at the bottom.

He kissed down the side of my neck, and I closed my eyes, letting my pajamas fall out of my hand. I felt his heart beating in his chest as it pressed into my back. He slid the other strap of my dress down as his lips worked their way to my shoulder.

Breathless, I reached up and wrapped my fingers around the back of his neck. "Only if you provoke me."

His mouth moved to my ear. "Challenge accepted."

SEVEN

RAINA

"Stop stressing. Michael knows better than to let his guard down around Luke," I said, reassuring Natalie.

She looked up from the seat next to me and blinked.

I hadn't said over two sentences to her all morning, but I couldn't take her twisting her hair around her finger a second longer. For thirty minutes, I'd witnessed her wrap a strand around her index finger and then slowly unwind it again. She'd repeated it over and over while sitting there, staring off into space, and I couldn't imagine dealing with it the rest of the flight home. As much as I appreciated her caring about my brother, she was driving me absolutely crazy.

"I know," she replied quietly, not sounding convinced at all.

She glanced across the aisle to my dad. My gaze followed to find him sitting alone, looking out the window in the same position as the last time I'd checked on him, which had to have been at least twenty minutes ago.

It hurt to see him like that. He missed Mom, and even though he didn't talk about it, I knew, on some level, he blamed himself even though there was nothing he could've done differently.

"So, what happened after you left my room last night?" I asked Natalie, trying to not only distract her, but also myself.

Natalie's face turned as red as her hair.

Ew.

"Let me rephrase that." I didn't hide the fact that she had completely grossed me out. "Did you reach Becca after you went to sleep?"

Natalie sighed. "No. I tried four times throughout the night but couldn't connect with her. So, either Henley is still drugging her even though she's pregnant or she just wasn't asleep when I tried to reach her."

"I'm with Michael. I don't think Henley would risk the baby. She's too important to him." It still blew my mind that I was going to be an aunt. Although I knew nothing about how to fulfill the duty, I envisioned feeding her lots of sweets and then letting her stay up past bedtime. I could handle that.

"Michael told me about Henley's plan for you two to have a baby," she said, catching me off guard.

He told her, and she's still sitting here? Any sane person would've run for the hills after hearing that.

"Pretty twisted, huh?" The idea of having a baby with Michael was revolting. It didn't matter that we weren't blood-related. *He is my brother.* I'd never seen him any other way.

"He also told me that Henley was planning to kill you both if your child proved to be more powerful. I don't blame Luke for being afraid and leaving." She looked down, and I knew she worried about Becca, not that she'd ever admit it to me.

Becca's safety wasn't my concern. She'd been nothing but trouble since we'd rescued her from Henley. Logically, I knew they had brainwashed her into being the person I'd met. Natalie and Seth had insisted she was completely different before. Nevertheless, I'd never get past the fact that she'd murdered my mother regardless of who she used to be.

Natalie reached for her hair again, and I quickly intervened before she could resume her new nervous tic.

"You should try contacting her again," I said. "Maybe attempt a different time or something. Henley probably put her on a weird sleep schedule if he isn't drugging her, hoping to throw you off and keep you away from her."

She pondered it and then nodded. "Do you mind if I try to doze off? The sooner I connect with her and we know if Luke is lying, the sooner Michael can come home."

Finally, some peace.
I grinned. "Go for it."

Three hours later, we were home. Natalie hadn't been able to contact Becca, but she took some melatonin and went to bed to try again.

Dad was quiet on the drive back to the house. We finally told him about Mr. Weber and what was going on with Luke. Despite his concern, he didn't offer any advice on what to do. It was like Mom's death had paralyzed him from making those critical decisions that we had always depended on him for.

Before I could even close the front door, he was already retreating to his bedroom. He mumbled something about wanting to unpack, but I knew I wouldn't see him again until dinnertime. And that was even if he showed up for it.

With Natalie napping and Dad isolating himself in his bedroom, I meandered around the house, bored out of my mind. Normally, I'd convince Michael to go with me to grab a giant triple chocolate fudge cookie from our favorite bakery, but without him there, the treat lost its appeal.

I grabbed my keys off the counter and walked out the front door. I got into the car and started driving, telling myself that I didn't have a destination in mind despite knowing exactly where I'd end up.

Fifteen minutes later, I sat outside the fire station.

This is a bad idea.

J.T.'s truck was outside, but I didn't know if he had been serious about seeing me again. Still, talking to him was the only thing that sounded enjoyable to me.

I opened the door and got out of the car.

The door to the garage where they kept all the emergency vehicles was open. Inside, I spotted two fire trucks and an ambulance. I looked among the half-dozen guys working around the garage but didn't see J.T.

A guy that I recognized as his friend Hector from the bar spotted me and smiled.

"J.T.," he called out. "Your *girlfriend* is here to see you."

I stopped dead in my tracks. *His what?*

J.T. walked around from the other side of the ambulance, confusion all over his face until he saw me.

"I'm sorry," he bellowed as he approached. "My friend here is just jealous because the only female visitor he's ever received was his grandma."

The other guys in the garage laughed as J.T. guided me back outside.

When we were away from the others, J.T. stood there, clearly waiting for me to explain why I was there, but my mind went blank.

This is a mistake.

"Sorry ..." I said, squinching my face even though I knew it wasn't a flattering look for me. "I don't know why ..."

What am I doing here?

He grinned like it was completely normal for me to just randomly show up at his job and not even be able to articulate why. "You caught me just in time. My shift ends in five minutes. Want to grab a coffee or something?"

I loved coffee. It was one of my absolute favorite joys in life.

I shrugged nonchalantly. "Yeah, sure. I mean, if you want."

He snickered. "Okay. Wait here. Let me just change and grab my stuff."

I stood awkwardly out front, waiting for him. Several of his coworkers curiously glanced at me, and I eventually turned my back, so I didn't have to see them. They probably thought I was a total weirdo.

A few minutes later, I heard footsteps behind me.

"Do you want to just follow me?" he asked. "I know a great coffee shop."

"Sure." I pulled my keys out of my pocket as I noted the way his athletic shirt clung to his biceps. *Were his muscles that big the last time I saw him?*

"Wait, a minute." He turned to me, a serious expression on his face. "You'll be okay to drive yourself, right? You're not planning on ordering an Irish coffee or anything, are you?"

I fought the urge to laugh and scowled instead. "No," I replied, although a boozy coffee sounded delicious. I'd never tried one before, but I made a mental note to order it another time.

I followed him about two miles away until we pulled into a large shopping center containing at least ten different businesses. A coffee shop named Dee Dee's sat on the corner.

J.T. reached the door to Dee Dee's first, opened it, and stepped aside, waiting for me to pass through.

I motioned for him to continue ahead of me. "No, go ahead." It was a polite gesture, I guessed, but it wasn't like we were a couple or anything. I was more than capable of holding the door open for myself.

He raised his eyebrows and nudged his head toward the inside of the café. "Are you crazy? My mama would hunt me down if word got back to her."

I rolled my eyes and walked inside.

Dee Dee's was trendy with a rustic vibe to it. The back wall showcased exposed brick with two rows of shelves that housed various bags of coffee and syrups. The main coffee bar was mint green with a shabby-chic finish. An old bicycle hung on the wall above it, like a piece of art.

At the front of Dee Dee's was another narrow, skinny bar, where people could sit on stools and sip their coffee while looking out through the large glass windows. Scattered throughout the shop were a mixture of leather couches, wooden armchairs, and small, circular coffee tables.

We walked up to the main bar, and a woman greeted us. She had a sandy-brown shag haircut with bangs that were cut too short. But she made up for it by wearing a solid black tank top that exposed a myriad of black rose tattoos that ran down her shoulder and onto her forearm. The artistry was beautiful, and I wondered if it would look as good on me.

"What can I get you?" she asked, looking between me and J.T.

He gestured in my direction.

Knowing he'd make me order first, I decided not to waste my time arguing. "A large vanilla iced latte with extra sugar, six pumps of caramel, a chocolate drizzle, and whipped cream on top."

"Wow ... okay." He looked at me in awe before turning his attention back to the barista. "I'll have a small coffee. Black."

Even though J.T.'s puny coffee was only a dollar and mine was almost ten, he insisted on paying for both of ours.

"So, you like sugar," he said as we found two stools at the bar table by the window. "What else do you like?"

I shrugged. It wasn't like I had time for a lot of hobbies.

"How do you spend your time?" he asked, as if rephrasing the question would prevent me from having the most pathetic life on the planet.

I spent my time hiding from Henley and trying to stay alive, but it wasn't like I could tell him that. "I enjoy hanging out with my brother, although he ditches me most of the time for his girlfriend."

He took a sip of his coffee. "I take it, you're not a fan of hers?"

I frowned. "It's not that. I mean, she's okay. It's just that she's *always* there."

"You're jealous of the time he spends with her."

"What about you? Any brothers or sisters?" I asked, trying to take the heat off myself.

Dad had taught us at a young age that it was best to keep the conversation focused on the other person when they wanted too many details about our life. Most people enjoyed talking about themselves, so it worked like a charm the majority of the time.

"I have two brothers. I'm the youngest."

"Are you close?" I tasted my latte and immediately went back for another sip. It was heaven in a cup.

He nodded. "Yeah. They're my best friends. Both are still single, so maybe I'll be resentful like you someday when they get into serious relationships."

"I'm not resentful," I protested. *Am I?*

Two women approached, taking a seat at one of the leather couches just behind us. They wore tight-fitting workout clothes, like they'd just gotten out of yoga class or something.

"Can you believe it just exploded like that? It's a miracle no one died," one woman said.

I stiffened.

The other woman replied, "The news said there've been several explosions and they think they're all connected. The first one was at a house in McHenry. It killed some woman."

Some woman.

The image of my mom lying on the floor flashed into my mind, and I set my drink on the bar.

I'm going to be sick.

J.T. reached out to touch my arm. "We should go."

I wasn't sure if I could move. I felt paralyzed.

He stood up and gently tugged me to my feet before shepherding me out of the café.

As we stood outside, I contemplated getting in my car and heading home. Coming to the fire station had been a mistake. I was delusional to be out with J.T., pretending to be a normal girl, hanging out with him.

It was time for me to be honest with myself. There was no way he liked me, not like that. He pitied me, which was why he hadn't already told me to leave him alone. To him, I was the poor girl who'd lost her mother in a tragic accident. Nothing more.

I opened my mouth to rattle off one of my canned excuses for going home, but he cut me off before I could speak.

"I know what you need," he said. "Come on."

My brain screamed at me to just get in the car and leave well enough alone, but my feet followed him across the parking lot to the opposite end of the plaza.

"*Whizzing Balls*," I said aloud, reading the sign on the door. I raised an eyebrow at J.T. "This is a joke, right?"

"Just trust me." He opened the door and stood to the side. "You know the drill."

Instead of protesting, I let him hold the door for me as I went inside.

"We're … hitting baseballs," I said, taking in the rows of bats behind the counter and Chicago Cubs paraphernalia decorating the walls.

"Yep. It's the perfect way to get you out of your head. And I also had a feeling that you just might want to hit something."

"I've never hit a baseball before." *Or kicked a soccer ball or dribbled a basketball …*

He shrugged off my comment like it wasn't strange at all. "I'll teach you."

I silently followed him around as he rented our batting cage, picked out our bats, and fitted me for a helmet.

"Do I have to wear this thing?" No matter how I tried to adjust it, the helmet was uncomfortable.

He put his own helmet on and winked at me. "Yes. Not even your hard head is a match for a fifty-mile-per-hour baseball."

I scowled in response, which made him chuckle. His dimples pressed tightly into his cheeks, and when they faded, I tried to think of a way to make them reappear.

He led me out of the lobby and to the area with the batting cages. Well, they weren't cages exactly, more like thick black nets on all four sides and the ceiling. They had replaced the flooring with fake turf to give it the feel of a real baseball field.

He walked over to one cage, pulled a piece of the netting back, and stepped through it. He held it for me as I followed him inside.

"What's that?" I asked, pointing to a contraption at the far end of our cage.

"That machine will pitch the balls to you." He handed me a bat and motioned toward the corner of the cage. "Go stand over there, so you don't accidentally get hit. I'll let it pitch me a few, so you can see how it works before you try."

I retreated to the corner, eager to watch.

There was a metal box near the entrance with a large red button and a small black button. "The black one is to start the pitch. The red is an emergency stop," he said before hitting the button to begin.

The machine rumbled to life. He walked over to a white square painted on the fake turf and stood in the middle. He raised the bat and got into position to hit the ball. A red light appeared on the machine and then blinked three times before shooting a ball straight toward him.

He swung, making solid contact that sent the ball flying to the opposite end of the cage. The ball hit the net before dropping to the ground. The machine pitched him ten balls, and he hit each one perfectly every time.

When his turn was up, I clapped. "Wow. Where did you learn to do that?"

"My brothers and I always played, growing up. As a kid, I dreamed of playing for the Cubs someday."

"Why didn't you?" It wasn't because he didn't have talent.

He looked down at the bat in his hand and took a light swing at nothing. "Sometimes, things don't work out the way you want them to."

I sensed there was more to the story but decided not to push him. "Well, you set the bar awfully high."

"Nah," he replied with a modest grin. "Come over, and I'll show you."

I walked over to him and stood in the white square. He reached out and situated me in the same spot he'd been standing in. He stepped into the square with me, and I was suddenly aware of his proximity behind me.

His arms reached around, lifting mine up into the correct position to hold the bat. "Keep your back elbow up," he instructed, tapping on my right triceps. "So, when you swing, you go like this." He guided my arms into a slow practice swing.

"You try," he urged, letting go and stepping to the side.

I took another practice swing.

"Good. Now, when you swing, make sure you pivot your body a little." He demonstrated the motion I needed to take.

I attempted to imitate him, but he shook his head and stood behind me again.

"Like this," he said, placing his hands on my hips and rotating them in the motion they needed to go.

His touch sent a thrill of electricity through my body, and I hoped I could re-create the movement. It was as if my brain were short-circuiting.

He released me and stood to the side again.

"Ready to try hitting a ball?" he asked as I stared at him like an idiot.

I blinked and then nodded, feeling nervous and excited, all at once.

He hit the black button and then ducked into the corner, out of the way.

The machine roared again. I waited for the red light to come on and then held my breath. The light blinked three times, and the first ball flew out and zipped right past my head. I let out a squeal without even attempting to hit the ball. The pitch had been a lot faster than I'd expected. It looked different when it was coming directly at me.

"That's okay," J.T. said. "Now, you know what to expect on the second one."

The next ball popped out, and this time, I swung but unfortunately missed.

"Keep your eye on the ball. It'll help you make contact," he said.

Another ball came out, and I watched as it raced toward me. I swung and felt it make contact. I stood in shock as the ball sailed across the cage, hitting the top of the net.

I screamed with excitement and began jumping up and down in the square box. J.T. leaped from the corner, pumping his fist and cheering me on. He hit the stop button and then scooped me up into his arms. I let him lift me off the ground and spin me around.

"That was amazing!" he said. "You're a natural. It would've been a home run for sure."

I grinned ear to ear. I couldn't remember the last time I'd been this happy. And it was all because of J.T.

As he put me down, the excitement drained from my body. The sobering reality of who I was and how J.T. and I'd met flooded my thoughts.

What the hell am I doing?

It took J.T. a minute to register that my mood had completely shifted, and by the time he put the pieces together, I was already climbing through the net and out of the cage.

I heard him call after me as I took off my helmet and threw it on the floor. I sprinted through the lobby and out the front door. Once outside, I gasped in the fresh air.

I was halfway through the parking lot when he caught my arm.

He turned me around to face him. "What's wrong? What just happened?"

"I—I can't do this. I'm sorry."

He deserved an explanation, but I didn't have one. All I knew was that I needed to get out of there and away from him.

"I don't understand." He yanked off his helmet, never taking his pleading eyes off me. "We were having fun. What changed?"

"I don't deserve it," I blurted out.

She's dead, and I'm here, laughing and cheering.

His soft expression told me he understood. "Don't go. You shouldn't be alone right now."

"But I *am* alone." It was a weight that I hadn't realized I'd been carrying. And now that I was aware of it, I desperately needed it lifted off. "My mom's gone, my dad can't function without her, and my brother and I aren't getting along."

He furrowed his brows. "Well, I'm here."

"You wouldn't be if you really knew me." I was headed into dangerous territory, but I didn't care. "You're only here because you pity me and you think I'm pathetic."

His eyes assessed me as he took in everything I'd just unloaded on him. Finally, he replied, "I think you're a lot of things, Raina, but pathetic isn't one of them. Sure, you are moody as hell. And sarcastic. And stubborn." He flashed me a sly smile.

I looked away. All of those things were true, and I was positive the next thing out of his mouth would be *good-bye*.

"But do you know why I'm here?" he asked as I allowed my eyes to connect with his again. "Because you're also funny, tenacious, smart, and beautiful." He took a step closer as he listed out each attribute.

I wanted to run away, but I froze in place, mesmerized that a person like him would see those things in someone like me.

This thing with J.T.—whatever it was—would never work. I couldn't get into a relationship with him—or anyone. It'd be too dangerous to involve him, not to mention how horrified he'd be if he discovered the truth about where I'd come from and what powers I possessed. He was easygoing and accepting, but there was no way he'd be okay with all the baggage that came from being with me.

Sure, Michael had found somebody to love him the way he was, but I believed it was largely in part because Natalie had powers of her own. I'd never be so lucky.

J.T. searched my eyes, looking for a sign that maybe he'd changed my mind and I'd stay. Just as I was positive that I was going to let him down, run to my car, and never look back, I surprised myself. Instead of bolting away from him, I thrust myself toward him, taking his face into my hands. I wanted to kiss him but hesitated.

What if I'm bad at it?

Before I could overthink it, I pulled him toward me and pressed my lips to his. I expected him to be repulsed and push me away, but he didn't. Instead, he dropped his helmet to the ground, engulfed me in his brawny arms, and kissed me back.

His touch sent shock waves across my skin as his hand brushed against my back, down where my shirt had ridden up. Every nerve in my body lit up as I melted into him.

My phone buzzed in my back pocket, but I ignored it, not wanting the moment to end.

He pulled away slightly. "Do you need to get that?"

"No," I replied, breathless, kissing him again.

It vibrated again, and I sighed, dragging myself away. "Okay, maybe."

I pulled the phone out and realized I had two text messages from Natalie. The first asked me to come home. The second told me she'd "found something."

As much as I didn't want to leave, I knew if she was texting me, then she had good reason. We never texted each other outside of necessity and urgency.

I looked up regretfully at J.T. "I really have to go now, but it's not because I want to."

He smiled, flashing his dimples at me once again, as he scooped his helmet up off the ground. "Can I see you tomorrow?"

I didn't know how to answer him. I wanted to say yes, but with everything going on at home, I couldn't commit.

Seeing my hesitation, he reached out and tucked my hair back, letting his fingers linger by my ear. "Just stop by the station when you can."

Without making any promises, I kissed him one last time before sprinting to my car.

EIGHT

NATALIE

I yawned as I checked my phone. It had been fifteen minutes since Raina had texted back to say she was on her way home.

The house was quiet. Alexander was taking a nap. I'd poked my head in his room about an hour ago to see if he was hungry, but he hadn't stirred, so I'd decided to just let him rest. I made him a sandwich, wrapped it up, and placed it in the fridge, so he could eat it later.

I hoped he'd remembered to take his dream blocker before falling asleep. Frequently, when Michael or I asked him about it, he admitted to forgetting. Without it, he left himself vulnerable to Becca visiting his dreams, although I doubted that she was asleep at the moment anyway.

Since Luke's return, I'd attempted to contact Becca every time I dozed off. I resorted to taking sleep aids to nap, but the moment I realized I couldn't connect with her, I'd end up waking myself up, feeling disappointed and exhausted.

The pressure was on to confirm Luke's story, so Michael could come home. I hated the idea of him being so far away, especially when we didn't know if it was a lie to separate and then trap us.

My phone chimed, notifying me of a new text. I checked it, thinking it was Raina, but it was Steven, confirming he'd received the message I'd sent to him earlier, letting him know I needed to cancel our sessions this week. With everything going on, I didn't think it'd be wise to have him around.

I set my phone back down and contemplated trying to doze off again for a few minutes until I heard Raina's car pull up in the driveway. I sat up straight on the couch, eager to talk to her.

She rushed through the door, her cheeks flushed.

"What?" she asked defensively.

I shook my head, knowing better than to ask her where she'd been. We weren't friends, so she probably wouldn't tell me anyway.

She tossed her keys onto the coffee table. "Did you connect with Becca?"

"No," I replied. "But I have some news."

She plopped down on the love seat and looked at me expectantly.

I folded my hands in my lap, unsure of how this interaction would go with her. Normally, we had Michael as a buffer. "I did some research on Dr. Rees."

"And?"

I scooted to the edge of my seat. "Her name is Elaine Rees, and she's one of the most renowned infectiologists in the country."

She shrugged, unimpressed. "Okay … but I don't understand what Henley would be doing with an infectious disease specialist."

"Think about it," I replied. "When I was at Henley, he tested all kinds of different illnesses on me. He'd need someone like her to pull it off. It's not like you can just run to the store and pick up a dose of avian flu."

She bobbed her head, considering it. "Yeah, I guess, but that doesn't mean she's involved with Henley now. Maybe he just got the goods and then cut ties with her."

I didn't have all the pieces of the puzzle put together, but Dr. Rees was connected to whatever he was planning. My intuition told me I was right.

"She's at a conference in Phoenix," I said. "I have her address, and from what I could tell, she probably lives alone."

She narrowed her eyes and tilted her head. "What are you suggesting?"

I hesitated but said it anyway. "I want to break into her house and see if she has any info on Henley."

"Wouldn't she keep that at work?" She was skeptical, but at least it wasn't an immediate *no*.

"She works in a research center," I said. "But something tells me that whatever her involvement is with Henley isn't legit, so I doubt she'd keep any information tracing her back to him at her job."

She sank back into the love seat, contemplating the scenario. I couldn't tell if she thought I was crazy or if I'd impressed her. "Michael's going to be pissed."

"He can't say I'm going rogue if you go with me." At least, I hoped Michael would see it that way when he eventually found out.

Raina ran her hand through her hair, tossing it from one side over to the other. "Okay, fine. But I'm driving."

There wasn't a single car parked outside Dr. Rees's house. I turned my head to look at it as Raina drove right past it.

"Where are you going?" I asked.

She stopped a block away and parallel parked on the street.

"It's too suspicious to park right outside." She turned off the car and looked at me. "Are you sure you want to do this?"

I nodded, although I'd be lying if I said I didn't have *some* reservations about breaking and entering. But with no way of knowing if I'd ever be able to contact Becca, this could be the only way to find out what Henley was up to.

We suspected Henley was using the explosions to divert our attention. It was possible he was doing it to keep us from learning about Becca's pregnancy, but that didn't explain Dr. Rees. Becca would need an obstetrician, not an infectious disease specialist.

We got out of the car, and I noticed Raina taking a quick surveillance of our surroundings. It was just past nine p.m., and the neighborhood was quiet. There was no one else outside as I casually followed Raina toward the house. We drifted off into the grass to avoid a streetlight.

As we got closer, I regretted not discussing a plan with her beforehand. Michael always insisted that we lay out a detailed approach before making a move. But Raina was more impulsive, like me, and that wasn't necessarily a good thing.

She confidently led me to the back door of Dr. Rees's home, like she broke into houses every day. Feeling a little paranoid, I looked at each window on the back side of the house, making sure all the lights were out. I couldn't find a trace of anyone being home.

Without hesitating, Raina walked up to the back door and pulled a credit card out of her back pocket. "Good."

"What?"

She looked at me, her expression implying it should be obvious. "No dead bolt."

She slid the card into the side of the door, catching the lock on the second try. The door opened, and I was ready to rush inside, but Raina held out her arm, stopping me. She listened for something, but I didn't know what.

Finally, she lowered her arm for me to pass. "No alarm system."

Inside, the house was dark, and I wanted to turn on the light to see where I was going. Raina saw me eyeing the light switch and nudged me. She activated the flashlight app on her phone. I pulled out mine and did the same.

"Don't shine it in any of the windows. We don't want any of her neighbors to see it," she said.

I nodded and started looking around. We were standing in Dr. Rees's kitchen, my light shining on her cherry cabinets.

We made our way out of the kitchen and into the living room, which was tidy and organized but devoid of evidence that an actual human being lived there. She had an abstract painting above the fireplace, but the mantel and the rest of the walls were completely bare. There wasn't a single photograph on display or decor to give any insight into her taste or personality.

Raina disappeared down a hallway just off the living room. A minute later, she quietly called my name, so I followed. There were four doors down the hallway, but only one of them was open. I walked to it and found Raina standing in what appeared to be Dr. Rees's home office.

The room was narrow with a long desk to the left and a floor-to-ceiling bookcase to the right. Raina was already at the desk, so I quickly scanned the shelves.

As expected, there were dozens of medical books, the majority about viruses. I noticed a book on the bubonic plague, and it sent a chill down my spine. Henley had been planning to infect me with Yersinia pestis, the bacteria that had caused the plague, when he held me captive at his facility. Thankfully, I had gotten rescued before he had the chance, or I'd likely be dead.

Raina sucked in a sharp breath. I jumped, startled, and turned toward her. She was standing next to an open drawer, holding a folder.

"What?" I shone my light onto the paper, eager to see what she'd found.

"She locked it in this drawer. It's about the others—the ones who attacked you and Michael at the warehouse. There aren't just the two of them. There're *four*."

I scanned the paper, which confirmed there was one female and three males, and each had their own special powers. Headshots that reminded me more of mugshots accompanied their descriptions. The four of them wore blue scrubs, similar to the ones Luke had worn when he was there.

The female's name was Lovisa, and she had telekinesis, the same as Raina. Through her picture, I instantly recognized her as one of our attackers from the warehouse.

The first male listed was Viktor, and he had superior strength. According to his description, he didn't have any additional capabilities.

The second was Hemming, who could read minds and manipulate people's thoughts, like Luke.

The third was Rolf. He was huge—six foot five with the physique of a bodybuilder. His talent was an enhanced sense of hearing, not strength, but I didn't think it mattered. He was strong either way.

I hadn't gotten a good look at the second person who attacked us at the warehouse, but I was almost positive it was a guy, based on their build. If I had to narrow it down between one of the three listed on this sheet, I'd assume it was Viktor. Rolf's size would've stood out to me, and the assassin hadn't used mind manipulation, so it was likely not Hemming.

There was no mention of any of them having the ability to heal. Perhaps that was why Henley was so obsessed with Michael.

"They are older than us," Raina said, reading further down on the page. "By three years. They were born in a lab in Sweden."

Even more disturbing was what I read next. Not only were their first names listed, but so was their last. *Henley.*

Raina didn't notice as she moved on, rummaging through the drawer and pulling out another folder. She opened it, looked up at me, and frowned.

"What is it?" I asked.

"Information on the tests they ran on you."

I fought back bile as I recalled the needles they'd poked me with and how many times they'd cut me with a scalpel, each time without anesthetic. Sometimes, if I thought about it long enough, I could almost feel the blade glide across my skin. I remembered how it had been so sharp that it would take several seconds after being sliced for me to experience the pain.

"Jeez," she mumbled and then looked up at me. "No wonder you were so sick when we found you. There's at least a hundred listed here."

I didn't respond. Henley had cut, tortured, starved, poisoned, sickened, and mentally ripped me apart at his facility. My days there bled together in my memory, and I knew there were several that I wasn't even conscious of, especially toward the end of my stay.

She closed the folder and placed it back in the drawer. "We need to leave. We've been here about five minutes too long already."

"Okay."

She walked toward the door, and I made one last attempt to find something, anything, that could be useful. I shone my flashlight across Dr. Rees's desk as I trailed behind.

Despite how minimal and organized her home appeared, Dr. Rees's desk was another story. She had pens and random notes scattered across the top. As I followed Raina, the beam of light from my phone danced from sticky note to sticky note. Although Dr. Rees's handwriting was almost illegible, I could tell that she needed to return a phone call to someone named Dave. She'd also had a dentist appointment last week, and she needed laundry detergent from the store.

Then, I noticed a desktop calendar, buried among the notes. It was open to March, and every day within the first two weeks had at least two or three activities listed. She'd scribbled each one in black ink.

Dr. Rees had circled March 9 with a red marker. There were no activities listed for that day or for the rest of the month after it. It stood out like a bull's-eye.

Maybe she hasn't gotten around to updating her calendar? Perhaps that's the reason for all the sticky notes?

A knot formed in my stomach.

I grabbed Raina's arm, stopping her from leaving. She shone her flashlight on the desk while I scanned the dates on the sticky notes.

There was nothing after the 9th.

Raina ran her finger over the red circle; it stood out to her as well.

March 9 was only five days away. Was the date linked to Henley somehow?

The knot twisted tighter, my intuition confirming that something bad was going to happen.

"Let's go," I said.

I was pretty sure the pain in my stomach was a warning about the date, but just in case, we needed to get out of there. My intuition wasn't an exact science, and it often warned me of *immediate* impending danger. We couldn't take any chances.

We silently left the house the same way we'd entered. Raina relocked the door behind us. Concealed by the lack of light, we walked across Dr. Rees's yard, down the street, and back to the safety of Raina's car.

Raina tousled her hair but had said nothing since we'd left Dr. Rees's house.

I wasn't in the mood to talk to anyone, especially Raina, but I felt like we needed to talk through all that we'd discovered.

"Michael told me that Henley refused to name you after you were born," I said, breaking the silence.

"Mmhmm." She dropped her hand back to the steering wheel, staring straight ahead, perfectly content to avoid conversation on the ride home.

"I noticed in Dr. Rees's records that the other four—the ones born in Sweden—not only had first names, but also had Henley as their last," I said. "Why would he name them and not you and Michael?"

That got her attention. She pursed her lips together, contemplating it, before responding. "Who knows? I gave up on figuring out why Henley does the things he does a long time ago."

Something told me it bothered Raina more than she was letting on. Being deprived of a name was dehumanizing, and despite how unaffected she wanted to appear, it had to upset her to learn that Henley had treated them differently.

"Michael said that your names were the first thing you could choose for yourselves, which is why you keep them everywhere you go." I wasn't sure if my next question would be too intrusive, but I asked it anyway. "How did you choose your names?"

She shifted in her seat, her brows knitting together. "Dad helped us." She paused, waiting to see if that would satisfy my curiosity. When I remained silent, patiently waiting for her to continue, she did. "Michael asked him if he had a son, what would he name him? When Dad said Michael, that became a done deal. Luke said he thought it was stupid to pick names since we could only use them in private. Eventually, he told Dad to just give him a name, that he didn't care what it was. Dad named him Luke."

"And what about you? How did you choose Raina?" I didn't want her to feel interrogated, but it was past time for us to get to know each other better. We rarely had moments like this, alone on a car ride without Michael as a mutual distraction.

"Dad mentioned his wife from time to time. I'd never met her, but I could sense from the way he talked about her that he loved her. I wanted to be loved, too, so I told him I wanted my name to be Lorena as well." She ran her hand through her hair again, letting it fall over the left side of her face.

She changed lanes to pass a slow-moving car in front of us. "He tried to convince me to pick a different name, one that was unique to me, but I threw a fit." She laughed at the memory. "To compromise— because it would obviously be weird for me to have the same name as his wife—he suggested I take her middle name, Cecile. But once again, I dug in and refused. Then, he told me about how parents often named their children based on variations of their own name and proposed Lauren. I didn't think that was close enough, so I countered with Raina. It was similar enough to appease me, and he helped me spell it in a way that would really make it mine."

I leaned back against the headrest. I hadn't known she named herself after Lorena. Because of the difference in spelling, I'd never put two and two together. "I can't think of a better person to be named after," I said with complete sincerity.

She sat up straighter. "It sucks, you know? Getting attached to someone and then losing them."

I loved Lorena, too, but the grief I'd experienced when she died could never compare to how Raina and Michael felt.

"Can I ask you something?" There was something about their family that I'd always wondered about, but I didn't want to ask Michael because I worried he'd take it wrong.

"Depends on what it is."

I took that as a yes. "Why do you call your parents Mom and Dad, but Michael calls them by their first names?" I knew he loved them and acknowledged them as his parents, so there had to be a reason behind it.

"I'm surprised you never asked Michael," she replied. "It's just a preference. When Dad rescued us and brought us home, they gave us the choice of what to call them. At first, I called them by their first names, too, but over time, I changed it to Mom and Dad. After a while, it just sounded right."

"But Michael never did. Why?"

"He said it was because he never wanted to forget the sacrifice they'd made for us. They had no parental obligation, but they raised us and loved us even though it meant living their lives on the run."

I couldn't help but smile. "That sounds like Michael."

"My family is all I have. Without them ..." Her voice trailed off, and she hardened her face.

I understood where she was coming from, even more than she probably realized. Until I'd met Michael, the only people who truly knew and understood me were Becca and Seth. Even my own parents didn't. When Becca disappeared, I felt like my world had crumbled apart. All I had left was Seth, and I pushed him away for years because he reminded me of what I'd lost. Back then, I thought it was easier to just continue on alone.

Luckily, Seth never gave up on me and reached out at a time when I was finally ready to face my grief. And then I got to know Michael, and he taught me it was okay to let go of the pain and guilt and move on with my life. Despite the looming possibility of him having to leave me to evade capture, I'd taken a chance on loving him. It was a decision that I never regretted, no matter how challenging or complicated things got.

"Losing someone is scary," I agreed. "But the regret that comes with not opening yourself up to love is even scarier."

She looked over at me but only for a second, and I sensed she wanted to say something. I waited for her to continue, but she just gave me a small smile and then turned her attention back to the road.

NINE

NATALIE

Alexander rubbed his eyes, and despite having had two cups of coffee, he was fading. I'd woken him up when Raina and I returned from Dr. Rees's house to get his input on everything we'd found. I'd felt bad for waking him though because when I had, he'd told me he'd been dreaming of Lorena.

It was almost five a.m., and we'd gone over every detail about what we'd discovered in Dr. Rees's office at least a dozen times. Alexander was just as perplexed as we were.

"I suspected Henley had other children somewhere beyond the two who attacked you at the warehouse," Alexander said. "The fact that they are older means the scientist before me must have created them."

"Scientist before you?" I asked.

"I never met him," he replied, finishing his last sip of coffee. "I just inherited some of his notes."

"March 9th," Raina said, snapping her fingers. "Could that be Becca's due date? Is Project Josie code for her baby?"

It was an excellent theory, for sure—the best we'd come up with all night—but it still didn't quite fit. It didn't explain how Dr. Rees was involved.

"I need to get inside Becca's head," I said, feeling both mentally and physically drained.

Even if she didn't give us insight into what Henley was plotting, at least we'd know if Luke was lying, so Michael could come home. We needed his help in piecing all the clues together.

"Do you want me to give you something to help you sleep?" Alexander asked.

"No, thanks," I replied. "I'm exhausted, so I don't think I'll have a hard time dozing off. I just hope I can reach her."

Five a.m. was a time frame I hadn't tried yet. If Henley had her on a strange sleeping schedule, maybe that would be it.

A little while later, Alexander and Raina retired to their rooms, and I sat alone in mine, missing Michael. I wanted to call him but decided it would be best to wait until we had more information. All it would do was make him worry, and he already had his hands full, keeping tabs on Luke.

I changed into one of Michael's T-shirts and crawled into bed. I closed my eyes and allowed his familiar smell to comfort and relax me.

I felt myself slowly drifting into unconsciousness until I was standing in the woods.

Trees surrounded me on all sides, but one stood out in particular. I remembered it vividly even though my accident felt like it'd happened another lifetime ago. There was no sign of my wrecked car, but the trunk of the tree appeared damaged and charred.

Something on the tree glistened in the moonlight. I couldn't make out what it was, so I approached it to get a better look. Broken glass surrounded the base of the tree, and I was careful not to step on it with my bare feet.

I stood in front of the tree and leaned in, trying to make it out. The tree seemed wet, so I reached my hand out, letting my fingers run over it. As I lifted my hand, the taste of iron and salt hit my tongue before I could even see it, letting me know what the substance was. The memory of how it had tasted in my mouth after the accident made me want to gag.

I attempted to wipe the blood onto my pajamas, but it lingered on the tips of my fingers. My heart raced, and I felt the onset of panic. How did I get back here? *I glanced all around, hoping Michael was nearby to help me find my way out, but all I found was deafening silence.*

Then, a raven landed on the tree, just above my head. It looked down at me, similar to how it had appeared on the hood of my crumbled dashboard. The bird flitted its wings.

I shifted my eyes back down to the tree. A cloud must've passed from blocking the moon because the blood on the bark became easier to see, and now, I could make out the shape of letters.

Natalie.

The raven moved higher to another branch, and I looked back up. It stared at me, and as it did, the reality that I was dreaming set in.

"Becca?" I asked.

The raven turned its head, uninterested in me, and took flight over the trees and out of the woods. I waited for a moment to see if it would return, and when it didn't, I set my focus on trying to connect with Becca.

The trees faded away, and a thick fog appeared. As it evaporated, I stood among a sea of clouds. They surrounded me on all sides. I looked down at my feet, surprised to see that I wasn't floating. I was standing, still barefoot, on a pristine white tiled floor.

I reached toward the cloud directly in front of me, expecting my hand to just push through. It was thick and fluffy but solid, as if it were actually a giant cotton ball.

I pushed on the downy puff, and it easily moved out of my way, revealing a series of pink and gold balloons.

As I moved another cloud out of the way, I ran into something solid blocking my path from the waist down. I looked down and recognized it as the island in my parents' kitchen. Becca was dreaming of our parents' home.

A glittery gold balloon danced ahead, weaving in between the cotton balls, forging a path for me to escape. As I followed it, each cloud I passed turned a shade of stormy gray.

I pushed past the last one and entered my parents' living room, which appeared to be set up for a baby shower.

There was no one else in the room despite it being fully decorated for a party. An oversize gold half-moon hung from the ceiling, and spread across the fireplace mantel was a sign that read, It's a Girl. *Beneath it were dozens of gifts and a fully assembled vintage pink pram.*

"What are you doing here?" Becca asked.

I turned to find her standing at the bottom of the staircase, her fists clenched tightly at her sides. Between them was a pregnant belly hidden beneath a pink floral dress.

I remembered Michael's advice and pretended to be surprised. "You weren't planning to tell me?" I motioned to the pram and then back to her. "I'm your sister."

She took a step toward me. "You're nothing to me or to my baby."

Her words stung, although I should've expected them.

"When are you due?" I tried and failed to sound unfazed by her comment.

"Today." She placed her hands on her stomach.

If she was telling the truth, then that didn't align with the March 9 date in Dr. Rees's office. I was more convinced than ever that her baby had nothing to do with Project Josie.

She looked up at me, darkness in her eyes. "Do you want to know who the father is?"

I played dumb. "Don't tell me it's Henley. He's a little old for you, don't you think?"

She smiled, and the living room faded away. The staircase disappeared, and a mirrored wall took its place. My parents' taupe walls turned gray, and I realized she was taking me to Henley's facility.

As I looked around, I acknowledged I was back in my old room. I recognized the twin bed with the thin, scratchy blanket and the small metal table with two chairs that sat on the far-left side of the confined space.

The air suddenly felt thicker, and I tried not to gasp. I wanted to get out of there, but I had to force myself to calm down. There were still so many unanswered questions that I needed to resolve.

The door to the room opened, and instinctively, I cringed. I expected Henley or Tonya to come inside, but it wasn't either of them. It was Luke, wearing his blue scrubs.

"Natalie!" he said, fear laced in his voice.

I straightened, as if he were addressing me, but instead, he rushed past me to the other side of the room.

I turned to find him standing with another version of me, dressed in a set of gray scrubs. Everything about the setting appeared familiar, but I couldn't recall this exact moment.

I peered over at Becca, who was watching the scene unfold with a satisfied grin on her face.

This isn't my memory—she's showing me one of hers.

"You came," the other me said. "I wasn't sure you'd be happy to see me."

Becca's impersonation of me was flawless. She looked and sounded just like me. It was surreal.

"I'm not happy to see you in here," he replied. "What happened? How did they find you?"

"I came looking for you."

Luke seemed confused. "You did?"

My pretender nodded.

"I didn't think you'd ever want to see me again," he said.

"Why did you come back here?" she asked, changing the subject.

"I came to get info on Project Josie. I thought you'd forgive me if I did."

So far, Luke's story was checking out, but I stayed in Becca's dream anyway to see if I'd witness anything else of value.

Before my imposter answered, Luke stepped back, like he was going to leave. "I'll be back for you first thing tomorrow."

She reached out for him, forged vulnerability in her eyes. "Please don't leave me."

Her actions surprised him, and his face softened. He returned to her and pulled her into his arms, hugging her to his chest. "Don't worry. I'm going to get you out of here even if I have to kill everyone in the building to do it. I won't let them hurt you again."

Becca huffed beside me but didn't stop the memory from continuing in front of us.

The pretend version of me pulled back to look up at Luke. "Stay with me. I can't be alone in here tonight."

"I shouldn't."

"No one ever checks on me during the night. They'll never know you were here," she said.

"That's not it." With his eyes glued to her, he remained completely still, as if he were afraid of what might happen if he moved.

"Then, tell me why."

He swallowed hard. "You know why."

Her eyes lingered on his lips. "I need you to stay."

"What about Michael?" His voice was hoarse.

"It's over with Michael." She inched her face closer, making her intentions clear. "I was looking for you because I need you to know how I really feel about you. About us."

Luke refrained but only for a second before crushing his lips to hers.

She wasted no time. With her arms still wrapped around him, she reached for the bottom of his shirt, tugging it upward. Without hesitation, he parted with her to rip it over his head. He shuddered as she ran her hands over his bare chest and down to his abs.

"Are you sure?" he breathed as he reached for the bottom of her shirt.

She looked him in the eyes and nodded. "I want you, Luke."

He slowly lifted off her shirt and then tossed it to the floor. His eyes lingered on her body before he kissed her again, backing her up toward the bed. She lay down, pulling him on top of her.

He looked down at her—at me—with a tender expression that I'd never seen on him before. He brushed the hair from her face before bringing his mouth down to her neck. His fingers entwined in her auburn hair as she dug her nails into his back, making him moan.

I turned around, unable to watch anymore. Although I knew this wasn't really me giving myself to Luke, it was still wrong on so many levels. I wrapped my arms around myself, feeling vulnerable—and violated.

"You're such a prude," Becca scoffed at me. "You're missing a perfectly good show."

I closed my eyes, wanting it all to stop.

Maybe I should wake myself up. I wanted to confirm if there was truth to Luke's story, and I got what I had come for. I didn't sign up for *this*.

"He wasn't half bad," Becca said. "It makes me wonder what the other brother would be like."

I was grateful for the code words Michael and I had chosen. After seeing this, I wouldn't put it past her to make a move on him just to spite me.

"You're vile," I said, my voice shaking. I opened my eyes and forced myself to look at her.

My humiliation dwindled as anger welled in my chest. This was sick and twisted. She was out of control and needed to be stopped.

I focused my attention on the sordid memory unfolding in front of me and struggled to take possession of it.

I don't know if I can even do this.

"What are you doing?" Becca asked.

She tried to fight me, but I continued to push.

The image of me and Luke vanished, and the gray walls of Henley's facility subsided. In its place were the sage-green walls of her bedroom in our parents' house. Her favorite childhood teddy bear, Sonny, was in his usual place in her bay window as the sunlight beamed through.

A version of the real me, at thirteen years old, walked into her bedroom. She strolled over to Becca's dresser, quietly opened the top drawer, and pulled out Becca's new black shirt.

I'd already asked to borrow it, and she'd told me no on several occasions, but I knew that she'd eventually forgive me after she found out I'd taken it anyway.

Laughter poured in from the hallway. The younger version of me quickly tossed the shirt back in the drawer, closed it, and hid in her closet.

Becca came running through the door with Seth right behind her. They were both fifteen. Seth tackled her from behind, and they landed on the bed with a thump. He tickled her sides as she squealed and laughed.

I remembered seeing them through the slats in Becca's closet door. I'd stayed hidden, not wanting to get caught in her room.

I looked over at Becca, all grown up now, to gauge her reaction to this memory that she hadn't known I had. Her expression showed no emotion as she watched, but she'd stopped fighting me for control of her dream.

A part of her wants to see this.

Seth stopped and rolled over to his side, propping his head up on his elbow to look at her.

Teenage Becca reached up, grabbed the collar of his T-shirt, and pulled him toward her until their lips met. I'd always known their relationship was special and suspected it had taken a romantic turn. Witnessing their kiss confirmed those suspicions.

Becca released him. "We need to head back downstairs before Natalie finds us in here."

Seth sighed. "I thought you were going to tell her."

"I'm going to," she replied. "It's just …"

"What?" he asked, grinning ear to ear. "Are you worried that she won't approve of me?"

Becca giggled, but then her expression turned serious. "No, of course that's not it. But I worry about her. We're her two best friends. She doesn't open up to anyone else, and I don't want her to feel more like an outsider than she already does. Especially not with us."

I paused the memory and turned my attention to the Becca beside me. She didn't look away from my recollection of her and Seth, frozen in time. A part of me felt guilty for showing it to her because Seth was no longer hers, but I'd needed her to see the real her—the person she once had been. I wanted her to remember the girl who had been in love with her childhood best friend but worried about how her little sister would take the news. She'd been kind and empathetic, and I wanted so desperately to believe that she could find herself again.

Otherwise, what kind of mother would she be?

Becca closed her eyes tightly, and when she opened them, the room quickly shifted back to Henley's facility. She was back in bed with Luke, pretending to be me. He held her in his arms, snuggled under the gray blanket, and kissed her forehead.

My heart sank. She was back to trying to hurt me.

"I'm sorry about Becca," Luke told her, still thinking she was me.

She looked up at him but said nothing.

"I didn't know you when Henley ordered me to turn her against you," he continued. "It's not an excuse, but I wish I could go back in time and tell Henley to go to hell. If I had it to do all over again, I'd just let him torture me or do whatever out of retaliation. I shouldn't have let him use me to brainwash her."

She pulled away from him and sat straight up in bed. He slowly sat up and placed a hand on her back, realizing he'd upset her.

I turned my attention back to the Becca beside me—the one I was trying to influence into seeing the truth about what Henley had done to her.

She brought her palms up to her temples, as if she were going to squeeze through them to get to her brain.

"Becca ..."

Before I could utter another word, she screamed.

I flew backward, out of her dream and into the conscious world. I stirred awake and stared up into the ceiling fan spinning above me. The silence in the room felt substantial, given the chaos I'd just witnessed.

The clock on the nightstand said that it was just after ten a.m. I hadn't slept very long, but I knew there was no chance of going back to sleep. I reached for my cell phone and dialed Michael's number.

He picked up on the second ring, and I felt relieved to hear his voice.

"Everything okay?" he asked when I didn't respond.

I sighed. "Yes. I'm much better now that I'm talking to you."

"How's it going there?"

"There's a lot I need to fill you in on, but we can do it when you come home. I just left Becca's dream and confirmed Luke's telling the truth." I pulled the comforter up over my chest. "She seduced him, like he said. The baby's real, and she's due today."

As much as I wanted to tell him about Dr. Rees's office, the other four, and that I believed something was going to happen on the 9th, I wanted to wait until we were face-to-face.

"I'll be out on the first flight I can get today," he said.

"What about Luke?" As much as I didn't want to see Luke, I couldn't help but feel bad for him. What Becca had done to him was horrible, both physically and emotionally.

"You mean, I can't kill him?" he asked, but I knew he was kidding. "I'll bring him with me. I've already given Stan a heads-up that Luke might need a fake ID to get on the plane."

"Just keep your guard up. Becca's mind manipulation might even be better than Luke's." I shivered at the thought of her pretending to be me and seducing Michael next. "You remember our words, right?"

"Of course I do. I plan on using it as soon as I get home." There was a mischievous tone in his voice, and I knew he was trying to cheer me up. When I didn't respond, he turned serious again. "Are you sure you're okay?"

I closed my eyes and tried to pull myself together. He had so much on his mind already, and I didn't want to be another burden. "I just miss you." It was true, of course, but after Becca's dream, I craved the reassurance of being safe, of being *his*.

"I'll be home as soon as I can. I love you."

"I love you too," I replied, staying on the line until he hung up first.

TEN

MICHAEL

Luke opened the door to his hotel room, still half-asleep, although it was almost one p.m.

"Be downstairs in five minutes," I said, tossing his fake ID into his chest.

"Good morning to you too, brother," he replied, but I was already walking away, heading back to the elevator.

I paced around the lobby downstairs, waiting for him. I finally forced myself to sit down when I caught the hotel clerk looking at me. *Calm down. You're drawing attention.*

I was eager to get back to Natalie. Not only was I anxious to find out what she'd uncovered, but I could also tell she needed me. She hadn't sounded right, and running through the scenarios of what'd happened made me uneasy.

I glanced at my watch, and it had been ten minutes since I'd returned to the lobby. Just as I was contemplating going up to Luke's room and removing him by force, he stepped off the elevator.

All he carried was a backpack, and for that, I was grateful. I only had a carry-on suitcase, so at least we wouldn't need to stop and check bags.

The clerk looked up from the counter again and noticed Luke. He winked at her, and she batted her eyelashes at him in return. Without a doubt, she still believed he was some celebrity.

"Thanks for the hospitality, gorgeous," he said to her on the way out.

I didn't acknowledge him as we walked to the rental car and got in. The less we interacted, the better.

Unfortunately, conversing with Luke was all I'd done since everyone else had gone home. Well, interrogate might be a more accurate description. I'd made him recount his story at least a dozen times, looking for any inconsistencies. I'd found none, and now that Natalie had confirmed his story matched Becca's, I could at least go home.

For probably the first time, Luke was possibly telling the truth. And of course, it was about this. The idea of Luke believing Natalie would sleep with him made me want to reach across the car and punch him in the face. I couldn't stop dwelling on the fact that in his perverse, delusional mind, he *had*.

I looked down at my hands as they wrung the steering wheel and forced them to loosen. I seriously needed to cool off. As long as I was this mad, I wouldn't be as alert as I needed to be, and distractions were dangerous.

"If you ever show up in Natalie's room again, I'll break your jaw," I informed him, hoping that would make me feel better.

"She told you about that, huh?"

I scowled. "We're honest with each other, although I know that's a foreign concept to you."

"Fine. I deserve that," he said. "But you don't have to treat her like fragile glass. She's a lot more capable of taking care of herself than you give her credit for."

"I'm aware of that," I snapped, growing more agitated with him by the second.

If I had another option—other than bringing Luke home with me—I would take it in a heartbeat. The creep appeared to be fascinated with Natalie, and I didn't want him within a hundred miles of her, let alone under the same roof. Even if Natalie could defend herself, it didn't give Luke a right to put her in situations where she felt like she had to. I didn't know if he truly had a crush on her or if he just wanted her because I loved her. Either way, it didn't matter. I wanted him out of our lives as soon as possible.

Then, I remembered the baby, my niece, and realized that being rid of him also meant I would be without her too. I didn't want that regardless of who her parents were.

"Any idea where Henley is holding Becca now?" I asked.

We needed to formulate a strategy to save his daughter. I'd been so preoccupied with questioning Luke that I had given little thought to a plan.

"They are at the same facility where they held Natalie before."

That surprised me. I assumed Henley would've changed locations to make it harder for us to find Becca and the baby.

When we'd rescued Natalie from that facility, Raina had exchanged gunfire with one of their security guards. She was positive that she'd shot him. The story never made the news, so either she was mistaken or Henley had covered it up somehow. I was betting on the latter because, surely, someone would've at least heard the shots and reported it.

"How do you know they are still there?" I asked.

He casually turned down the air conditioner. "Because Becca has been contacting me in my dreams since I escaped."

I almost pulled over. *He's just now telling me this?*

Instead of reacting, I took a breath and let him continue.

"She's trying to use the baby to get me to rejoin them," he said. "I don't think Project Josie was just a figment of Natalie's imagination. I believe it's real, and whatever it is, it's so important to Henley that he wants the numbers on his side."

I debated on keeping my mouth shut but tested the waters. "Henley's been using Becca to create a bunch of explosions all over the state. Natalie and I think it's an attempt to distract us from whatever he's really planning."

Luke folded his arms across his chest. "No, that's probably Lovisa."

"Lovisa?" *Who the hell is Lovisa?*

"One of Henley's other children. I got the pleasure of meeting them when I returned. Let's just say, Lovisa makes Raina seem like a ray of sunshine."

"Blonde?" I recalled the woman who'd attacked me and Natalie at the warehouse.

"Yep."

There had been a man with Lovisa at the warehouse, but I hadn't gotten a good look at him.

"Did you meet any others like her?"

"I met four, close to our age, maybe older," he replied with a shrug.

I strangled the steering wheel again. I'd spent countless hours questioning Luke, and he'd waited to disclose this information on the car ride to the airport.

What else is he hiding?

He leaned his head back against the headrest. "Henley has a picture of a little girl on his desk. For the longest time, I assumed it was his kid, but I don't know. Maybe he has more like us, only younger."

I cleared my throat, determined to stay focused on getting as much information from him as possible. "Could it have been Lovisa as a child?"

"Doubtful. This girl had dark hair and freckles. They look nothing alike."

"I can't imagine Henley as a parent," I said, although I couldn't imagine Luke being one either.

He reclined his seat back, getting more comfortable. "I would've thought his obsession with us all having kids would be enough for him."

Luke's words lingered like a sour stench in the air, making my stomach turn. Sure, Henley had wanted me and Raina to have a child, so he could see if they were more powerful than us. Our escape denied him of that opportunity, which prompted him to shift that focus onto Luke and Becca. I hadn't considered that one child wouldn't be enough for him. He'd want them *all*.

I realized that if Natalie and I ever had children of our own, Henley would hunt them as well. In fact, he'd likely chase them even more aggressively than he pursued us, believing their powers would evolve far beyond what either of us was capable of. It'd be wrong of us to bring an innocent kid into that life.

"Natalie said Becca is due today. Do you think there's a chance that she cares about your baby enough to leave Henley on her own?" It was a long shot, but it sure would be easier to save someone who *wanted* to be rescued.

I expected Luke to shoot my idea down instantly, but he pondered it for a moment. "Maybe ..."

"What makes you say that?"

"After we—" He cleared his throat, realizing he'd better adjust his choice of words. "When I still thought Becca was Natalie, I apologized for brainwashing Becca. It caught her so off guard that it broke the guise. I didn't let on that I'd discovered it was really her because I didn't want to lose my advantage to escape."

"You planted doubt in Becca's mind about the lies Henley had been feeding her?"

"By accident, but yeah, potentially."

"Natalie visited Becca in her dream, so we'll see if she believes there's hope in getting through to her."

I wished there were a way, but I was hesitant to have the conversation with Natalie. We'd attempted many times to undo the damage done to Becca, but we'd been unsuccessful. I hated to see each failure result in Natalie's disappointment. Not to mention the fact that the longer it dragged out, the more dangerous Becca became.

"Natalie told me about Lorena," he said, interrupting my thoughts. "That sucks."

It might have been the first genuine thing my brother had ever said to me. I didn't know how to respond, so I just nodded to accept his condolences.

The taxi pulled up in front of our house, and I groaned.

"What?" Luke asked.

I paid the driver, and we got out of the car. "Just go along with whatever I say," I told Luke as we walked past Detective Thompson's car in the driveway.

I opened the front door and stepped inside with Luke right behind me. Natalie, Raina, and Alexander sat on the couch while Detective Thompson sat directly across from them in an armchair, sipping on a cup of coffee. It appeared to be three on one, but it was clear who had the upper hand.

The detective's back was to me, but the second he heard the door open, he stood up and turned around. Natalie shot me a nervous look.

"You finally made it home," Detective Thompson greeted me, a false friendliness in his tone. "Natalie told me you decided to spend an extra day in St. Augustine."

He was baiting me to talk, to explain why I had been in St. Augustine, hoping to catch me contradicting Natalie's story. When most people were nervous or lying, they tended to overexplain. Thankfully, Alexander had trained me well.

"How can I help you, Detective?" I asked, turning the conversation back to him.

"I'm in town, and I thought I'd stop by to make sure everyone made it back safely. And, of course, to see if Natalie recalled any details from the pub explosion that she forgot to mention the other day."

How did he figure out that Natalie was there to witness it? Maybe he didn't, and this is just a test to trip us up.

I opened my mouth, not sure how to respond to him, when Natalie jumped in.

"I explained to the detective how disoriented and shaken up I was from the whole thing, which was why I left and came home instead of staying and giving a statement."

"So, we're all settled then?" I asked, looking expectantly at Detective Thompson.

He smiled tightly. "Apparently, she was so upset that she completely forgot to mention it when I stopped by that same night."

I kept my expression indifferent, refusing to give him the reaction he was looking for. "This has been very difficult for her."

He noticed Luke standing quietly behind me and extended his hand. "I don't believe we've met. I'm Detective Ray Thompson."

"That's Luke," I intervened, not wanting Luke to say anything if I could help it.

Luke narrowed his eyes as he shook his hand, and I realized he was probably reading the detective's mind.

I stepped around Luke and opened the front door, giving Detective Thompson a not-so-subtle hint that it was time for him to go. He didn't have a warrant, so he and I both knew he couldn't stay if I flat-out asked him to leave.

The detective placed his mug down on the coffee table and walked to the door. He stopped in the doorway to give Natalie one last knowing look. The second he cleared the threshold, I closed the door behind him.

"What the—" Luke said, but I held up my hand, cutting him off.

I listened for the detective's car to start, pull out of the driveway, and head down the street. Then, I lowered my hand. We couldn't risk him being outside, eavesdropping.

I ignored Luke and focused instead on Natalie. "How did he know?"

She frowned. "A traffic camera recorded me and Jen leaving the bridal shop and walking to the pub when it blew up. Then, it showed us getting in the car and leaving. At least, that's what he claimed anyway."

"He thinks you're involved," Luke told her.

"I know ..." she replied and then quickly diverted her eyes from Luke. She crossed her arms protectively over her chest as color rushed to her cheeks.

"Raina, can you show Luke to his room?" I asked, wanting to put some distance between him and Natalie. Clearly, his presence made her uncomfortable.

Without saying a word or acknowledging Luke, Raina got up and started walking toward the stairs. Luke raised his eyebrows but followed her without protest.

Alexander stood up and grabbed the detective's empty mug off the table. "I'll be in the kitchen if you need me."

He was trying to give me and Natalie a minute alone, and I appreciated him for it.

I sat down next to her on the couch and put my arm around her shoulders. She leaned into me, wrapping her arms tightly around my waist, and I planted a kiss on the top of her head.

"I'm so glad you're home," she said with a deep sigh.

"You and me both." I hated being away from her, especially when there was so much crap going on around us. "What did you find out? Anything about Project Josie?"

"I discovered Dr. Rees is an infectiologist, and I think something's going to happen on the 9th," she replied. "I just don't know what."

"Why the 9th?"

She peeked up at me. "I saw it circled in red on Dr. Rees's calendar."

I didn't understand. "Where did you find that?"

She cringed. "In Dr. Rees's home office."

What?

I forced myself not to overreact. I recalled Luke's comment from earlier and promptly reminded myself that Natalie wasn't fragile. She could take care of herself, and the fact that she was sitting here with me now was proof of that.

"Did you go alone?"

She shook her head. "No, Raina went with me. Don't be mad at her though. It was my idea."

I made a mental note to deal with Raina later. "What else did you find?"

"Um, information on Henley's tetrad." She sat up straight and faced me. "At least, that's what Raina and I are calling his other children."

"Lovisa …"

Her eyes grew wide. "You know about her?"

I nodded. "Yes. Luke told me about her and the other three."

She explained to me what she'd found out about them—how they were older than us and each had their own powers, very much like me, Raina, and Luke.

"But none of them have the ability to heal," she said. "I think that explains Henley's obsession with you. You're different from them."

"So are you," I reminded her. I had been born in a lab, but she had these abilities naturally. Me saving her life had only unleashed the dormant powers that she'd already possessed. That made her more valuable to Henley than any of us.

She frowned. "And apparently, Becca is now too."

As much as I didn't want to admit it, I was to blame for that. Without thinking about the consequences, I'd healed Becca after she slashed her own throat. All I could think about was how much it would hurt Natalie if Becca died, so I acted on instinct and healed her.

It never dawned on me that Becca had the same latent abilities as Natalie and I'd activate them by saving her. I hadn't understood the magnitude of what I'd done until I realized she'd escaped, murdered Lorena, and attempted to kill Jen.

If I'd chosen differently and just let Becca pass away by her own doing, she'd no longer be a threat to us, and Lorena would still be alive. But being a healer, it wasn't my natural reaction to just let people die.

Natalie pulled away from me. She ran her hands over her face and then stood up. "I need to talk to Luke. Will you come with me?"

I stood up without hesitation. I knew Natalie could handle Luke on her own, but I still didn't like the idea of her being alone with him. Not to mention, she was asking me to go, which meant she felt uneasy in his presence.

"I'm hoping Luke can shed some light on what we found in Dr. Rees's house," she said as I followed her up the stairs to Seth's old room.

The door was slightly open, but Natalie paused in the doorway, knocking instead of just barging in.

Luke was standing at the dresser, unloading clothing from his backpack. He smiled when he saw her, but it quickly disappeared when he saw me walk into the room behind her.

He leaned up against the wall next to the dresser. He folded his hands in front and then quickly crossed his arms across his chest. "What's up?"

Natalie walked over to the bed as if she was going to sit down but then appeared to change her mind and continued to stand. "What can you tell me about Dr. Rees?" she asked Luke.

He shrugged. "She's a doctor who works for Henley part-time. She used to come in about once a week, but I think she might be full-time now."

"What makes you think that?" Natalie asked.

"She was there every day after I returned to Henley."

"Why?"

Luke tilted his head, confused by her line of questioning. "I assumed it had something to do with the runaways. There were more of them when I returned. About three times the amount as compared to before."

Natalie had told me all about the teenage runaways. Henley would bring them to his facility, make them sick, and then test his *miracle cure* on them—the one capable of healing any condition. His experiment wasn't working though, and according to Natalie, it was actually killing them.

"Why so many?" Natalie asked.

"Henley must think he's close to creating his cure," I replied. "I wonder if Dr. Rees is playing a role in developing it."

"Or she's the one making them sick in the first place," Luke said. "She brought in the different diseases to infect Natalie."

Natalie nodded. "I was afraid of that. Are you aware of anything happening at Henley on March 9th?"

Her mentioning the date to Luke surprised me. Whatever had happened in Becca's dream must've made her confident that he was on our side and not Henley's.

Luke dropped his arms to his sides. "That's the deadline Becca gave me to return to Henley." He leaned his head back against the wall and looked up at the ceiling. "They threatened me and told me I had until midnight on the 9th."

It all made sense. The diversion and now this. Henley wanted to ensure none of us was a threat to stop whatever he was plotting. Whether we were preoccupied or recaptured, he was trying to stay in control. If neither of those tactics worked, I was positive he'd just kill us instead.

"What did Becca say would happen if you didn't comply?" Natalie asked.

He kept his eyes fixed on the ceiling. "She said I would never meet my daughter."

Natalie wandered over to the window and pulled back the white curtain, so she could look outside. "We have to find out what's happening on that date. Whatever it is, it's tied to Project Josie. My intuition can sense it."

"Do you think Becca will tell you if you visit her again?" I asked.

She watched a squirrel climb up the tree outside the window. "No. Henley will expect that, especially since I already contacted her."

"Then, what are you proposing?" I could tell she was already coming up with a plan.

"I need to go to the last place Henley would expect me to check, the one place he'd be unprepared." She let go of the curtain and turned to look at me. "I want to visit Henley's dream."

ELEVEN

RAINA

I kicked my legs out as I looked down at my black sneakers. The white soles were dirtier than I'd thought when I put them on, and I regretted not opting for my boots instead.

J.T. swung past me. The frame of the swing set creaked with each shift of his body.

"I haven't done this since I was a kid," he said. "I hope this thing can handle my big-boy weight."

After Luke had gotten settled, I'd snuck away to see J.T. I wasn't ready to tell Michael about us yet, so I left a note on the refrigerator, saying I was going out to run errands, and slipped out the door. I drove to the fire station, thinking I'd just stop by to say hi to J.T., but lucked out because he was about to go on break. To avoid the attention of his coworkers, he'd suggested we walk over to the park across the street.

He brought his swing to a halt and leaned in closer to me.

"I was hoping I'd see you today," he said, giving me a peck on the lips.

My lips warmed upon contact with his and wanted more.

He hopped up off the swing. "What have you been up to since yesterday?"

He reached down for my hands, and I let him pull me up.

Oh, you know, breaking and entering, lying to the police, trying to stop the evil plans of a crazed lunatic—the usual.

I shrugged. "Not much. Just hanging out."

For the first time in my life, I regretted lying about it. I'd never felt bad before because I knew deep down that it was a necessity in order to protect myself and my family. But it was different with J.T. These lies created barriers in our relationship even if he didn't realize it.

"Are things getting any better with your brother?" he asked.

He led me over to the empty merry-go-round and released my hand, so he could give it a good spin. I half-expected him to hop on it, but he didn't. Instead, he just watched it turn, as if curious to see how fast it would go.

"Things are okay, I guess. He just got back into town today, so he's hanging out with his girlfriend."

"The one you don't like."

"She's not *that* bad," I replied. "She just isn't my family."

"Not yet anyway," he said. "But you should figure out how to get along with her just in case that changes someday."

His comment caught me off guard, although it shouldn't have. Of course, it was likely that Michael and Natalie would get married one day. But even then, it didn't mean she'd consider herself to be *my* family. I hadn't exactly given her much reason to like me.

"What's irking you so much about her?" He pulled the merry-go-round to a sudden stop and then leaned against the railing, giving me his full attention.

I didn't know how to put it into words. It wasn't like I'd explored the feeling much myself.

"Well, I guess it's because it's just been the four of us for so long. My dad, my mom, me, and Michael. It was us against"—I almost said Henley but corrected myself in time—"the world. Now, all of that has changed. Right from the start of their relationship, they all just accepted her as if she were one of us, like she'd just been there the entire time."

They all trusted her, loved her, and would do anything for her. I wasn't there yet, and I didn't know how to be. It felt like my family had made this incredible shift without me.

"Cut yourself some slack," he said. "Not all relationships develop on the same schedule. Sounds like you two just need some more time."

Deep down, I suspected he was right. Natalie wasn't a bad person, and the fact that she'd gone to Henley to rescue Michael proved how much she loved him. I was clueless about how to build a relationship with her though, one where I accepted her like a sister. It wasn't like

I'd figured out how to have a decent bond with Luke, and he was my actual brother.

"Enough about me," I said, changing the subject. Thinking about my problems was exhausting. "What did you end up doing last night?"

"My brother came into town," he said nonchalantly.

"Is that a bad thing?"

He shook his head. "No, not at all. It's just that he has to work, so I won't get to spend too much time with him."

"Well, I happen to know someone who's willing to keep you entertained," I said, surprising even myself. I'd never experienced this version of myself—fun and flirty.

A smile spread across his lips as he pulled me closer, wrapping his arm around my waist.

I leaned in and kissed him, letting my mouth linger for a moment. As I pulled away, I rested my hands on his shoulders. My fingertips drifted over a hard line beneath his shirt on his right shoulder. It wasn't a seam because it was only on the one side.

"My scar," he said. "Rotator cuff surgery."

I moved my hands up and looped them around the back of his neck. "Is that why you stopped playing baseball?"

He frowned. "It happened senior year of high school. I had a full scholarship to Louisiana State University but tore it while pitching a doubleheader."

I rubbed the back of his neck, a slight gesture to show him how much I cared even if I didn't know what to say. I'd never had a passion in life, a dream, but I still couldn't imagine the heartbreak of having one and then it being taken away.

"I can't be too bitter though." He managed a smile. "Things work out for a reason. As much as I love baseball, I also enjoy having a job that allows me to help people."

"What made you decide to become a paramedic?"

As tragic as the injury was to his baseball career, I was glad that he'd found something else to give him purpose. It gave me hope that maybe one day, I'd find mine.

There has to be more to life than running from Henley and just trying to survive.

"About two months after my surgery, my brother got shot. A paramedic saved his life. I'd never been so grateful for another human being before."

For someone who appeared to have a normal life, he'd sure been through a lot.

He let out a soft laugh.

"What's funny?"

He shook his head. "Nothing. Just a joke between me and my brother."

I grinned, wanting to know more. "Tell me."

"My brother wanted me to follow in his footsteps and go into law enforcement."

I tilted my head in confusion, still not getting the humor in it.

"Because of my name," he explained.

"Oh?" It suddenly dawned on me that I didn't know J.T.'s actual name.

"Justice," he replied, recognizing that I had no clue. "Justice Thompson, but everyone's always called me J.T. for short."

The smile dropped from my face. "What?" Surely, I'd heard him wrong.

"Justice," he repeated. "Ray still teases me about it to this day, telling me it's not too late for me to change my mind."

My hands shifted back to his chest, this time pushing him away from me. I needed to distance myself. "Your brother is *Detective* Ray Thompson?" The words spilled out of my mouth in a hurried panic.

"Yeah, so? You already knew that."

I gave him another shove. "No, I didn't."

He reached for me to bring me back to him, but I jerked away.

"What's wrong?" He sounded confused, but he wasn't fooling me. He'd deliberately manipulated me.

"Don't play dumb with me." I didn't hide my irritation. "He's investigating my family."

I can't believe I fell for this … for him.

"He's investigating the person who killed your mother." He tried again to touch me.

"Get away from me!" I yelled.

He quickly retracted and put his arms up defensively.

"How could I have been so stupid?" I asked myself aloud as I pivoted around and started walking back toward the fire station, to my car.

J.T. kept pace with me. "Can we talk about this?"

When I didn't answer, he stopped walking. "Fine. But for the record, I'm not the one who's constantly running away."

I halted and spun to face him. "Are you seriously going to pretend like this wasn't all some trick to get me talking?" Before he could answer, I continued, "All of those questions about Natalie. You don't care about me; you were just using me to get dirt on her."

His nostrils flared. "I asked you about Natalie because you obviously have some kind of issue with her. I was trying to help you."

"Yeah?" I stepped an inch closer. "I think you're full of crap. I've been opening up to you, and you've been running back to give your brother intel on my family."

"Ray's work is his business, not mine."

I huffed. "You really expect me to believe that this is all just a coincidence then? Do you think I'm that naive?"

"All right," he said. "Maybe I should've double-checked to make sure that you knew I was related to Ray, but I still don't get why you're *this* mad. What are you afraid of?" He narrowed his eyes as he looked deep into mine. "What are you hiding?"

I glared back at him, unable to look away and unwilling to show him how he really affected me.

He leaned closer. "Raina, do you know who killed your mother?"

There it was. The question he'd been dying to ask me since his brother had put him up to the task.

I remained firm, unmoving and refusing to answer. His assumption that I'd confess was infuriating.

As he watched me, the tension left his body, and both his posture and his expression softened. "Are you in some kind of trouble?"

His warm brown eyes pleaded with me to trust him. As much as a part of me wanted to, the wiser part wanted me to run away and never lay eyes on him again.

"I'll help you—with or without Ray—if you just level with me about what's going on," he said.

I wanted to believe him. The thought of having someone out there, beyond my family, who loved me and wanted to protect me was a desire I hadn't even known I possessed. Just a few minutes earlier, I'd empathized with J.T. about how he never got to live out his dream. Now, I found myself in the same boat, and it was excruciating.

"We're done," I said, my voice strangled. Without waiting for a response, I turned and sprinted out of the park, across the street, and to my car.

I jumped into the driver's seat and pulled out of the parking lot, making a conscious effort not to look back at J.T. He'd used me to help his brother gather information on my family, and for that, I'd never forgive him.

Less than a mile down the road, I pulled off onto the shoulder and put the car in park. I just sat there, unsure of what to do next. My heart wanted me to turn around and talk it out with him. More than anything, I wanted him to convince me I had it all wrong and that he truly cared about me the way I'd allowed myself to care about him. My mind, however, reminded me that my heart was an idiot with really poor judgment.

The night J.T. had approached me in the bar, had he planned that out in advance? Perhaps his brother had tailed me and asked J.T. to stop there after work. J.T. had played it off like he was just concerned about my well-being, but what were the odds that I'd run into him right after his brother came to the house and unsuccessfully interrogated us?

I gripped the steering wheel as I screamed at the top of my lungs. Hot tears streamed down my face, and I didn't know who I was angrier with—J.T. for using me or myself for allowing him to.

The glass on a nearby lamppost burst, sending tiny sparks of fire raining toward the ground.

I knew better than this.

My parents and Michael had always warned me about getting too close to people. They'd told me how dangerous it was to let my guard down, to reveal too much.

I attempted to run through every conversation I'd had with J.T., searching for interactions where I'd slipped up and said something I shouldn't have, but my mind wouldn't cooperate. Every time I pictured him, all I could see were his dimples and the kindness in his eyes.

It was all a lie.

I didn't know how long I sat there, but at some point, I decided it was time to go home and face the music. As much as I wanted to put it all behind me and never think of J.T. again, it wasn't the right thing to do. I needed to come clean about it all. I had to swallow my pride and tell Michael.

And I thought he was mad at me before.

When I got to the house, Luke was the only one in the living room. He was watching TV.

"What's up, sis?" he greeted me.

I stiffened. "Where is everyone?"

"Alexander is in his room, Natalie is getting ready for bed upstairs, and Michael is in the kitchen." He flipped off the television. "And I think I'm going to call it a night too."

Without saying another word, I left him and headed into the kitchen.

Michael was sitting at the kitchen table, staring at a piece of pecan pie. He had a fork in his hand, but he wasn't eating.

"Do you want this?" he asked when he saw me enter the room. "I'm not hungry."

Pecan pie was one of my favorites, but just the idea of food made me feel nauseated. I shook my head.

Michael eyed me as he put the fork down on the plate. "What's wrong?"

As much as I didn't want to tell him about J.T. and admit that he'd been right about me getting involved with a stranger, I had to. We were in more danger because of my carelessness.

"I wasn't running errands," I said. "I went to see J.T."

He sat back in his chair, surprised by my revelation. "Okay ..."

I straightened my back, preparing for the worst. "I just found out that he's Detective Thompson's brother."

He rubbed his hand over his face and then glared at me. Without saying a word, I knew he was thinking, *I told you so.*

"It's over," I said, as if it would offer some bit of comfort. "I won't see him again."

"What does he know?"

"Nothing." It annoyed me how Michael had immediately assumed I'd spilled all of our family secrets to J.T. at the first opportunity. "He asked some questions about Natalie, but I didn't tell him anything that would give his brother any ammunition against us."

He pushed his chair out and stood up. He threw away the slice of pie and then dropped his empty plate into the sink. The clank of it hitting the stainless steel was so hard that it surprised me it hadn't shattered. "Seriously, Raina, I don't need this right now, not from you. *You know better.*"

I wanted to argue with him, but he was right. I'd been aware of the risk and let my guard down anyway.

He turned to face me and rested his hands on the sink behind him. "I understand you're going through a lot. We all are. But that doesn't give you an excuse to go against everything Alexander taught us."

As the words came out of his mouth, my cheeks grew hot.

"So, don't tell anyone our secrets? I'm pretty sure you broke that one when you told Natalie *everything*. And then she turned around and told Seth and Jen," I replied. "We always stick together, no matter what, and you took Natalie to her aunt's house instead of leaving St. Augustine with us. We agreed not to use our powers on strangers, and yet you healed Natalie and Becca." I held up a finger as I listed each infraction. "So, please, tell me the part again where it's important to follow all the rules. Or is it only acceptable when you break them?"

He slammed his hand on the ledge of the sink. "I'm doing the best I can. Do you think any of those decisions were easy for me?"

"Do you think my life is painless?" I asked, my voice cracking. "You have no clue how terrifying it is to realize that I have no future, no purpose, no career, and no hope of ever getting married and having a family of my own. I'm destined to spend the rest of my life living on the run, in fear, and all alone."

My heart ached as I said the words aloud. But it was true. I'd just been shielding myself from the pain of my reality for so long.

"You're not alone." His tone was softer, borderline regretful. "But you have to open up to us, not to some person off the street. And if it makes you feel any better, I won't have any of those things either."

I shook my head, defeated, certain that he was missing my point. "You have Natalie."

He glanced toward the stairs, and I assumed it was to make sure we were still alone. "I can't give her an actual future. Not the one she deserves anyway."

"What?" *He can't be saying what I think he's saying.*

"I need to let her go. It's for the best."

I stared at him, dumbfounded. "You brought her into all of this just to abandon her? That isn't fair. I thought you loved her."

I didn't care where Natalie and I stood. What Michael was proposing was wrong.

"I do, more than I ever thought possible, but she's upstairs right now, getting ready to go into Henley's dreams, and I can't ignore the fact that I've dragged her into a life of misery. I won't let her do this forever." He roughly raked his hand through his hair. "I'm going to get her out of this mess somehow. She deserves a normal, safe, and happy life. And the first opportunity I have to give that to her, I'm going to take it."

TWELVE

NATALIE

I'd just finished slipping on a tank top and pajama shorts when I heard a knock on my bedroom door.

"Come in."

The door opened a crack, and Luke poked his head inside. "I can't. Your boyfriend threatened to rearrange my face if I do."

Of course he did.

"I'll come to you," I said as I tossed my dirty clothes into the hamper.

I stepped out into the hallway and took a quick look around. It was quiet, so I assumed Michael was downstairs and Raina was still out, running errands.

He leaned his shoulder against the wall as he faced me. "About this whole Henley dream-creeping thing, I don't want you to do it."

"Why is that?" I wondered if it was because he had something else to hide.

He sighed. "I've lived with Henley my entire life, and he's ..."

"Evil?"

"Well, yeah," he agreed. "His mind is going to be a dark place. Are you sure you really want to explore it?"

He didn't have to tell me how disturbing and twisted someone's dreams could be. I'd found that out all too well during my last encounter with Becca. The memory made my cheeks flush, and I wrapped my arms around my waist, suddenly aware of how much skin I was showing.

He looked me over. "What's with you? You've been acting strange since I got here."

As much as I didn't want to discuss it, I knew we had to. With the baby coming, I needed to clear the air with him and move past this whole uncomfortable situation.

I gestured to his bedroom, and he raised his eyebrows skeptically in response.

"I'd rather talk in private," I said. "Michael can't blame you if it was my idea."

Luke didn't seem convinced of my logic, but he led the way to his room anyway.

As if things weren't awkward enough, I shut the door behind us.

The last thing I wanted was to be in a room alone with Luke. I also didn't want to give him the wrong impression; plus, I knew it would upset Michael if he found out. But we needed to talk, and it was a conversation that needed to be had in private.

I deliberately stood on the opposite side of the room, away from him, as he watched me curiously.

"There's no easy way to say this, but Becca showed me what happened," I said. "Her pretending to be me, with you. She did it mainly to hurt me, I think."

"How much did you see exactly?"

I cringed, knowing it was likely embarrassing for him too. "Pretty much everything."

He creased his forehead. "Well, that explains a lot."

I stood there, mortified and unsure of what to say next.

"Look," he said, breaking the painful silence that had settled in the room. "I don't want things to be weird between us. You're …" He looked up, as if searching for the words to appear in the air. "You're the only person who doesn't hate me one hundred percent of the time."

I relaxed a little. "No, it's only about ninety-nine percent."

He grinned. "That's fair."

My cheeks felt hot again. "I should go."

"Can I ask you something?" Luke blurted out as I started toward the door.

I stopped. "Sure."

He swallowed hard, as if the words were stuck in his throat. "I know you're in love with my brother, but what would've happened if you'd met me first? Would you have thought of me differently?"

It was an impossible scenario for me to speculate on, but for Luke's sake, I tried. "Maybe." He deserved my honesty even if it wasn't the response I *should* give him. Michael definitely wouldn't appreciate it. "But that's not the reality of our situation, is it?"

"No, I guess not." He watched me thoughtfully.

I opened my mouth, ready to reassure him that I cared for him as a friend despite everything we'd been through. I wanted him to know that I had forgiven him for brainwashing Becca when I heard his heartfelt apology in her memory.

Before I could say anything, he cut me off. "You should go before Michael finds you in here."

Unable to tell him what he wanted to hear, I turned back toward the door.

"Be careful," he warned as I reached for the handle. "Whatever you do, don't let Henley discover you're in his head."

I gave him a nod of acknowledgment, and then I left and walked back to my room.

Once alone, I turned out the lights and lay down in bed. I stared up at the outline of the ceiling fan, just as I'd done after waking up from Becca's dream.

My mind wandered back to the conversation with Luke, and I wondered if I should've handled things differently. Maybe I shouldn't have told him about Becca's dream and tried to work past the discomfort on my own.

I hadn't decided yet if I would tell Michael about what Becca had shown me. He was already on guard around Luke, and telling him would only make it worse. I didn't even know what I would say exactly.

It was easier for Michael to think Luke wanted me out of spite. That was what I had believed too—that his attraction to me was nothing more than a twisted form of revenge for all the bad blood between the two of them. But after viewing it myself in Becca's memory, the situation was much more complicated than that. As I recalled the way he'd fervently gazed at me on the bed, I knew he genuinely had feelings for me. It was something I hadn't seriously considered before.

I rolled over to my side, hoping to shut out my own thoughts. My issues with Luke would have to wait. I needed to clear my head, so I could complete my task of gaining access to Henley's thoughts.

No, I didn't want to see behind the curtain, into Henley's twisted mind, but I needed to. The stakes were higher than ever, especially now that my niece was in the picture. Henley needed to be stopped before he could carry out whatever awful thing Project Josie really was. I just hoped he wasn't taking dream blockers similar to the ones Alexander had created for us. If he was, I'd never connect with him.

Surely, Henley wouldn't think I'd be bold enough to invade his dreams. After having me in captivity, he'd appreciated that I feared him and taken joy in giving me reasons to. But Henley always had and probably always would disregard my persistence and dedication. He likely thought I'd written off Becca after the attack, but he was wrong. I still loved my sister, and he underestimated the determination I possessed to get her back.

I yawned but planned to stay awake until Michael came in to say good night. Earlier, he'd said he'd stay with me to make sure I was okay when I woke up. But as I lay there, forcing thoughts of Luke out of my head and focusing only on what needed to be done, my eyelids became heavy as my mind prepared to dive into the unknown.

I closed my eyes and felt myself drifting off. Before my consciousness could talk me out of it, I sought Henley in the darkness.

I stood at the bottom of a grand staircase in a dimly lit foyer. A massive crystal chandelier that was at least six feet in diameter hung from the ceiling of someone's home. Beneath my bare feet was a cold marble floor.

The sound of a piano playing in a nearby room interrupted the silence. Because my dad was a classical music fan, I instantly identified it as Beethoven's "Moonlight Sonata."

I followed the music, listening as it grew louder with each step, until I stood in the entryway of a study. The room was situated with several tall bookshelves and two floral chenille jacquard upholstered armchairs. A round pedestal table sat between them.

The chairs, although empty, faced the ebony-finished grand piano.

Seated at the piano, almost hidden in the shadows, was a boy, no older than twelve years old. Even in the low lighting, I could make out the squareness of his jaw and the sharpness of his eyes. As the realization hit, I dipped back into the hall, lingering just outside the door. I didn't want him to know I was there.

THE AWAKENING

Peering from around the corner, I stole another glimpse of this adolescent version of Henley. He focused on his performance, lost in the music, which he played with expert precision.

As if an eclipse had come through the room, I watched as a deeper shadow took over, inch by inch. Henley must've noticed it, too, because he stopped playing and folded his hands in his lap.

A man wearing a perfectly tailored gray suit passed by without noticing me and entered the room. He was a middle-aged man with an intense stride, similar to the adult version of Chad Henley.

"Did I tell you to stop playing?" the man asked as he loomed over Henley.

Henley looked up at him with fearful eyes. I'd never seen him look intimidated before. He placed his hands back on the keys, ready to resume.

The man scoffed. "Never mind. You've never played it right anyway. Despite thousands of dollars in lessons, you continue to be inadequate. Do you have any idea how disappointing that is?"

Henley kept his eyes fixed on the sheet music in front of him but failed to hide the terror written on his face.

The man stomped an inch closer to Henley. "Look at me, boy."

Henley swallowed and then trailed his gaze to look at the man in front of him.

"Play Chopin's Prelude in E Minor," the man said. "And if I hear one mistake, I'll put you in the cellar."

Henley cowered before flipping through his sheet music. His trembling hands touched the keys, but when he pressed them, they played a string of sour notes.

The man reached out, grabbed Henley by the shirt collar, and yanked him up from the bench. Henley let out a wail before the room turned pitch-black.

I forced myself to stand still, wondering what had happened, afraid to move. Henley, the more intimidating version I knew, could emerge at any moment.

I am in his mind after all.

Over the sound of my heavy breathing, I heard orchestra music play in the distance, playing the song the man had demanded from Henley. I turned back toward the foyer and realized it was coming from upstairs.

Step by step, I followed the music. As I ascended the stairway, the house faded, and in its place was an elegant ballroom. Men in tuxedos and women in sparkling evening gowns mingled as they sipped champagne. I looked down at my attire to find I was still in the pajamas I'd gone to bed in.

Worried that Henley would easily spot me because my clothing was so out of place, I tried changing it. I wasn't sure of how that worked—or if it would at all—but I made an attempt. The first dress that came to mind was a one-shouldered, floor-length scarlet gown that I'd seen in a magazine once. I remembered thinking it was the most beautiful dress I'd ever seen but couldn't fathom a situation where I'd ever wear it.

As I recalled the details of the dress, how the fabric gathered at the right shoulder and then draped down the back, my pajamas faded into this much more appropriate attire.

Able to blend in with the crowd, I searched for Henley among them. I wouldn't approach him, of course, but I needed eyes on him. His reaction to the things going on inside his own head was the key to understanding him. He was dreaming of all this for a reason.

"Know your enemy. Anticipate their next move," Steven had told me. "Staying ahead keeps them from having the upper hand."

No one in Henley's dream noticed me as I moved about, looking for him. I tried to listen in on their conversations, to gain some insight into what Henley was thinking, but I couldn't decipher their muddled words. Henley wasn't dreaming of them having actual conversations. It was just the general sounds you'd expect from a large gathering of people.

The music halted, and Henley's voice filled the room. "Ladies and gentlemen, may I have your attention, please?"

The inaudible chatter stopped, and everyone turned their attention toward him.

On the other side of the room, Henley stood center stage, alone, in front of a microphone. He wore a black tuxedo as he smiled confidently at the crowd. "It is now time for our grand finale of the evening. It's a moment that I've been waiting a very long time for, and without a doubt, it's one that will go down in history."

He paused as clear Plexiglas walls emerged from the floor of the stage. He stood still and unalarmed as they formed four walls and a ceiling above him until it completely boxed him in. His friendly smile transitioned into one that was far more sinister, and I realized something bad was about to happen.

I heard a few coughs scatter across the room. Within seconds, it spread, and the gagging intensified. I turned around, viewing from every direction as the other partygoers struggled to breathe. They choked on their own breath and grabbed on to each other for support before collapsing to the ground, one by one. A man clawed at his bow tie, frantically trying to get it opened before falling on the floor right at my feet. I jumped out of the way to avoid him landing directly on top of me.

I watched in horror as the woman next to me turned blue. The blood vessels broke around her hazel eyes, turning them a deep red before she dropped to the floor.

I wondered if I should throw myself on the ground and pretend to be one of them. It wasn't a rational thought, but a part of me panicked and worried that if I did, I'd die too.

"Chaddy!" a child's voice called out.

I spun around to see a little girl standing in the doorway to the ballroom. I froze as I realized it was the same girl I'd dreamed of. The one who had claimed to be Josie, the one who had almost led me and Michael to our graves as we tried to save her.

She was approximately six years old with shoulder-length dark brown hair. But it was her eyes that made me confident she was the same person. I'd never forget those round blue eyes and how terrified they'd been as she begged me to save her.

Josie wore a pale pink dress with ruffles that trailed down the skirt and white tights. It reminded me of the type of dress my mother would make me wear for family photos when I was her age.

My first instinct was to go to Josie and protect her from Henley, but I forced myself to remain still.

This is just a dream, and Henley can't really hurt her—not here anyway.

Then, it sank in that she'd called him by name—and a friendly version of his name at that. She hadn't called him Henley or even Chad. She'd called him Chaddy. It wasn't the name you called someone you were afraid of.

As the last of the partygoers collapsed around me, Henley didn't seem to notice. His attention was only on Josie.

She placed one foot, adorned with a sparkly pink shoe the same shade as her dress, on the ballroom floor.

"No, Josie!" Henley called out, his arms stretched out, as if trying to reach her through the clear wall. "Stay there."

She paused and looked at him curiously.

"Listen to me," he said. "Go home to Shirley. It's not safe here. You'll get very sick."

She considered his words and then shrugged. "But I already am."

She brought her foot forward until she was fully standing in the ballroom with us. Within seconds, she began to heave, her tiny shoulders bobbing up and down.

"Josie, no!" Henley placed his hands against the glass, horrified at what he was seeing.

She grabbed at her throat as she looked at Henley.

It was hard enough to view adults suffer in Henley's twisted thoughts, but watching a child struggle to breathe was unbearable. To my surprise, Henley seemed to think so too. He pounded on the glass, throwing his body weight into it, trying to break through it.

But it was too late. We watched as she crumbled to the floor. Her little body just lay there, motionless, in a pink dress that almost seemed too large for her now.

Henley fell to his knees. "No," he wailed, slamming his fist against the clear wall one last time. He seemed to be in such distress that I expected him to wake himself up.

He leaned his forehead against the glass, defeated. He actually cared for Josie, whoever she was. It was a side of Henley that I hadn't realized existed.

His grief distracted him, and I knew I should leave. But I was absorbed in this bizarre nightmare he'd concocted, and I needed to stay and figure out what it all meant.

Is Josie his child? Luke had once told me he thought Henley had a family.

Henley's eyes met mine the second I looked up at him. His nostrils flared as he stared me down. I wasn't sure what'd just happened to Josie or any of the other people in the room, but I got the distinct impression that Henley blamed me. Or at the very least, he planned to make me pay for it.

Relax, Natalie. He doesn't know you're really here. This isn't real. Just play along and let him think you are part of his dream.

Henley's despair diminished, and his ominous smile returned.

The protective walls shattered around Henley, hitting the stage floor and breaking into smaller pieces. He hadn't hit the glass; it had broken under the pressure of his glare.

I had a choice to make. I could either force myself to wake up or choose to remain there with him. If I allowed myself to wake, Henley might realize I'd invaded his dream. In that case, we'd lose our advantage over him. There was no way he'd allow me to have another chance to explore his mind.

I stood my ground, trying not to give anything away in my face despite being petrified.

He hopped off the stage with ease and stormed toward me. I wanted to retreat, run, do anything, except stand there and face him, but I forced my legs to remain planted where they were.

Inches from my face, he surveyed me. Then, he circled, like a shark inspecting its prey before attacking. He stopped behind me, and I braced for the worst.

I expected him to hurt me, but his breath skimmed my ear instead. "We're about to have a little fun."

Before I could react, Henley squeezed my shoulder, and the room melted away, like hot wax against a flame.

In its place were the gray walls that often haunted my own dreams. I looked down and realized that I was no longer in my beautiful gown. I was in my standard Henley uniform—gray scrubs.

Henley's hand continued to push me down until I sat in a metal chair. I knew where this was going.

My heart pounded against my chest. Every fiber in my being screamed at me to bolt, to wake myself up before any of his torture games started, but the stubborn voice in the back of my mind urged me to stay. It negotiated with me, assuring me I wouldn't actually experience the pain. Not physically anyway.

Metal clamps appeared out of the arms and legs of the chair and wrapped firmly around my wrists and ankles. Even though I couldn't feel them touching my skin, they locked me in place.

Henley stood in front of me, and I noticed the mirrored two-way glass wall behind him. Next to him was a cart with a tray of medical tools. I immediately spotted the scalpel.

He followed my gaze and seemed amused as he picked it up. "It never would've come to this if you'd just cooperated in the first place."

Despite my best attempts, I couldn't take my eyes off the weapon in his hand as he approached.

Without hesitation, he ran the blade across my arm. It didn't hurt, but it was like my brain remembered the sensation and tricked me into believing it was real. As panic took over, I inhaled a deep breath, determined to stay in his dream.

Henley stood silently, watching my wound heal itself.

"You're brave and obstinate," he said. "But what you'll come to realize is that I always get what I want, one way or another."

As if he'd flipped an invisible switch, the mirror in front of us disappeared, revealing the room on the other side. Only it wasn't an observation room, as I'd expected it to be. It was a morgue.

Dr. Leeman, the man responsible for delivering the majority of both my torture and care at Henley's facility, stood inside the morgue. To his right were four gurneys, each containing a body covered by a sheet.

"You can continue to test me," Henley said as Dr. Leeman lifted the sheet off the one closest to him.

It was Lorena, as lifeless as she'd been when the ambulance carried her away to the real-life morgue. The sight of her made my heart ache all over again.

"But I always win," Henley continued.

Dr. Leeman pulled the sheet off the next body, revealing Alexander beneath it. I fought the urge to scream. Lorena and Alexander were like parents to me. The idea of losing both of them was unbearable.

As Dr. Leeman removed the sheet from the third body, I looked away the second I realized it was Raina's.

This isn't real.

Henley smiled at my torment. "You know who the last one is already, don't you?"

I heard Dr. Leeman rip the sheet from the last gurney, and I couldn't bring myself to lay eyes on him.

"Look," Henley demanded. When I refused, he reached down, pinching my chin between his fingers and forcing my head to turn.

Michael's body was so cold that it was almost purple. His eyes were open, staring blankly at the ceiling. The whites of his eyes were red, overshadowing the blue hue that I loved so much. Hot tears stung my cheeks.

"What do you want from me?" I asked through gritted teeth. I should've remained silent, but my emotions had taken on a life of their own.

Henley released me as he tilted his head curiously. His lips curled into a snarl. "Your blood, of course." And with that, he flicked the scalpel across my throat, slicing it open.

The wound didn't hurt, but streams of blood poured from my neck and down my shirt. It oozed over my abdomen and down my legs, flooding the floor.

I closed my eyes tightly. This isn't real. I'm alive, and I'm safe.

It surprised me that the terror hadn't yet forced me awake. But I couldn't stay there any longer. Not after this.

In my own nightmares, I could change the course of it once I realized I was dreaming. I didn't know if I could do that in someone else's, but I had to try. That would be my only chance of getting out of there undetected and with my sanity. I'd been able to show Becca a memory in hers, so maybe it would work.

I opened my eyes and stared down at the clamps around my wrists, refusing to become distracted by the red droplets that splashed against the floor. Instead, I focused on the cuffs and tried to force them open.

I felt Henley fighting for control of the dream. It was like a heavy weight pushing on my thoughts, but I resisted against it, shoving back with all my might until the restraints broke free. They released first from my hands and then my ankles. With shaking legs, I stood up from the chair.

Henley seemed shocked, but I couldn't tell if he suspected me. For all he knew, this was his own dream, taking an unforeseen turn.

A part of me wanted to lunge at him, to hurt him as much as he wanted to hurt me and those I loved, but I bolted for the door instead.

I slid on a puddle of my own blood, falling to the ground. Soaked and shivering, I got right back up and continued to run. I ran as if the devil was chasing me.

Because he was.

Thirteen

Michael

A scream echoed from upstairs.

Natalie.

I bolted out of the kitchen and to the stairs. I flew past Raina, who was sitting in the living room, alone.

Luke had been in the living room right before Raina came home. It concerned me he wasn't there now. Eager to get to Natalie, I took the stairs two at a time until I reached the top.

If he so much as laid a finger on her …

The door to Natalie's room was open, and my eyes landed on Luke the second I passed the threshold. He sat on the side of her bed with his hand on top of hers. As soon as he registered I was in the room, he stood up.

I shoved him. "What do you think you're doing?"

"Me?" He caught himself and charged back toward me, stopping inches away from my face. "I'm doing *your* job. She screamed, and I came in here to check on her."

I clenched my hands at my sides, unsure yet if they'd remain there. "I told you to stay out of her room."

He gritted his teeth and stepped around me, intentionally bumping into my shoulder as he passed.

Raina stood in the doorway, eyeing Luke, but she moved to the side to let him leave.

Luke paused in the hallway. He turned his head slightly but didn't make eye contact with me. "The next time your girlfriend goes into the mind of a psychopath, maybe you should try keeping your word and be there for her when she wakes up." He took a breath and then calmly walked back to his room.

When I heard his door shut, I turned to Natalie. She stared off into nothing as she trembled. I didn't need her to confirm that she'd connected with Henley. Her body language said it all.

I hurried to her side, feeling like a failure for not being there when she came out of the nightmare. I'd intended to, but I hadn't realized she'd gone to bed so soon. Time must have gotten away from me.

Before I could apologize to her, she closed her eyes, as if in pain. "My blood ... so much blood."

"What?" I asked, alarmed.

There wasn't any blood on her face or arms, but I promptly yanked the covers down to look her over.

I didn't see any traces of blood on her pajamas or legs and let out a sigh of relief as I sat down beside her on the bed.

"You're okay." I pulled the blanket back over her. "I don't think you're injured."

Her teeth chattered, so I wrapped my arm around her, trying to warm and comfort her.

"You're safe," I whispered, lowering my lips to kiss the top of her head.

I shot a wary glance at Raina, who stared back at me with mirrored concern.

"It was awful," she said as I continued to rub my hand up and down her arm.

I waited for Natalie to stop shaking and for her breathing to become even again before urging her to tell us what had happened. "It's probably a good idea to talk about the dream before too many details slip away." As much as I didn't want her to have to think about it, I also didn't want the entire experience to have been for nothing.

She took a deep breath before going into every gory, unpleasant detail. She told us about the man she believed to be Henley's father, then about the ballroom where all the guests and Josie mysteriously died, and then how Henley noticed her and took her to his facility. When she got to the part where Dr. Leeman revealed our dead bodies, Raina turned her face away, trying to hide the emotions it stirred up in her. I did my best to remain silent and strong for Natalie as she recapped how Henley slit her throat and she had to take control of the dream in order to escape.

"The blood was everywhere," Natalie said with a shudder. "It seemed so real."

We sat in silence for a moment as Natalie laid her head on my chest. I stroked her hair, wanting to soothe her but knowing I could never take away the horrifying things she'd seen in Henley's mind.

I shouldn't have let her do this.

What made Henley's dream so frightening was, we knew this was what he really wanted to do to us. It wasn't a surprise. He'd do it in a heartbeat. Henley wanted me and my family out of the way, so he could have Natalie all to himself. She was special, and her natural gifts made her particularly valuable to him. Without a doubt, he'd steal every last drop of blood from her if given the chance.

"Josie is a real person," Natalie said. "And whoever she is, Henley cares about her."

"Henley doesn't care about anyone, except himself," Raina replied.

Natalie lifted her head. "Henley was different with her. The idea of her getting hurt terrified him." She looked between me and Raina. "Is it possible that Josie is Henley's daughter?"

I almost shook my head but then recalled the conversation I'd had with Luke in the car. "Luke told me he saw a picture of a little girl on Henley's desk. I wonder if it's her."

"I remember Luke telling me that, too, when I was with him at Henley's facility," Natalie replied. "But even if she is his daughter, I don't understand her connection to all of this."

I rubbed my head, trying to figure it out. "I don't either. But she *has* to be … somehow."

The next morning, I turned over in bed, searching to make sure Natalie was safely beside me. My hand landed on her back, and I let it rest on top.

She stirred.

"Sorry," I said. "I didn't mean to wake you."

She rolled over onto her side and opened her eyes to look at me.

"Did you get some sleep?" I asked.

She nodded. "Yes, but not much. Every time I realized I was dreaming, I'd force myself to wake up. I know I can't accidentally end up in Henley's dream, but I worried *I'd* have a nightmare about it ... if that makes sense."

"It does." I understood because it was all I'd dreamed about throughout the night. Every time I'd closed my eyes, I'd see Henley hurting Natalie and me being powerless to stop him.

I hated putting Natalie through the torment of seeing what was inside Henley's mind. If I could have done it myself, I would have. Regardless of whether it was in the conscious or the unconscious world, I didn't like her being anywhere near Henley. Clearly, he had the power to hurt her either way, and I consistently failed to protect her.

She deserves better.

She lifted her hand and laced it into my hair. I felt the strands stretch and then fall freely between her fingers.

I'd give anything to wake up next to her every morning for the rest of my life. As I let the thought linger, a sadness crept over me. That wouldn't be how our story ended, not if I wanted to keep her safe. If Henley got his hands on her, there'd be no guarantee that I could stop him from hurting her. My best bet was to get her somewhere secure before he got his chance.

I gently pulled away and sat up, sensing her confusion as I turned away.

She took a small breath, and just when I thought she'd ask me what was wrong, the doorbell rang.

It was probably just a solicitor, but we couldn't take any chances. I jumped off the bed, still fully dressed from the night before, and hurried downstairs.

As I approached the front door, I braced myself, as I always did, for the worst-case scenario. If it was Henley or one of his people, I had to be prepared. I'd need to react quickly and be ready to fight.

In the back of my head, I heard Natalie say, *Henley wouldn't be polite enough to knock.* That was the primary reason I always insisted on beating her to the door.

As I placed my hand on the knob, I realized it could be Detective Thompson coming back to question us some more. After Raina's recent lapse in judgment, there was no telling what his brother had told him about us.

I opened the door to find two friendly faces that I never would've expected to see. Well, not this soon anyway.

"Surprise!" Jen squealed, throwing her arms around me.

"What are you doing here?" I asked, hugging her back. Without a doubt, I was glad to see her and Seth, but I couldn't help but think about how they should be on their honeymoon, far away from all the danger.

She released me, and I exchanged a fist bump with Seth before moving to let them inside the house.

"Well, we landed in St. Croix, had one overpriced fruity cocktail, and realized that even though we were in paradise, we wouldn't enjoy it, knowing you guys were here, dealing with, you know, *everything*," Seth said.

"Oh my gosh!" Natalie said as she ran down the stairs and straight into Seth's arms. She held on to him, squeezing him tight. "I'm so glad you're here."

He gave me a concerned look before she released him. As she hugged Jen, I shook my head, letting him know I'd fill him in later.

Raina trailed slowly down the stairs. She stopped at the bottom of the staircase and exchanged a chin nod with Seth.

The doorbell must've woken Alexander up because he came out of his room. His eyes were still heavy from sleep as he greeted them.

Luke appeared at the top of the stairs, and Seth and Jen paused, as if they weren't sure what they were seeing was true.

Seth looked at Natalie. "What the ..."

Natalie sighed. "It's a long story. I was going to tell you but not while you were on your honeymoon."

"We're here now, so what's going on?" Without a doubt, Seth imagined the worst.

Natalie motioned for him and Jen to sit down on the couch in the living room. The rest of us found seats as well, except for Luke, who wisely stood by the front door in case he needed a quick escape.

"Before I tell you this, I need you to understand it wasn't Luke's fault," Natalie told Seth.

I stiffened, not completely agreeing with her statement.

Seth wasn't a fan of Luke's either. He shot daggers in Luke's direction before turning his attention back to Natalie. "Just tell me what's going on."

"Becca's pregnant, and Luke is the father," she said, concise and straightforward. "They're having a girl."

Seth glared at Luke, imagining exactly what I had at first—that Luke had seduced Becca in her unstable condition. Even though Seth wasn't in love with Becca anymore, he still cared about her and wouldn't want anyone to hurt her.

"This is Becca's doing though," Natalie said. "She tricked Luke into thinking she was someone else."

Natalie hadn't told Seth that she was the "someone else," but her face flushed with embarrassment. I decided not to clarify the point either. It didn't need to be said aloud more than it already had.

"So, you have a niece coming," Jen said, breaking the tension with her optimism. "If nothing else, that's something to be happy about, right?"

Natalie nodded, but her face was solemn, not happy. "Yes, but we can't let her grow up at Henley."

"Of course." Jen's smile faded as she considered our niece's fate. "Obviously."

"Things are going to get ugly around here," I said. "Henley has something planned for the 9th, but we don't know exactly what yet. We think it has something to do with Project Josie though. Between dealing with that and rescuing the baby ..." I let my voice trail off, unwilling to say what was on the tip of my tongue. *We probably won't survive.* "No one will blame you if you change your mind and go back to St. Croix. I think that would be the safest place for you right now."

Seth turned and looked at Jen. They seemed to have a silent conversation between them before Jen replied, "We aren't going anywhere. We want to help."

"Detective Thompson is all over us," I added, purposely keeping my eyes off Raina. "More so than ever before."

As angry as I was with her, I wouldn't throw her under the bus. There'd be a time and a place to tell everyone what had happened. And it really didn't matter anyway. Detective Thompson had already been suspicious, and I knew Raina wouldn't flat-out admit our secrets to J.T. Without a confession, everything was still circumstantial.

"We're staying," Seth insisted.

With that, Natalie filled them in on what they'd missed. She apologized for leaving the reception early to follow William but explained how it wasn't a wasted effort because she'd learned about

Dr. Rees. She described what she and Raina found in Dr. Rees's house and then recapped Henley's dream.

I noticed she'd mentioned very little about Becca's dream and then realized she hadn't given me any details about it either. All I knew was that she'd confirmed Luke's story was true. She seemed uncomfortable every time the subject came up, so I'd wait and ask her sometime when we were alone.

Jen stood up and turned to Seth. "Let's grab our stuff out of the car. I need my laptop to get to work. If Josie is real, I'm going to figure out who she is."

We unloaded their luggage, placing it all back in Jen's old room, which she'd primarily used as an office to work remotely. After the attack, she'd taken a break from on-air reporting in order to give herself time to heal and shifted into a role focused on researching and editing their written content. Her desk was still there, and Jen placed her laptop on top of it, ready to dive in.

Wanting to give her some space, the rest of us walked back downstairs and gathered around the kitchen table. Alexander made a pot of coffee while Raina pulled out mugs and a container of sugar.

As we took our seats, I noticed Luke wisely sat at the opposite end, away from me and Natalie.

"Where do we start?" Seth asked, clapping his hands together. "What's the plan?"

"First, I think we need to come up with a strategy to rescue the baby once we get confirmation she's been born."

"She's been born," Luke said.

"How do you know that?" Natalie asked, her eyes wide. "And why didn't you say anything earlier?"

He frowned. "Becca visited me last night, trying again to get me to rejoin them, and she wasn't pregnant anymore."

He didn't address the second part of Natalie's question, but I decided to just write it off as typical Luke hiding information until *he* deemed it the right time to reveal it.

"So, do we go in there, all action movie–style, or what?" Seth asked.

Raina rolled her eyes, but I caught a hint of a smile on her face. Seth didn't annoy her as much as she liked to pretend.

"I want to try contacting Becca one more time," Natalie announced. "The last time I did, I showed her a memory from her past. I think it resonated with her because she screamed so hard, she forced me out of her dream. Maybe she's having doubts about Henley and questioning who the real bad guys are. What if I can get her to come around?"

Seth shook his head. "I know you want to believe that, Nat, but even if you contact her and it seems like she agrees, how can you trust her? She might just lead you right into another trap."

As much as I wanted to be on Natalie's side, Seth was right. Although it was feasible Becca was having second thoughts about Henley, we couldn't risk letting our guard down and her turning on us. If she'd proven anything, it was that she was both conniving and convincing, and that was a dangerous combination.

"We need to keep the element of surprise," I said. "That's what's always worked for us in the past."

"Breaking in there a third time won't work," Alexander warned. "Honestly, I can't believe we've gotten in there twice already. Security will be on high alert, especially if Henley is planning something in a few days."

"But Henley thinks we're distracted," Natalie challenged. "That was the whole point of the explosions. He still believes he's in control. He might not even realize that Luke came to us for help."

There was no way for us to know that for sure. But I trusted my instincts, which told me to exclude Becca from our plans and try something Henley wouldn't expect.

"Becca knows that Natalie and I had a falling-out," Luke said. "They assume I wouldn't go to her for help or else they wouldn't be trying to get me to rejoin them."

Raina took a sip of coffee and then lowered her mug back to the table. "I still don't see how we'd get in there though."

Luke leaned back in his chair and shot me a cautious glance.

"What?" I asked, my patience with him wearing thin.

"I have an idea," he replied. "But you have to promise not to rip my head off."

I glared at him, refusing to promise anything. "Just say it."

He shifted uncomfortably under everyone's attention. "Natalie and I have the best chance of getting in there, undetected, if we go alone."

My leg bounced under the table as I tried to contain the urge to lunge at him. "If you think I'm letting her go anywhere alone with you, you're out of your mind."

"Hear me out." He sat up straight and stretched his arms out on the table. "I can make people believe I'm someone else. Becca also has that ability, which means Natalie probably does too. If she and I can get in there by pretending to be other people, we might get through without raising suspicion."

Alexander shook his head. "We already used that approach when we rescued Natalie. Henley will expect it."

"Not if we make him think we already belong there," Luke said. "When you rescued Natalie, I made them believe you were Henley and a team coming to get her. It was out of the norm, but they basically just handed her over anyway. This time, we need to make it seem like any other night."

"How do we do that?" Natalie asked. The determination in her voice frightened me. Eager to help, she was totally buying into this idea.

"They'll have a shift change at seven p.m. tonight. It used to be at six, but I noticed they'd changed up their routine when I returned. I'll pretend to be the security guard coming on duty, and you'll pretend to be Tonya. She'll be working tonight."

"I'm coming with you," I said.

Natalie placed her hand on top of mine. "It'll break the ruse. How would we explain having another person with us? Luke is right. If we're going to sneak in under the radar, then they need to believe it's just an ordinary night."

I searched my brain, trying to figure out a way to talk her out of it.

"If we agree to do this, I'll need you guys to stop the real security guard and Tonya from making it to work. You'll also need to prevent them from calling into work—at least until we're out of there," Luke said.

"How do we do that?" Raina asked, shooting me an apologetic look.

"We empty their cars of just enough gas to where they break down a few miles from their houses and then use a cell phone jammer to stop them from making outbound calls," Seth replied matter-of-factly.

We all turned to stare at him in awe.

He shrugged. "I saw it on a TV show."

Raina raised her eyebrows. "It's so absurd that it might actually work."

All eyes shifted to me, as if waiting for me to give the final approval. Every cell in my body screamed at me to push back on Luke's idea. We'd fought so hard to get Natalie out of Henley's facility that I couldn't imagine just allowing her to walk back in there. But the objective part of me saw that Luke's plan might pan out. We needed to hurry, for the baby's sake, and I didn't have a better strategy to offer.

Alexander pulled his phone out of his pocket and paused, awaiting my response. Reluctantly, I gave him a nod, and he began typing out a message. I didn't have to ask to know he was contacting Stan.

Alexander's phone chimed. "Everything we need will be here before noon."

"You don't have to do this," I told Natalie as she laced up her sneakers.

She stood up and pulled on her jacket before turning to me. "I don't see another option. Henley has our niece, and we have to get her out of there before he moves forward with Project Josie. We can't risk her being caught in the middle of whatever it is."

I knew she was right, but I still didn't like it.

"Are you positive that Luke isn't in cahoots with Becca and Henley?" I asked, praying that her intuition would warn her if he was setting her up.

"I'm sure," she replied, looking away. "Luke's telling the truth about Becca."

As I walked her downstairs, I wished I could go back in time and change things. I wouldn't alter my decision to save her life—I'd do that again in a heartbeat—but I'd avoid being captured by Henley in Philadelphia. If that hadn't happened, Natalie wouldn't have sought me out to rescue me. She'd still be living in Kentucky, safe with her aunt, where I'd originally left her. It wasn't an option to send her back there though. Now that we knew Becca was alive, it would be too easy for Natalie to be discovered.

Natalie and I were the first ones outside, so I took her hand and spun her around to face me.

Regardless of how many hours we'd spent rehashing the details of our plan, I still felt uneasy. Luke was confident that Natalie had tapped into her mind manipulation ability, but there was still the possibility of something going wrong, and if it did, I wouldn't be there to protect her.

"Be careful. *Please*," I said.

"I will."

I wanted to believe her, but her desire to help Becca often clouded her judgment.

I wrapped my arms around her, pulled her close, and kissed her good-bye. When the front door opened behind us, she pulled away.

I turned to see Luke standing there with a look of disdain on his face, knowing he'd just interrupted us.

Natalie's face reddened as she quietly parted from me and walked to the car.

The others piled outside, everyone set with their missions. Natalie and Luke would go to Henley's facility while Alexander and I took care of the security guard and Raina and Seth went for Tonya. Thanks to Jen, we had both of their home addresses. Jen would stay behind and continue to research the real Josie.

As everyone scattered to get into the cars, I stopped Luke, pulling him aside. He said nothing but looked at me, contempt still written all over his face.

"Natalie insists she can trust you," I said. "But that doesn't mean I do. If *anything* happens to her, I'm holding you responsible. I don't care how long it takes, but I swear I'll hunt you down."

"Your threats are getting a little old, brother," he replied, trying to jerk away from me. I was stronger though and refused to release him.

"Anything," I reiterated before letting go. "I mean it."

He smirked at me. "For someone who brags about what an honest relationship you have, you sure are in the dark. Aren't you the least bit curious about why she suddenly trusts me?"

I narrowed my eyes at him as he took a bold step closer.

"It's because Becca showed her *everything* about that night." His voice was low, as if he didn't want others to overhear him. "I want her because I love her, and she knows it."

Natalie talked to Luke about this? My eyes darted to her, but she was busy saying good-bye to Seth and was oblivious to our conversation.

Luke assessed the confusion written on my face. "Do you want to know why she didn't tell you? Why she gets so embarrassed whenever it comes up?"

I glared at him but didn't respond.

He sneered. "It's because every time she looks at me, she's reminded of that dream, and even though she doesn't want to admit it, a part of her wants me too."

FOURTEEN

NATALIE

"Do you want to practice again before we get there?" Luke asked from the passenger seat.

I shook my head. "No, I think I've got the hang of it."

Luke had coached me on how to impersonate Tonya. Mind manipulation only worked when the other person didn't expect it, so I wasn't able to test it on anyone at the house. But when I attempted to morph my persona into hers, I felt different, more attentive, and it gave me hope that I'd be successful at pulling it off.

"Just give me a heads-up if you feel yourself coming out of it," he said. "It's a sensation similar to losing focus when you've been concentrating on something for too long. Your mind will get hazy right before."

I nodded, trying to grasp what that might feel like so I'd recognize it if it happened. At least with Luke there, he could cover us both, if needed. But my being able to warn him ahead of time, before anyone grew suspicious, was key.

My phone chimed, and I handed it to Luke, so I could keep my eyes on the road. It was likely either Michael or Raina, completing their checkpoint. Our plan was to have Raina and Seth go to Tonya's house, drain her gas, and then text us when it was complete before initiating the cell phone blocker. Michael and Alexander planned to do the same to the night-shift security guard, Don.

Luke stared at the phone, puzzled, as he tried to remember how to check the message. I'd forgotten that there were so many things he had to learn about the real world, outside of Henley's walls. He'd offered to drive, telling me he'd done it a handful of times and gotten the hang of it already, but I'd declined. As much as I hated driving, I needed to keep myself preoccupied with something other than my nerves.

"Do you want me to do it?" I nodded to the phone in his hand.

"I've got it." He opened and closed a few windows before finally getting to the message. "Raina says they're done."

"Good. Now, we just wait for Michael."

We were about five minutes away from Henley's facility. Just when I got concerned that Michael and Alexander had run into a problem, the phone chimed again.

"Michael's done. It's a go," Luke said.

"What if the tetrad is there?" I asked, recalling how Michael and I'd barely escaped Lovisa and Viktor back in the warehouse.

"They don't live at the facility, but if they are there, mind manipulation works on them. Don't worry. I've tested the waters already on that. How do you think I escaped?"

"How *did* you escape? And how did you even find us?"

"I pretended to be Dr. Leeman and walked right out of there," he replied. "Then, when I got out, I returned to the house, but you had already moved. So, I called the only connection I still had to you."

"You contacted Mr. Weber?" I asked, surprised, because Mr. Weber hadn't let on that he'd spoken with Luke when I read his mind.

"That was the plan, but he changed his phone number. I guess to put distance between himself and Henley. Luckily, I'd also stolen his address, so I hitchhiked to Virginia, and when I got there, his housekeeper told me he'd just left to attend his son's wedding in St. Augustine, Florida." He glanced at me. "I figured you'd be there."

For someone without a lot of experience in the outside world, Luke had sure adapted in order to get what he needed. As upsetting as his manipulations could be, it comforted me, knowing he'd be able to use those skills to provide for my niece.

"Have you thought about a name?" I asked, changing the subject.

He blinked at me, as if he hadn't even considered it. "A name?"

I couldn't help but let out a laugh. "Yes, Luke, your daughter needs a name."

"I—I don't know ..." He looked out the window, deep in thought. "I can't think of one. Do you have any ideas?"

I felt a twinge of guilt for putting him on the spot like that. Of course he didn't have a name picked out. He'd come from a place that refused to let him have his own. If it wasn't for Alexander, he still wouldn't have one.

"Becca always liked the name Willow," I said, remembering how she'd picked that name when we were kids but made me pinkie swear never to tell anyone. I felt like it was okay to break that promise now though since I was telling her baby's father.

"Willow," he repeated. "I like it."

I wasn't sure if he meant it or just didn't know how to come up with something he liked better.

"I'll tell you what," I said. "When you meet her, you decide. If she doesn't seem like a Willow to you, I'll help you find another name that suits her."

He nodded and flashed me a nervous smile.

Henley's facility came into view, still disguised as G.G. Armand Designs. I wouldn't have recognized it though if it wasn't from the signs out front. I'd been unconscious when Henley's men brought me here. And I had barely been coherent when I got rescued. I vaguely remembered being in the back of a car with Alexander trying to figure out how to keep me alive.

"Pull over there," Luke said, pointing toward the side of the building. "I don't want the receptionist to notice we're coming out of the same car. Don and Tonya wouldn't ride together."

I followed his instructions, and as I put the car in park, I noticed my hands were shaking. I felt edgy, much like the time Seth and I had snuck in to rescue Michael. Only now, I was more terrified because I knew firsthand what Henley was capable of. I closed my eyes, remembering his dream and how he'd like nothing more than to slash my throat open.

"Hey, hey," Luke said, touching my shoulder to get my attention. "You've got to get it together, okay?"

I opened my eyes and robotically nodded my head.

He gave me a squeeze before letting go. "If you let yourself get distracted, the disguise won't work."

"I know," I replied, trying to stop the racing thoughts going through my head.

"We need to go in separately, but I'll go in first and wait for you," he said, reminding me of the plan. "I won't let anything happen to you, all right?"

My intuition told me he was sincere and that I should trust him.

I took a breath and nodded again. *I can do this.*

As we'd planned, I stayed in the car and watched Luke enter the building. I counted to ten, and then I got out and focused on making myself into Tonya. I recalled all the details I could remember about her—from the tight bun on her head to the deep wrinkle that appeared between her eyebrows when she got angry.

My hands were full of random medical books as I approached the door to G.G. Armand Designs. I hit the handicap accessible button with my elbow to open the doors for me.

As soon as I entered the lobby, I spotted Luke chatting with the receptionist, as planned. He still looked like Luke to me, but the receptionist seemed relaxed, so I assumed she believed he was Don.

"Hi, Tonya," Luke greeted me.

I scowled at him, as I imagined the real Tonya would do, and looked at the receptionist. "Do you mind?" I motioned my head toward the door.

"Oh, sure," she replied, flustered. She hit the button to unlock and automatically open the door, heading back toward Henley's real facility.

My impersonation worked.

I stomped through the door without thanking her because Tonya wouldn't bother to be grateful.

Behind me, I heard Luke say to the receptionist, "I'd better get clocked in too. See you later, Ashley."

Luke slipped through the door behind me right before it closed.

He rushed past me, and I followed about ten paces behind to the nurses' station, where I set down all the books.

We took a quick look around, and all was quiet. No one else was in sight.

"Come on," he said.

I trailed Luke down the hallway to a room that served as both a kitchen and employee break area. As we walked inside, I recognized the security guard sitting at the table, watching the news. It was Chuck, the guard Seth had knocked unconscious when we rescued Michael. I recalled how he'd punched Seth in the stomach in retaliation, dropping him to the ground in pain. I froze.

Luke discreetly nudged me, prompting me to concentrate on the task at hand. Chuck glanced up at us, and Luke walked over to chat with him. I didn't listen to what they were saying as I made my way over to the fridge and pulled out a tray of food. It was right where Luke had said it would be.

I took the tray without so much as acknowledging Chuck and strolled out of the room. I paused just outside the door, and right on cue, Luke came out a moment later.

Again, Luke walked ahead, just in case someone saw us in the hallway. We passed several patient rooms, similar to the one they'd held me in, until Luke stopped in front of one. We'd reached Becca's room.

He nodded at me before I went inside, looking for confirmation that I was good. I nodded back, resolved to see it through. We'd made it this far, and I couldn't let Willow—or him—down.

Without knocking, I barged into Becca's room, as Tonya would do. The door wasn't locked, but we hadn't expected it to be. Becca wasn't a prisoner. She wanted to be there with Henley.

Once again, I focused on being Tonya. I kept my shoulders back the way she would—confident—when Henley wasn't around. The only time she ever slumped was when she was in trouble with him. She was tall and proud until she sensed his displeasure. Then, she'd try to shrink herself up as tiny as possible.

Becca lay, propped up on her fully made bed, gazing at the wall. She turned when she heard me enter and watched as I set the tray of food down on the table.

It surprised me how similar her room was to the one they'd held me in. It had the same layout and furniture.

I stole a glance at Becca and confirmed she no longer appeared to be pregnant. Then, I scanned the room but found no trace of the baby.

"Where's her bottle?" Becca asked, looking at me expectantly.

Her glare made me nervous, but I willed myself not to break the guise.

"I was told it already ate," I replied, hiding the cringe I felt at referring to my niece as *it*, but I needed to sound like Tonya.

"Shelia's an idiot," she scoffed.

I assumed Shelia was another nurse Henley had added to his staff.

"I'll go feed it," I said, rolling my eyes like I'd seen Tonya do dozens of times.

"You can bring her to me, and I'll do it." Becca looked me up and down, and I got the feeling it wasn't because she doubted I was Tonya. I sensed it was because she thought I *was* Tonya and didn't want me near her child any longer than necessary.

I gave her a curt nod before leaving the room.

Once outside the door, I walked away, unsure of where I was going. Luke glanced around, and when he established we were still alone, he stepped to my side.

"Where would they keep the baby?" I asked him. "She's not in there with Becca."

"One of the empty rooms, if I had to guess." He stepped ahead of me again, moving faster this time.

As I followed, I felt myself growing angry at the idea of my niece in one of the awful gray rooms, all by herself, out of earshot of everyone when she cried.

Why isn't Becca insisting on having the crib set up in the room with her?

He passed two rooms before stopping. He gestured for me to stay put before slowly opening the door. I held my breath, unsure of what he might find on the other side.

His shoulders sank as he peeked around the door. He looked back at me and shook his head before quietly closing it.

We walked by another room before stopping again. I continued to maintain my distance as he opened the door and looked inside.

He staggered back a step, and then he quickly regained his composure and smiled.

We've found her.

I hurried into the room behind him, closing the door. He practically leaped to her crib and stood there, unsure of what to do.

"You should hold her first," I said.

The plan was for me to carry her out while Luke gave me extra cover to make it seem like I was carrying the pile of books back out of the building, but it only seemed right that he got to hold his daughter before I did.

I stood beside him and gazed at my niece for the first time. She was sleeping peacefully despite being tightly swaddled in a scratchy gray blanket. A streak of red hair ran across the top of her head, like a mini Mohawk.

He reached for her but then stopped. "She's so tiny. I don't want to break her."

"You won't," I said. "Scoop her up with one hand while the other steadies her head. Her neck isn't strong yet, so make sure you keep it supported."

His hands hovered over her for a second, but then he moved, doing exactly what I'd told him. He lifted her out of the crib and to his chest, holding her firmly and gently, all at once.

"See? You're a natural."

He looked at me with glistening eyes. "Wow. I get it now."

"Get what?" I asked, curious to know what was going through his mind in this life-changing moment.

"The kind of love you described to me once. You said it was being selfless for the sake of someone else. I didn't really understand it before."

I nodded but didn't reply. I wanted him to savor this experience with his daughter.

He sniffled and blinked away the mist from his eyes, and then he turned his attention back to our mission. "We should get out of here."

I refocused on being Tonya, and just as he was about to hand his daughter over to me, the door flew open, and Becca barged in.

"What are you doing?" Her tone was full of accusation and suspicion, and I couldn't tell if she believed we were Tonya and Don or if she'd figured out who we really were.

My mind was blank, trying to think of a response.

Luke remained composed. "She was crying, so I offered to hold her until Tonya came back with her bottle."

Becca narrowed her eyes and looked at her baby sleeping in Luke's arms. "Give her to me." She reached out, ready to take her.

"Don't wake it up yet," I said. "It just went back to sleep. Let me grab the bottle first. Otherwise, all it'll do is scream again." I was grasping at straws, trying to keep up the illusion.

I walked past Becca and toward the door. She let me go without giving me a second glance. Instead, she watched Luke, who was still pretending to be Don. I could tell her brain still hadn't reconciled why Don would hold her baby.

Why would Don even be in here at all?

She suspected something was off about the whole situation, and it wouldn't take her long to figure it out. And when she did, the illusion would shatter. We were running out of time.

"You know what? Just give her to me," I said, sounding inconvenienced, like Tonya would. "I'll feed her and bring her back to your room."

As Luke approached me, I watched Becca's head tilt slightly to the side. Then, I realized I'd referred to the baby as *her*. Becca's eyes widened, and I knew in that moment that she'd figured it out.

"*You*," she said.

She stepped toward me, but I used my powers to push her back. The impact wasn't forceful, but it was enough to stop her in her tracks and give Luke time to slip past her.

"I'm trying to help her—to help you," I said, trying to rationalize with Becca before this escalated further. "You can come with us. You don't have to stay here if you don't want to."

She screamed, releasing a burst of energy that sent me flying backward. I slammed against the wall in the hallway and then came crashing down onto my front. Before I hit the ground, I pushed my hands out and just barely avoided smacking my face on the tiled floor. My wrists cracked, and I instantly felt the pain radiate up my arms as I scrambled to sit up on my knees.

Becca shrieked as the bones in my wrists fought to mend themselves. Luke reached a hand under my arm to help me up. As I came to my feet, I saw Becca pacing just inside the room, like a wild animal. There wasn't anything to prevent her from pushing past the threshold, but she must've thought there was because every time she got too close, she'd stop and retreat.

I glanced at Luke, who carefully held the baby with one arm and steadied me with the other, all while watching the doorway. He was making her see something that wasn't really there in order to hold her back.

"I'm good," I said, flexing my healed wrists. "Let's get out of here."

Without a doubt, Chuck or someone else had heard the commotion and was on their way.

I used my powers to slam the door closed, hoping to drown out Becca's voice as Luke and I dashed down the hall toward the reception area. At any moment, she'd realize she could just open the door and leave.

We burst through the double doors, making Ashley jump at the sound. She stood up, as if expecting danger and wondering if she should run too. Confusion ripped through her face as she took in the sight of us with the baby. We were no longer pretending to be Tonya and Don, and Ashley knew we didn't belong there. She reached across her desk.

"The door!" Luke yelled, and I used my powers to force the main doors to the building open.

The receptionist hit a button, one that I assumed was to lock us in, but it was useless against my powers, which fought to keep the doors ajar.

We ran out of the building, and I fumbled for the car keys in my pocket.

"Hurry," Luke yelled, his hand holding the back of his daughter's head in place so it didn't bounce around as he ran.

I found the keys and hit the unlock button, and we jumped into the car. He held her in his arms as he slammed the passenger door shut.

As we drove by the front of the building to exit the parking lot, I saw Chuck run outside, but it was too late. We'd already escaped.

FIFTEEN

NATALIE

I pulled up to the house and looked in the rearview mirror, into the backseat. My niece was securely in her car seat as Luke sat beside her. Alexander had installed it before we left. He'd also been kind enough to pack us a diaper bag, including a bottle in case she got hungry.

About an hour after we had stopped at a rest area to feed, burp, and change her, Luke had decided the name Willow suited her.

Luke and I emerged from the car. I stretched my legs while Luke got Willow out.

The front door opened, and Michael stepped outside. I saw the look of relief on his face and could tell he'd been listening out for us to arrive home.

"Meet your niece, Willow," I said.

Luke closed the passenger door and carried Willow in her baby carrier.

Michael walked over to Luke and reached down, delicately touching her wispy red hair. "She's beautiful. Congratulations."

"Thanks," Luke replied, beaming. "I'm going to bring her inside and let Alexander check her out." He walked past me and hurried into the house.

She looked healthy to me, but I agreed it was best to let Alexander look her over to make sure.

Michael took my hand and pulled me toward him, hugging me tightly to his chest.

"I'm glad you're back. Did everything go as planned?" he asked, his face buried in my hair.

"Of course not. It never does," I replied with a bitter laugh. "Becca figured out who we were and attacked me, but Luke stopped her long enough, so we could escape."

He squeezed tighter.

"He made her believe a wall of fire had trapped her in her room," I said. Luke had explained his tactic to me in the car, and I was still in awe. *Can I do that?* I couldn't even imagine it.

"There's been no sign of Henley or his people," Michael said, pulling back. "We've been on high alert, and we'll take shifts tonight to keep watch in case they show up, looking for her."

"We're not leaving?" I asked, surprised. I'd just assumed we'd change houses. Surely, Becca and Henley would attempt to get Willow back.

Michael shook his head. "We can't. I haven't told the others just yet, but Raina befriended Detective Thompson's brother. Apparently, he was asking some questions about you before she realized the relation. If we leave, the detective will think it was because of that, which will make us look even guiltier."

I thought about my conversation in the car with Raina after we'd broken into Dr. Rees's house. She'd seemed more vulnerable than I'd ever seen her before, and I recalled how she'd looked at me after I told her not to have regrets about opening herself up to love. She'd wanted to say something to me—I could feel it—but she'd stopped herself. I didn't think Detective Thompson's brother was just a friend to her. Without a doubt, he was much more.

"Go easy on her," I said. "She deserves the opportunity to find happiness."

"She literally couldn't have picked a worse person." He clenched his jaw.

I shrugged. "The heart doesn't always give you a choice when it comes to love. Sometimes, it's complicated."

He creased his brow as his eyes searched mine, and I feared he was angry with me for siding with Raina. I waited for him to say whatever was on his mind, but he turned back toward the house.

"We should get inside. It's not safe out here," he said.

I followed Michael into the house and found everyone gathered in the living room. We watched as Alexander finished examining Willow.

"She seems perfectly healthy," Alexander said.

Luke grinned ear to ear and looked at me to see my reaction, which mirrored his.

"While we were waiting for you to return, I went to the store and bought her some clothes," Jen told Luke. "I could show you how to dress her, if you'd like. We could get her into something less ... depressing."

"That'd be great," Luke replied, looking down at Willow in her solid gray onesie.

Luke and Jen took Willow upstairs, and I plopped down in Jen's spot on the couch next to Seth, feeling exhausted.

I glanced at Seth. "She looks exactly like Becca in her baby pictures. It's crazy."

He gave me a bittersweet smile but didn't reply. He'd noticed it too.

"I don't want them to leave," I said. "But they have to. I wish we could go with them."

"The important thing is to keep Willow safe," Seth replied. "Do you think Luke can do that?"

I nodded. "Without a doubt. It's incredible to see how much he loves her in such a short amount of time. And he really stepped up today. Becca figured us out, and he saved both me and Willow while keeping her away. He has his faults, but I think, deep down, he has a good heart."

Michael crossed his arms over his chest, clearly disagreeing with my opinion of his brother.

I noticed Jen's laptop open on the coffee table in front of me, and I sat up straighter to get a better look at it. "Did you find something?"

The browser window was open to an obituary. I scrolled to the top of the page and found a picture of Josie, the same girl from both my and Henley's dreams.

"Josie was Henley's sister," Michael replied. "She died of leukemia forty years ago on March 9. She was six years old."

I looked up at him in shock. "That can't be a coincidence."

Seth reached across me and tapped the keyboard to show a newspaper article open in a different window. "According to this story written ten years ago, Henley's dad donated millions of dollars toward cancer research. In the interview, he mentions he did it in memory of his daughter, Josephine. He never mentions a son though. We only found out about Chad Henley through the obituary."

"The newspaper included a quote from Josie's nanny, Shirley Higgins," Alexander said.

"Henley mentioned Shirley in his dream," I said, the details gradually coming back to me. He'd told Josie to go home to Shirley.

Michael shifted his feet. "Shirley's in her seventies now and still alive. We're going to visit her tomorrow."

"Do you think that's wise?" I asked. "What if she still talks to Henley and tips him off?"

"Alexander spoke with her granddaughter briefly, and she said Shirley hasn't been in contact with Henley for many years but agreed to let us meet with her," he replied. "It's still a risk but one worth taking if we can gather some more information."

I nodded. If Michael felt it was worth it, then I trusted him. Even if Shirley hadn't seen Henley in years, maybe she could still offer us some kind of insight into what Henley was planning. It felt like we were close to having all the puzzle pieces, and now, we just had to figure out how they fit together.

Later that evening, after dinner, Michael offered to help Luke set up a bassinet in his room for Willow to sleep in. Luke would need to take it down again in the morning, so he could transport it with them when they left, but at least he'd already know how to get it assembled when they reached their next destination.

Alexander had already contacted Stan to help get things arranged for their departure. I was dreading saying good-bye, but it was for the best. Willow was a defenseless baby, and we couldn't put her in jeopardy of getting recaptured, hurt, or worse.

Michael came back downstairs as Jen, Seth, and I finished cleaning up the kitchen.

"I'm going to run up and say good night to Willow," I said, tossing the dishrag onto the counter.

Michael watched as I left, and I half-expected him to follow me, but he didn't.

Maybe he's finally coming around to Luke now that he's leaving.

When I got to Luke's room, I paused in the doorway. He was standing over Willow, admiring her while she slept.

"Remember, she'll need to be fed every two to three hours," I said. "Do you want me to take shifts with you?" I walked into the room and stood at his side.

He smiled and shook his head. "No. I've got this. I know it sounds crazy, but I don't want to miss any opportunity that I have to be near her."

"It doesn't sound crazy."

It was sweet how much he cared for her, and it gave me the reassurance I needed that she'd be in the best possible care once they left us.

"She looks comfortable in her bassinet," I said. "Did you and Michael get some bonding time in?"

I'd meant the last part as a joke, but he looked over at me skeptically.

"What time are we leaving tomorrow?" he asked, changing the subject and shifting his eyes back to Willow.

"Stan said the car will arrive at noon. I'm going to take you to the drop-off location while Michael, Raina, and Alexander interview Shirley." I wished I could go with them to hear what she had to say firsthand, but I wanted to make sure that Luke and Willow left safely.

"You could come with us," he said, eyeing me.

I looked at him, confused. "I am."

He held my gaze. "I mean, *leave with us*."

I slowly shook my head. "I can't do that."

"I know they need you, but we do too."

I shifted my eyes away from him and down to Willow. She was asleep, safe, and content. My heart ached at the thought of her growing up without me.

"I should go," I whispered, feeling a sting in my eyes. "I don't want to wake her up."

Luke took a seat in his room, staying close to Willow. He watched me as I stepped into the hall and shut the door.

My heart felt heavy as I wandered back downstairs. I stepped into the living room to find Seth sitting on the couch, drinking a large cup of coffee and watching television. He'd offered to take the first shift and stay up all night to keep watch.

"Where is everyone?" I asked, looking around the empty living room.

"In bed or getting ready for bed," he replied. "Except Michael. He's in the kitchen."

"You good?" I asked, realizing Seth's eyes were bloodshot.

He nodded. "I'm fine. Get some rest."

"Just wake us up if you see or hear anything suspicious or if you need a break," I said as I made my way into the kitchen to see if Michael was ready to go to bed.

I found him hovering over the coffeemaker, zoned out.

"Hey," I said, making him jump in response. "Sorry, I didn't mean to startle you."

He picked up the cord to the coffeemaker and plugged it into the wall. "Raina made a cup of coffee for Seth, and now, this thing won't turn on." He flipped the power switch, but nothing happened. Frustrated, he unplugged it and slammed the cord against the counter.

"I'm sure she didn't mean to break it," I said.

He turned around, eyeing me, as if debating on whether he wanted to respond.

"What?" My heart sank as I realized something was wrong and it had nothing to do with the coffeemaker.

He opened his mouth to speak and then hesitated.

Just as I was about to tell him he didn't have to get into it if he didn't want to, he asked, "Why didn't you tell me about Becca's dream?"

I froze, immediately knowing which part he was referring to. *How does he know about that?*

"Because the entire situation makes me incredibly uncomfortable," I replied, finding my voice and trying to be as honest with him as possible.

"Why is that?" he asked, but it felt like a loaded question.

"Why do you think?" I felt a twinge of annoyance. All I wanted was to put the ordeal behind me, but I couldn't seem to escape it. "Because my sister pretended to be me so she could seduce your brother into impregnating her. And now, I feel like every time he sees me, he's picturing what I look like naked or something. That's why."

"He's in love with you." His eyes searched mine, looking for a response.

"That's ridiculous," I scoffed, but he didn't waver.

156

"Do you have feelings for him?"

"Seriously?" I couldn't believe he'd pose such a question.

"Do you?"

"No," I replied firmly. "Not like that anyway."

Michael's cool demeanor made me anxious. He calmly folded his arms across his chest. "Then, like what?" His tone was more curious than accusatory.

I laughed—the kind you made when you were nervous and you couldn't believe how incredulous someone was being. "Like a *friend*, Michael."

As he approached me, his gaze grew more intense—with purpose rather than anger. "Could you be happy with him?"

I leaned on the counter, the pressure of his question and scrutiny making me unbalanced. "What's that supposed to mean?" I hated answering his absurd question with another, but I didn't understand what he was trying to accomplish. If he was asking me if I was in love with Luke, the answer was no, and I'd already confirmed that.

"I've been thinking a lot about us," he said, "about our future and what that looks like, and I'm not sure I can give you what you want."

I felt like I'd been sucker-punched. *Where is this coming from?*

"What I want? I want *you*," I said.

He closed his eyes and then reopened them, as if what he was about to say would hurt him as much as it would me. "You deserve a future that includes marriage, kids, a career, and anything else you ever dreamed about before you met me."

I dramatically shrugged my shoulders to emphasize the point I was about to make. "Okay. I can have all of those things. *You and I* can have all of it."

He shook his head. "I can't guarantee that."

"Well, there are no guarantees in life. No matter what the circumstances are." I suddenly felt desperate to change the direction I feared the conversation was heading. "You said whatever happens, we'd face it together. Do you remember that?"

The frown on his face said it all. He remembered, but he was going back on his promise.

"Are you breaking up with me?" I asked, not believing the question as it came out of my mouth.

Of course he isn't. Right?

He ran his hand through his hair, and I could tell he was battling with himself. "I want you to be happy and safe."

That's not a no.

We stared at each other, waiting for the other to say something—anything—but I was incapable of it. His comment sucked the air from my lungs, and I wondered how I was still standing.

I'd been perfectly happy before this conversation. Sure, we had a lot of stress in our lives, and danger lurked in every corner, but I could deal with all of it with Michael by my side.

Why doesn't he feel the same about me?

He approached, and I instinctively recoiled, moving away from the counter and away from him. My reaction stopped him in his tracks. At first, he appeared hurt, and then he took a deep breath and seemed relieved.

"I thought you loved me," I said, my voice quivering.

His face softened. "I do."

"Then, why are you leaving me again?" I recalled how after I'd rescued him from Henley back in Charlotte, he'd reassured me he wouldn't leave me.

"I'm not. I'm asking you to consider leaving me to go have a real life away from all of this."

I gestured out with my arms. "This is my life. Here with you."

"Luke is leaving tomorrow." The statement came too quickly, as if it was something he'd already thought through and not a spur-of-the-moment idea that he'd retract. "If you think there's a chance you'd be happy, raising Willow with him, I want you to leave with them."

Hot tears stung at my eyes, but I refused to release them. "So, you claim to love me, but you're willing to just give me away to someone else—to *Luke*." My voice unleashed every piece of bitterness I felt in my heart.

Michael despised Luke but was perfectly content to pawn me off on him.

He isn't just throwing our relationship away; he's throwing me away.

He rubbed his hand over his face. "I think he's capable of protecting you. The chances of us ever defeating Henley are slim to none, especially now that he has Becca and his tetrad."

"So, you're just going to give up," I concluded. "On stopping Henley and on us."

"I'm not giving up on anything. *I love you.* I just want you to reconsider if this is the life you want. A life on the run, always in danger and losing people you care about. You won't be able to have children of your own because this monster will try to take them from you." His shaky voice and furrowed brow confirmed that he truly believed everything he was saying. "You deserve so much better than that. Than *me.*"

I could tell there was no changing his mind. He wanted me to choose a life outside of him. In fact, he was begging me to.

I batted away a tear as it escaped down my cheek. Unable to continue the conversation with him, I marched out of the room and up the stairs without giving him another word.

Once in the safety of my room, I threw myself down on the bed, buried my face in my pillow, and sobbed. I didn't want to wake anyone up, especially Willow, but despite my best attempts to be quiet, someone must have heard me because there was a soft knock on the door.

I didn't move or respond, hoping they'd give up and go away.

A moment later, I felt someone sit beside me on the bed.

I lifted my head, assuming I'd see Seth or Jen sitting there, but to my surprise, it was Raina.

She was wearing black pajamas with her hair pulled back into a ponytail. Her eyes were puffy, and I couldn't tell if I'd woken her up or if she'd been crying herself.

I tensed. The last thing I wanted was an argument with her.

"For the record, I think my brother is being an idiot," she said. "I told him so when he mentioned this whole stupid idea to me."

I sat up, facing her, hoping she could shed some light on what'd just happened. "I thought he loved me, and I don't understand what changed."

"He does love you."

"Then, why is he doing this?" It made little sense.

"I think he's worried about not doing the right thing," she said. "In case you haven't noticed, he has this innate desire to be the hero."

I knew that was true about Michael, but I had a hard time fathoming that he thought the right thing was to push me toward someone else. "He wants me to leave with Luke tomorrow." As I said it, I realized Michael must've discussed it with him when they were putting together Willow's bassinet. That was why Luke had brought up the idea of me leaving with them. He had been feeling me out.

Raina rolled her eyes. "He doesn't really want that. He just isn't thinking clearly." She shook her head. "And men say women are the complicated ones."

I wiped the tears from my face, remembering that she was going through her own heartache. I wanted to ask her about it, but I wasn't sure if she'd be mad that Michael had told me. Instead, I asked her, "What do you think I should do?"

She looked me over, thinking through my question before responding. "I think you should decide for yourself what you want for your future. You know what this life offers, but Michael's giving you the option to start over. With your abilities, there's no reason that you and Luke couldn't have a fresh start. You have such an advantage by being able to pretend to be someone else. I'd give anything to have the option to be someone else."

I took a breath, trying to think rationally about the advice she was offering. It was both objective and sincere.

"I don't believe your sister is going to come around," she said, looking away. "So, other than Michael, what's really keeping you tied to this life?"

I nodded, knowing that she wasn't trying to hurt me with her comment. She just didn't want me to make my decision based solely on Michael or Becca.

If I stayed and Michael still didn't want to be with me, would I regret not leaving with Luke? I didn't have the answer, but that was the lens I needed to put on the situation. It was a decision that needed to be balanced by both my heart and my mind.

"Thanks," I said. "I'll think about it."

Raina stood up. "For what it's worth, I'm cool with it if you choose to stay. You're less annoying than you used to be."

I realized that was a compliment, coming from her.

She left me to contemplate my options.

I glanced at the clock. It was after ten p.m. That gave me less than fourteen hours to make a pivotal decision that would impact the rest of my life. If I stayed, I'd have to say good-bye to Willow, and unless we defeated Henley, I'd need to stay away from her forever. If I elected to leave, I'd put everyone else I cared about at a disadvantage in defeating Henley.

Henley had Becca and his tetrad, which meant he had the numbers on his side. From what I'd witnessed at the warehouse, Lovisa was skilled at using her abilities, so it was safe to assume Hemming, Viktor, and Rolf were as well. Without me, that left only Michael and Raina to take them on. Alexander was good with a gun, but even that was no match for their abilities.

Seth and Jen would likely remain even if I didn't. Although they'd originally gotten involved to help me, I knew they deeply cared for Michael, Alexander, and Raina. We'd become a family, ready to face unfavorable odds over and over in order to protect each other.

I also needed to consider Willow and what was best for her. She was just an infant, who fiercely needed to be protected from the evils of Henley and, sadly, her own mother. Becca might never recover, but having Willow in my life meant that I could still keep a part of my sister close.

Luke would protect Willow—I was convinced of that—but he was still learning to navigate the world on his own. Plus, he needed to figure out how to be a single parent and earn a living to support them both. It would be a much smoother transition for them if I was there to help.

If this were merely a decision of the heart, a choice between Michael and Luke, it would be an easy one for me. It fully belonged to Michael—whether or not he wanted it anymore.

I didn't know how I felt about Luke. If asked about him a month ago, I would've said I despised him for what he had done to Becca. But now, I was back to believing that he had redeeming qualities. With the anger gone, I could tell he had a big heart. He just rarely allowed himself to be vulnerable enough to use it. I'd witnessed how loving he could be earlier today when he held Willow for the first time.

And even though it made me uncomfortable to think about it, I'd seen the real him, with his defenses lowered, in Becca's dream.

Michael had told me that Luke loved me, and I'd brushed it off, not wanting to believe it was true. Not wanting Michael to think it was true. But as I lay there in the dark, curled up alone in bed, I knew deep down that it was. Luke had all but told me already himself. I just hadn't wanted to admit it to myself because of how it would complicate everything.

Although Michael didn't have competition in my heart, I had to consider what a life with Luke would be like if I left with him. Of course, opting to go didn't put me under any obligation to be his girlfriend or anything, but would romantic feelings just naturally evolve?

Luke had asked me if things would've been different between us if I'd met him before Michael. His question had caught me off guard, and I still wasn't certain how to answer it.

Now, I found myself faced with a different question: Could things be different between us *after* Michael?

I didn't have a straightforward answer. Without a doubt, saying good-bye to Michael for a third time would destroy me because this separation would be permanent. There'd be no going back. The stakes were higher than ever, and I couldn't risk Willow's safety just to satisfy my selfish desire to come out of hiding to see him.

Once I decided, there'd be no turning back.

SIXTEEN

MICHAEL

N atalie walked into the kitchen as I sat at the table, eating breakfast
with Raina and Seth. She stared straight ahead, refusing to look
at me as she went to the fridge and opened it. I wanted to clear the air,
but I didn't know what else to say to make her understand. I wasn't
trying to reject her, but I couldn't live with myself if she sacrificed
everything—her future, dreams, and safety—for me.

Raina kicked me under the table as Natalie poured herself a glass
of apple juice. I shot Raina a look of annoyance, but she replied by
nudging her head toward Natalie, wanting me to go talk to her.

I shifted in my seat, stalling, unsure of how to even approach the
conversation with her. As much as I wanted to know if she was
planning to leave, I also feared what that answer would be. And it
didn't matter which option she chose. Either would cause me to feel a
mix of relief and dread.

I stood up from the table, and Natalie noticed the movement. She
didn't acknowledge me as she picked up her glass and stormed out of
the room. A moment later, I heard footsteps charging back up the
stairs.

"What was that all about?" Seth asked, dropping his spoon back
into the giant bowl of cereal he'd just devoured.

Raina looked at me expectantly. "Are you going to tell him, or
should I?"

I sighed, frustrated with my sister for butting in and regretting ever
saying anything to her about my plan.

When I didn't reply, Raina turned her attention to Seth. "My brother told Natalie that she should move away with Luke and go play house with him."

Seth's eyes grew to the size of golf balls. "What the hell, dude? You don't even like the guy."

I snatched my and Seth's empty bowls off the table and dropped them in the sink. "I don't, but it will give her a chance to start over. He can protect her."

Seth got up from the table and walked over to me. "You should be the one doing that."

"What if I can't?" I replied, my jaw tight. "What if I get her killed? She's in this mess because of me. I'm trying to do what's right for her. Keeping her here to die or to watch the people she loves perish would be the selfish thing to do."

He seemed taken aback by my response. Then, his face fell, showing he understood my point.

"Why don't you all just leave town? Why does she have to go with Luke?"

He was trying to find a solution to something that wasn't solvable. I'd already mulled that over in my mind repeatedly. This was the best option I could come up with.

"Raina, Alexander, and I hold her back," I explained. "With Luke, she can morph into anyone in the blink of an eye. They have a much better chance of disappearing and never getting caught."

This is the right thing to do even if losing her will kill me.

Raina pushed up from the table, shot me a dirty look, and left in the same direction as Natalie.

"Good morning!" Jen replied cheerfully, carrying Willow in her arms as she passed Raina on her way into the kitchen. Luke was right behind them.

It was clear from the frilly dress and matching headband on Willow's head that Jen had taken it upon herself to play dress-up with her again this morning.

Luke eyed me as Jen set Willow down in her baby carrier and began preparing her a bottle.

"How did it go?" he asked.

I looked over at Jen. "Do you mind watching Willow for a sec?"

She smiled back, oblivious to what was going on. "Of course."

I motioned toward the garage and followed Luke inside.

He stood there a moment, taking in all the training equipment that we housed there instead of the typical things you might expect to find in a garage.

"I don't know if she's going with you," I said. "She hasn't spoken to me this morning."

He frowned. "It's only a matter of time before Henley makes a move."

"Why do you think I'm trying to get her to leave?"

I still couldn't believe out of all the people in the world, I'd ended up asking Luke to take care of her. It had crossed my mind to ask Seth and Jen. Without a doubt, they'd do everything in their power to keep her safe, but I knew they couldn't. I wanted them out of town as well before things got worse, and asking them to take Natalie along would be a death sentence.

Luke, on the other hand, was like a cockroach. The apocalypse could happen, and he'd survive. Heck, he'd thrive. That was the type of person I needed watching over Natalie even if I didn't like it.

He shook his head and laughed.

"What?"

He lifted his head, peering at me. "I just can't figure you out. One second, you're threatening me to stay away from her, and now, you're asking me to replace you."

I cringed as the words came out of his mouth. No, I didn't want him *replacing* me. The thought of him touching her made me want to put his head through the drywall.

Done with talking to Luke, I walked back into the house and glanced at the clock. We needed to leave soon if we were going to make it to Shirley's house on time.

Jen held Willow, feeding her a bottle. A part of me wanted to ask if I could take over, spend whatever bonding time I had left with my niece, but I'd never been around a baby before, much less held or fed one.

Alexander entered the kitchen, showered and dressed. Even though he looked exhausted, he'd at least shaved. "Ready to go?" he asked me.

"Almost." There was one thing I needed to do first. "Give me five."

I hurried out of the kitchen and up the stairs.

When I reached the top, I noticed the door to Natalie's bedroom was closed. I took a breath and knocked on it.

A moment later, she appeared. Her face hardened as her bloodshot eyes landed on me. Instead of inviting me in, she stepped out into the hallway.

"We are leaving in a few, and I just wanted to come and say good-bye in case …" I couldn't say, *In case I never see you again.* As I thought the words, my head screamed at me to apologize for everything I'd said last night and beg her to stay.

Looking over her shoulder, I noticed a duffel bag sitting on her bedroom floor. I swallowed a lump in my throat as I reminded myself that it was for the best. I'd *asked* her to do this.

Natalie stood there, awkwardly avoiding eye contact.

Instinctively, I wrapped my arms around her, hugging her tightly. "I want you to know that I love you, and I never meant to hurt you. But this is the only way I can save you from what is about to come."

She loosely gripped me back. "I'm not leaving." Her voice was flat, without a trace of emotion.

I released her and glanced back at the bag.

She followed my gaze. "I packed up Willow's clothes for Luke. I couldn't let all of those cute outfits Jen bought go to waste."

I opened my mouth, debating if I should try again to convince her to leave, but she held up a hand, clearly not wanting to argue.

"I'm staying here to see this through. You need my help to stop Henley, and you can't talk me out of it." She tilted her chin up, confident in her decision. "Regardless of where we stand, that is what I want."

Regardless of where we stand. The words turned over and over in my head as I tried to process them.

"You'd better get going, or you're going to be late," she said, pushing past me to walk downstairs.

She had every right to be upset with me. When I returned later this afternoon, I'd sit her down and try to find the right words to convey exactly why I'd suggested she leave. I needed her to understand that I could accept whatever might happen to me if I knew she was somewhere safe. That had been my only intention. It wasn't because I didn't want her anymore.

As I trailed down the stairs behind Natalie, I found Raina and Alexander waiting for me by the front door. Raina eyed us, trying to figure out what had happened.

"Be safe," Natalie told them, giving Alexander a hug good-bye.

She didn't try to hug Raina but gave her a small pat on the arm instead. Natalie looked at me, and I could sense she wanted to say more, but she frowned and walked toward the kitchen.

Alexander opened the front door, and I threw one last glance back at Natalie before leaving. She entered the kitchen and smiled the second she saw Willow.

I needed to prepare myself for the possibility of her changing her mind. She still had plenty of time to reconsider her decision before dropping off Luke and Willow. And just as I'd tried to convince her to leave, he would surely do the same.

I was quiet on the twenty-minute drive to Shirley's home in Franklinville. As Raina drove, I listened from the backseat as she and Alexander reviewed the list of questions Jen had prepared for us. Being the expert interviewer that she was, Jen had offered to come with us, but we'd told her no. Even though Alexander had spoken with Shirley's granddaughter briefly on the phone and she'd seemed genuine to him, we had no guarantees. For all we knew, Shirley might have told Henley about us, and they planned to ambush us. Jen had been through enough because of us, and we refused to put her in unnecessary danger.

Alexander hadn't told Shirley's granddaughter who we really were. With Jen's help, he'd concocted a story about him being a reporter for the same newspaper that had done the feature story on Henley's father years ago. Alexander had told Shirley's granddaughter it was a follow-up article that would now focus on Chad Henley and all the charitable contributions he'd made to the community over the years.

It still amazed me that Henley had so many people fooled. Sure, C. Henley Labs Incorporated had donated a significant amount of money over the last several years to fight childhood leukemia. But it was all a show to distract from the fact that he was running such an unethical business behind the scenes.

Shirley's house was a modest single-story yellow home in the suburbs. As Raina pulled into her driveway, I sat up straight in my seat, suddenly more alert, looking for any traces of a threat.

We sat there with the car running, but everything appeared quiet and normal. The neighbor across the street was mowing his yard, and a woman passed by as she walked her beagle. Aside from ours, there was only one other car in Shirley's driveway—an old, beat-up Dodge Caravan with a handicap permit hanging from the rearview mirror.

"I think we're good," I said, looking at Alexander. "Are you sure you're up for this?"

He nodded and opened his door.

Raina and I followed Alexander up onto the front stoop. There wasn't a doorbell, so he used the brass knocker instead.

A moment later, the door opened, and a young woman, not much older than me, answered. She was tall and lean with slightly downturned brown eyes. She smiled warmly at Alexander.

"Mr. Miller?" she asked, using the fake name Alexander had given her when he called.

He stepped past me, extending his hand to the woman. "Nice to meet you in person, Erica." He gestured to me and Raina. "These are my interns. I hope you don't mind that I brought them along."

Erica smiled politely. "Not at all." She stepped to the side, so we could enter. The inside of the house was minimal and spotless. As Erica closed the door behind us, I detected the scent of bleach. "She's a little under the weather today, but she still wanted to meet with you. I'll take you back to meet her."

We followed Erica through the living room and down a hall until we reached Shirley's bedroom. Erica knocked lightly on the partially open door, and we heard a faint voice say, "Come in."

Erica motioned for us to go inside.

Alexander entered first with Raina and me close behind. Shirley was lying in bed, propped up on two pillows. She pulled a frail arm from beneath the covers and brought it to her mouth, coughing roughly into her fist.

A metal folding chair, like the kind you'd set up at a poker table, sat next to her bed. Alexander went to Shirley's side and sat down.

"Would you like me to grab a few more chairs?" Erica asked me while Alexander introduced himself to Shirley.

I shook my head. "No, thank you. We're okay with standing."

We weren't planning to be there very long—ten to fifteen minutes, tops—not that Erica was privy to that.

Raina diligently pulled a notebook and pen out of her purse. Her job was to take notes—or at least give the illusion that she was.

Erica left us alone, and I lingered close to the doorway. Raina was the notetaker, Alexander was the interviewer, and it was my responsibility to keep watch and look out for signs of an ambush.

"What can I help you with today, Mr. Miller?" Shirley asked, tucking her arm back under the blanket with a shiver.

"We won't take much of your time," Alexander replied. "As I explained on the phone, we're doing an article on Chad Henley, and we were hoping you'd be able to give us a more personal angle about who he is. I didn't see any record of him having family nearby."

Shirley frowned. "Well, he doesn't have any family. Not anymore. His father, Charles, was all he had left, and he died about eight years ago."

Alexander leaned forward slightly, seeming empathetic, but he said nothing in response. Jen had instructed him to say as little as possible and just guide the conversation. If he asked too many direct questions, she'd feel like she was being interrogated.

"The trick is to get her to talk to you like a friend," Jen had told him. "Everyone has something that they're just dying to get off their chest. Make her feel safe to talk freely about anything she wants regarding Henley."

Right on cue, Shirley continued, "They weren't close. Charles was a hard man. I worked for him for over ten years, and I don't think I ever saw him smile. Not once."

"That must've been difficult," Alexander acknowledged. "Even more so for Chad."

"He was all business," she said. "I think that's why Chad became a workaholic. That and wanting to prove his father wrong."

"Prove him wrong?" Alexander asked.

Shirley glanced at me and Raina and then back at Alexander. "He could be very hard on Chad. It got worse when Josephine got sick."

Raina stopped scribbling in the notebook and looked up. Shirley didn't notice.

"They diagnosed Josephine with leukemia when she was three years old. Chad was ten. Poor girl spent most of her life in and out of the hospital. She died a few years later. Chad was thirteen then."

"Did Chad have an interest in science as a young boy?" Alexander asked.

Shirley let out a small laugh. "Hardly. Chad was in love with music, and he played the piano brilliantly. He got into science, particularly physiology, about a year before Josephine passed. He became quite knowledgeable on the subject, especially for his age. In fact, toward the end, he was trying to tell the doctors how to do their jobs."

It was hard for me to wrap my head around Henley as a kid. I'd only known him to be this predator who was always on the hunt, trying to destroy us.

Alexander smiled, mirroring Shirley's demeanor, gaining her trust. Although he hated Henley as much as I did.

"He was so angry with Josephine's doctor," Shirley said, wincing as if it was a painful memory. "There weren't as many treatment options back then as there are now, but Henley had researched an experimental treatment that he wanted them to try on Josephine as a last-ditch effort to extend her life."

"What happened?" Alexander asked.

"The doctor refused," Shirley said. "He didn't believe it would work. I remember Chad arguing with him, trying to bribe him with his father's money, asking, 'Why not try? What could it hurt to try?' Josephine died less than a month later. Chad always blamed her doctor for not exploring every viable option to keep her alive."

"How sad," Alexander said.

"Well, I think he eventually got over his anger," Shirley said nonchalantly.

"Why do you say that?" Alexander inquisitively tilted his head to the side.

Shirley shrugged. "Because I heard he's presenting the doctor with a lifetime achievement award in two days."

Raina and I exchanged a look.

Alexander shifted in his seat, trying to remain composed even though we'd just uncovered something big. "On the 9th?" he asked, making absolutely sure he'd heard her correctly.

Shirley nodded.

The 9th was not only the anniversary of Josie's passing, but also the same day he was giving her doctor—the one he blamed for her death—an award. When Natalie had visited Henley's dream, she'd seen a party of some sort.

Henley's planning to execute his attack at the event.

We needed to find out exactly what kind of attack, so we'd know what we were up against. The way Natalie had described Henley's dream, it sounded like he'd poisoned them or something.

"Can you confirm the doctor's name?" Raina asked. "For the article."

"Milford Crouse," Shirley replied. Her health might have been fading, but her mind was still sharp as a whip.

Raina nodded and wrote the name in her notebook.

Erica walked back to the room, stopping in the doorway next to me. "Are we almost finished? She really needs her rest."

Alexander stood up and smiled kindly at Shirley. "Thank you for your time."

Shirley creased her brows together. "You haven't asked me the most important question yet, Mr. Miller."

"What's that?" Alexander's smile faded.

"You haven't asked me about who Chad Henley really is, what kind of person he is."

It was an odd comment that made my hair stand on end.

Alexander took a breath. "What kind of person is Chad Henley?"

Shirley glanced around the room, as if Henley could appear out of thin air. She leaned forward slightly, her body trembling with the effort. "An *evil* one. The worst of the worst," she whispered. "Just like his father."

It wasn't anything we hadn't already known, but for his childhood nanny to have seen it firsthand meant the cruelty he exhibited at his facility extended beyond those walls. Just like in his dream, he'd hurt anyone who stood in his way. Something had happened in his past to make Shirley realize what he was capable of.

Alexander nodded in acknowledgment. "We should let you rest. Thank you again, Ms. Higgins."

SEVENTEEN

RAINA

"We have to find out where that charity event is taking place," I said, pulling out of Shirley's driveway. As I looked in the rearview mirror, I saw Michael bring his phone to his ear.

"Hey. I need you to find out anything you can on a Dr. Milford ..." His eyes met mine.

"Crouse," I said, and he repeated it back into the phone.

He had to be on the phone with Jen, requesting that she lend us her research skills once more.

"Turn here," Dad told me, pointing to the right. "I want to take this back road on the way home."

We'd taken the main highway to get to Shirley's, but Dad must've assumed it would be safer to shake up our route on the way back.

"He's receiving some kind of lifetime achievement award on the 9th, and we need to know where it's taking place," Michael said to Jen. "We think that's when Henley's going to strike." He paused for a moment and then added, "Okay, thanks. Call me if you find anything." He hung up the phone.

"Even though Shirley says she hasn't spoken to Henley in years, I think she suspects he's up to something," Dad said. "I got the impression her warning at the end was an attempt to create some kind of record about Henley's true character, just in case he tried to hurt Dr. Crouse. Especially since everything in the media has always been so positive about him."

I took a breath, feeling anxious about it all. The clock was ticking, and we only had two days to figure out where and how Henley was planning to attack Dr. Crouse, so we could stop him. If Henley was going to do it at the awards ceremony, it was because he wanted an audience and a larger population to hurt. Besides Dr. Crouse, there was no telling how many other innocent people's lives were at stake.

"Did Natalie decide to leave with Luke?" I asked Michael. I'd been waiting all morning for him to bring it up, but he hadn't. It was important to know if we should include her in our plans though.

"No," he replied, but I couldn't tell if he was happy or disappointed.

Of course, he didn't really want her to go. He was being stubborn about wanting to do "the right thing" and had unfortunately gone about it all wrong. After everything she'd been through with our family, I couldn't blame her for being pissed.

Dad turned around to look at Michael. "Why would Natalie consider leaving with Luke?"

I could tell by Michael's silence that he was likely shooting daggers into the back of my head.

Whatever. He shouldn't have been acting stupid in the first place.

"I suggested it to her," he replied, his voice tight with agitation. "But she decided this morning to stay to help us stop Henley."

Dad nodded and turned back around. He didn't need to say it, but he disapproved of Michael's approach as well.

"Do you think Natalie would be willing to pay Henley another visit?" I asked, throwing a cautious glance at my brother. I knew he wouldn't like my question, especially since he probably thought I'd just attempted to stir the pot by asking if Natalie had left with Luke. Still, we had an obligation to explore every avenue to defeat Henley.

Michael winced. "I really don't want her going back in there if we can help it. One time was traumatic enough for her."

I pursed my lips together, resisting the urge to remind him that *we might not have a choice.*

"Stop the car!" Dad yelled.

I slammed on the brakes with no regard for who might be behind me. Luckily, the back road had very little traffic, and no one was there to rear-end us.

Before I could assess the rest of our surroundings or ask Dad what was going on, he leaped out of the car. He just stood there in shock with the passenger door still open. "You're really here. Just like you promised."

I followed his gaze to a silver car parked on the side of the road with its hazard lights on. Standing next to it, staring back at him, was my mother.

It can't be ...

I blinked, not believing my eyes, as the image of her lying dead on the living room floor flooded my mind. My body turned to ice.

"What the ..." Michael mumbled, leaning forward between the two front seats to get a better view.

Dad stumbled toward her in awe.

My heart leaped into my throat. *That's not Mom.*

As if reading my mind, Michael yelled, "Wait, no!" before jumping out of the car after him.

The mirage of Mom faded, and in her place was Becca. As Dad approached her, still under the illusion, Becca smiled.

A man, tall and blond with a lanky build, got out of their car and pulled something out of his jacket pocket. I recognized Hemming from his photograph.

A second man, with dark hair protruding from beneath a baseball cap, emerged from the other side of their vehicle. Based on his massive size, I realized it was Rolf.

It all happened so fast that my brain could barely process one event before the next occurred. There was a loud pop, followed by several more. In an instant, Dad fell to the ground. Michael ran toward him but stopped as his body jerked, and he fell backward.

I ran from the driver's side of the car, and as soon as I saw the pool of blood around Dad, a fire ignited inside me, and instinct took over. Hemming turned his attention toward me, but I focused on all three of our attackers. I let the hurt of losing Mom wash over me and the fear of losing Dad convert into a burning rage that I unleashed back at them.

Becca and the two men flew backward, as if an imaginary blast had taken them off the road. They tumbled down the steep shoulder and into the trees that lined the road. The car tilted on its side and rolled down after them.

Unsure of how badly injured they were, if at all, or how long it would take them to reemerge, I ran to my father, who was unresponsive. My adrenaline was in full effect as I lifted him under his arms and dragged him back to the car. I hoisted him up onto the seat, slamming the door behind him.

Michael was bleeding, but I couldn't tell where it was coming from. He was mobile though and hurled himself into the backseat.

"Move," he said, inhaling sharp breaths through the pain.

Despite a burning stitch in my side, I sprinted back to the driver's side and climbed in. I threw the car in drive and sped off, making the tires squeal. As I looked back, I saw three figures emerge back onto the road. Without their car, they wouldn't be able to catch us. I continued to speed up, putting more distance between them and us.

"Dad," I said, my voice trembling. With one hand on the wheel, I shook him with the other, but his body was limp. "Dad?"

Michael let out a rasp as he reached around the seat, pressing his hand to Dad's bare arm. Nothing happened. Dad didn't move.

"He's not responding," I said.

"I'm shot," Michael replied, dropping his hand and leaning back. "I must not have enough energy to heal him."

"Hold on." I pushed my foot down harder on the gas pedal.

I grabbed my cell phone from the console and fumbled to unlock it. With one eye on the road and the other on my phone, I sent a text to Natalie, Seth, and Jen, that read, *Found.*

They'd understand, and they'd quickly drop everything to meet us at the safe house. Not that there was such a place anymore. Regardless, I'd needed to warn them. Lovisa and Viktor were unaccounted for and could be on their way to confront them.

I swallowed a lump in my throat as I recalled the panic I'd felt when we returned home to find Mom and Jen after they were attacked. The initial shock of it all, followed by the acute awareness of how grave the situation had been, would haunt me for the rest of my life.

"Michael?" I asked, sounding like a kid looking for reassurance.

I couldn't see him in the rearview mirror. Despite the increasing pain from the cramp in my side, I turned to peek into the backseat. He was unconscious, leaning against the door and slumped over. Blood soaked through the front of his shirt.

Running off the road twice, I picked my phone back up and dialed J.T.'s number. I needed a backup plan just in case Natalie had left with Luke after all.

The phone rang twice, and I worried that J.T. might not pick up. He might not want to talk to me.

Just when I was about to hang up, he answered.

"I need your help," I blurted out.

There was a confused pause.

"Raina? Are you okay?"

"No. Can I trust you?"

"Of course you can," he said, and every instinct within me told me to believe him.

I needed to trust him. I couldn't take Dad and Michael to the hospital like a normal person. It would be too easy for Henley to find them there and finish the job.

"Meet me at 144 Chapel Road," I said. "And bring your medical supplies."

Without waiting for him to respond, I hung up. As I tossed the phone back into the console, I noticed blood smeared all over the screen. I must've gotten Dad's blood on my hands when I pulled him into the car.

The silence in the car was unnerving as I drove to the safe house. I felt exhausted from it all but pushed myself to get them to safety, praying that Natalie would be there to heal them.

They said most of the things you worried about never actually came true. For me, that wasn't the case. I was living my worst nightmare. Losing my family had always been my greatest fear, and now, it felt like they were being taken away from me, one by one.

Fifteen agonizing minutes later, the car skidded as I turned right onto Chapel Road.

I let out an audible sigh of relief when I saw Natalie's and Seth's cars parked at the end of the street. We knew better than to park directly in front of the safe house, but her car being there meant she'd already arrived.

After Michael recovered, I'd have to rub it in that I'd been right about not sending Natalie away. He'd made her one of us, and now, she was here to stay. We *needed* her.

For a moment, I wondered what had shifted to make me feel that way. One minute, I had whined to J.T. about how I couldn't accept Natalie as my family, and the next, I was fighting with my brother to keep her.

I pulled into the driveway of the safe house, and although this was against protocol, I didn't have a choice. There'd be no other way to get

Dad and Michael out of the car. Now that my adrenaline had worn off, I was so drained that I could barely move.

I threw the car in park and pushed the driver's door open despite it feeling like it weighed a hundred pounds.

The front door to the house opened, and Natalie emerged with Seth and Jen close behind her.

Natalie looked at Dad, unconscious in the front seat. Her eyes darted to the back door of the car, and when it didn't open, horror took over her expression. She ran to it and carefully pulled it open, propping Michael up with one arm so he didn't fall out.

"What happened?" she asked.

"They attacked us on our way home," I said, clutching my side.

Seth and Jen hurried toward Dad as I clumsily climbed out of the car.

Michael was still out cold, but Natalie leaned in the car, laying her hand on his cheek. When he didn't respond, she shoved her hand under his shirt, pressing it directly to his wound.

Behind me, I heard gravel kicking up beneath the tires of an approaching vehicle and turned around. I was ready to kill Becca or the tetrad, not that I was confident I'd have the strength or powers to pull it off.

To my relief, the approaching noise was an ambulance without the lights or sirens on.

The ambulance stopped in the street, and J.T. hopped out, running toward me. Despite the direness of the situation, his presence gave me a small sense of relief.

The passenger door of the ambulance opened, and Detective Thompson got out. He paused momentarily, taking in the situation before hurrying after J.T.

"Are you all right?" J.T. asked, grasping the sides of my arms as he looked me over.

"I'm fine. It's my dad and Michael who need your help."

"You're injured." J.T. pointed to the bottom of my shirt, which was soaked in blood.

I pushed him toward the car, leaving a bloody handprint on his sleeve. "Help them! *Please.*"

Detective Thompson's hand rested on his gun. For a moment, I worried he might arrest me—or worse, believe I posed a threat and open fire. "Is the perpetrator nearby?"

I shook my head. "No. I don't think they followed us here."

Seth and Jen struggled to get Dad out of the car. Detective Thompson noticed and rushed to help them. J.T. ran back to the ambulance and retrieved a gurney.

After several minutes, we got Dad and Michael into the house. Luckily, the place Stan had selected didn't have many neighboring homes. The neighborhood was quiet, so I assumed the surrounding homeowners were likely at work, which was a good thing. If they hadn't been, surely, someone would've noticed the commotion and either come outside or called the police.

We laid Dad out on a hunter-green sofa in the living room but left Michael on the gurney in the foyer. Having him close by made it easier for us to bounce back and forth to take care of them both.

I stood by Michael, checking to make sure he was still breathing. He was unconscious but hanging in there. Everyone else's attention had shifted to Dad, whose condition appeared to be more critical.

Natalie knelt on the floor next to Dad. She had one hand on his arm, the other on his forehead. All the color had drained from his face as he lay there, completely still.

Jen couldn't watch and buried her face in Seth's chest as he clung tightly to her.

I stifled a cry, taking in the sight of Dad's open shirt that revealed several bullet wounds. They'd already attempted to revive him with a defibrillator, but it hadn't worked. Natalie was making one last attempt to heal him.

J.T. and his brother watched her curiously. I half-expected them to freak out and demand to know what was going on, but they didn't.

Natalie moved her hand from Dad's forehead to his chest, but still, there was no response. J.T. laid his hand on her shoulder, and she looked up at him with wet eyes.

I swayed back and forth, feeling woozy.

I shouldn't have stopped the car. If I'd kept driving, none of this would've happened.

J.T. turned to look at me. His face softened and then blurred.

I saw him mouth my name, but I couldn't hear. It was as if my head were being held underwater, clogging my ears. My legs wobbled beneath me as I submerged further and further into darkness.

J.T. leaped toward me right before everything went black.

Michael sat silently as Alexander stitched up the cut on his arm. He was used to it by now. About a year ago, he'd even stopped flinching when they cut him open. Me, on the other hand, I could never look directly at the needle as it pierced into Michael's skin, mending the wounds Henley had inflicted on him. Instead, I stared at the wall until Alexander was finished.

"All done," Alexander announced, more for my benefit than Michael's.

I peeked over at my brother, who was brave-faced as usual.

I was the lucky one of the two of us, and I knew it. When Henley or one of the doctors cut me open, Michael would heal me as soon as he got the chance. Thankfully for Alexander, he always made sure that was sooner rather than later.

Not that I had an easy life by any means. I still had testing of my own to complete every day, and if I failed to do as Henley instructed, I faced my own set of consequences. Henley had learned a long time ago that putting me in isolation, away from Michael, was an effective motivation tactic for me. On more than one occasion, when I dared not to follow exact orders, Henley had me placed in solitary confinement. No visitors, no food, only water. The worst time was when he'd placed me there for three days. At least, that was how long Michael said I was gone. I'd lost track.

Alexander gathered up his supplies and placed them back on the steel tray. He glanced up at the two-way mirror on the wall. "I have something I want to ask you." He looked at Michael and then at me.

Michael lifted his arm from the table and folded his hands in his lap. He didn't have to say it, but he was preparing himself for something awful.

"It's not bad," Alexander said, knowing Michael almost as well as I did. "But you have to promise me that you won't tell anyone about our conversation."

I looked at Michael, waiting for his reply. When he nodded, I did as well.

"I know things are tough here for you," Alexander said. "What would you think about leaving?"

His question made me nervous. Does he know about how we almost snuck out when the power was out? Did Luke tell him?

"We aren't allowed to leave," Michael replied, not giving away anything about our near escape.

Alexander cared about us. We knew that. But at the same time, I wasn't sure if he'd be mad at us if he knew we'd thought about running away.

Alexander nodded. "Yes, that's true. But what if someone took you out of here? Would you go with them?"

Michael narrowed his eyes, thinking through the question. "I guess it would depend on who was taking us."

"What if that person was me?" Alexander glanced at me, but I just stared back at him.

Surely, I hadn't heard him right.

Michael opened his mouth but then quickly closed it. He hadn't expected Alexander's response either.

"It's important to me that you have a choice. A life outside of these walls won't be easy either. Henley will look for us, and we'll have to take precautions to avoid him. But my wife and I want to be your parents. We want to try to give you some semblance of a normal life. We want to keep you safe."

My chin dropped. I wanted to jump out of my chair, throw my arms around Alexander, and accept his offer. But I wouldn't leave unless Michael wanted to. There was no way I was going anywhere without him.

Michael stared down at the table, deep in thought. When he finally lifted his eyes and smiled back at Alexander, I felt my heart leap out of my chest.

I was finally going to get the family I'd always dreamed of.

A warm hand held mine as the thumb traced circles in my palm.

I moaned, not because I was in pain, but because, as I woke up, I remembered the reality of my situation.

Both of my parents are dead.

"Raina," J.T. whispered, squeezing my hand.

I opened my eyes and found him sitting on the side of my bed. I wanted to see his friendly smile, the dimples in his cheeks, but his expression was one of concern, almost agony.

"You're here." My voice was rough, not sounding like me at all.

"Of course I am. Where else would I be?" He gently guided my shoulder back down with his free hand as I tried to sit up. "You took a bullet, too, and you need to rest."

"What's the date?" I asked, unaware of how long I'd been asleep. I prayed we hadn't missed our opportunity to stop Henley.

"It's March 8."

I sighed with momentary relief before recalling the events that had led us to being attacked. The image of Dad dropping to the ground after being shot burned into my memory. I closed my eyes as I thought of his limp, unresponsive body in the passenger seat of the car and willed myself to hold it together.

As if reading my mind, J.T. squeezed my hand again. "I'm so sorry about your dad. We did everything we could to save him."

"Where is he now?" The thought of him dead and still in the house was unfathomable.

"I loaded him into the ambulance, and Ray and I took him to the morgue."

The word *morgue* made my stomach turn.

"What about Michael? Is he ..." I couldn't finish the question, but I opened my eyes, needing to see J.T.'s reaction. If he told me Michael had died too, I was certain I'd crumble into a million pieces.

"He's going to be fine. Natalie and I gave him a blood transfusion. You got one too. You'd both lost a lot of blood."

I let out a small sigh, relieved that I still had my brother. "A blood transfusion?"

"You're lucky that she's a universal donor and you have a boyfriend in the medical field."

"Boyfriend? That's a little presumptuous." I couldn't believe that he was still sitting there with me. I would've thought he'd run for the hills by now.

It could still happen. I haven't told him anything yet.

Even with a faint smile on his lips, his dimples pressed into his cheeks. "Still playing hard to get, I see."

"After everything that's happened, I can't believe you came."

He tilted his head, his expression serious again. "I know we haven't known each other for very long, but I care about you, Raina. I don't know what's been going on in your life, but I've never spoken to Ray about you or your family. Not until today."

His brother had seen too much, and I wasn't sure that he'd be on our side. "Is he still here?"

"Yeah."

Great.

"Is he going to arrest us?" For all I knew, he'd already arrested Natalie and Michael, and he was just waiting for me to wake up, so he could arrest me too.

J.T. creased his brows. "No, of course not."

"I don't understand," I replied. "He was all over us, looking for evidence that we'd done something wrong. What changed?"

"Well, a lot." J.T. sat up straighter but kept my hand tightly in his. "He and I were having lunch when you called. I could tell it was an emergency by how panicked you were, so he insisted on coming with me. At first, he wanted to call it in, but I begged him to just trust me and assess the situation before he did."

"Did he make the call?"

The house was silent at the moment, but that didn't mean cops wouldn't be arriving at any second.

"No, but he wants to talk to you."

I sighed, wishing Dad were here to tell me what to do.

J.T. showing up today had reestablished my confidence in him. He cared about me, but I didn't know if I could trust Detective Thompson. J.T. did though, and maybe that was enough.

"I'll talk to him," I said. "But I want you to hear the complete story too. You deserve the truth."

J.T. stood up, his hand holding mine a little longer than necessary before letting it go. "I'll be right back."

After he left, I propped up on my elbows until I was in a sitting position with my back against the headboard. To my surprise, I didn't have any pain in my side from where the gunshot wound had been. I actually felt okay, healthy even.

A moment later, J.T. returned with Detective Thompson behind him. The detective watched me skeptically. I did my best to appear calm and confident despite thinking of all the negative consequences that could happen because of my confession. Telling them the truth could cause us to be arrested for obstruction of justice in Mom's death. At a minimum, I expected J.T. to conclude I was a total nutcase. I was confident that after this, he'd never want to see me again.

J.T. sat back down on the bed while Detective Thompson sat in a chair across the room. He was deliberately keeping a safe distance from me.

I hesitated, waiting to see if the detective would start the conversation but he didn't. Instead, he just sat there, assessing me.

I cleared my throat. "Detective Thompson, I get that this looks bad."

"Call me Ray."

"Ray, I understand it might seem like we're the bad guys, but we aren't."

"Chad Henley is," Ray said confidently.

I gaped at him in surprise but managed a nod.

He shifted in his seat, his shoulders relaxing. "I asked Natalie who executed the attack on you, and she named him. It doesn't surprise me though. While investigating the deaths of several missing teens in the area, I got a lead that pointed to Chad Henley. My informant turned up dead, and shortly after, my superior removed me from the case. The situation never sat right with me."

"He's killed dozens of runaways," I said. "He's conducting medical experiments on them."

"That explains the inconsistencies found in their autopsies." Ray sighed. "I began looking into Henley again when your mother's case came up."

"You did? What made you connect it to him?"

Henley had been so meticulous not to slip up that I couldn't imagine him leaving behind any evidence.

"The explosion at your previous residence was so uncommon because there were no obvious causes. There was no fire and no evidence of a bomb or gas leak," he said. "So, I began pulling police reports of all explosions with unknown causes from the past five years, and I found one that occurred at one of his laboratories in Charlotte, North Carolina. It looked like someone in the Charlotte PD had attempted to sweep it under the rug, but they hadn't done a good enough job."

I knew exactly which one he was referring to. That was the lab where Henley had held Michael, and Natalie had used her powers to blow out the wall of his office for them to escape.

"After my last visit to your house, I submitted a request for a search warrant of Henley's headquarters. Then, without warning, I got put on administrative leave." Ray folded his arms across his broad chest. "They took my badge and my gun."

I recalled seeing him reach for his gun earlier, and my eyes trailed to the one sitting in a holster on his hip, partially concealed by his jacket.

He followed my gaze. "This is my personal weapon. After what happened to my informant, I've been carrying it for safety reasons."

Dad had always warned us about the reach of Henley's power. It was the sole reason we could never go to the police for protection. We never knew who would turn us in. It turned out, Dad was right, as usual.

"What else did Natalie tell you about our situation and Henley?" I asked.

Ray glanced at J.T. and then back at me. "Nothing. She asked if we could wait for you to wake up. She thought you'd want to be the one to tell J.T. your story."

Huh.

I took a breath and decided it was now or never. I'd never told someone about the real me before, but it was time I did. As scary as it was, I needed J.T. to hear the truth even if it drove him away. If I was going to open up to someone for the first time, at least it'd be to someone who really mattered to me.

J.T. and Ray listened attentively, making no attempt to interrupt me while I told them *everything*. I explained who I was, where I'd come from, and what I could do. J.T. raised his eyebrows as I explained how I had telekinesis and that was how I'd escaped the ambush alive. Ray, however, remained apathetic through every detail.

I told them the truth about Mom's death and how it was Natalie's brainwashed sister who'd killed her. I explained all about Henley's experiments, how we'd been on the run from him for years, and why we suspected he was planning an attack.

When I finished, I watched J.T., expecting him to call me crazy, or repulsive, or any of the things I feared before running out of the room. But he didn't. He just sat there, thinking it through.

I glanced at Ray, still expressionless, and wondered if he'd call the local mental hospital and have me carted away in a straitjacket.

"Say something," I said, looking at J.T. I sounded desperate, but I didn't care.

I needed to understand where his head was at. If he was going to condemn me, I needed him to just get it over with.

"You realize how far-fetched it sounds, right?"

I stiffened. *Here it comes. He's going to leave.*

"But your bullet wound healed up when Natalie touched you. I saw it with my own eyes, and you can't just make that up." He smiled at me reassuringly.

I turned my eyes to Ray, who was rubbing his chin.

"Do you know how many drug addicts I've had over the years who told me they could move objects with their minds?" he asked.

"I'm not on drugs."

"You saw it, Ray. Natalie healed Raina with just the touch of her hand. They're telling the truth," J.T. told him.

Ray remained unconvinced. "Con artists have a way of making you believe things that aren't really there."

I looked around the room, determined to come up with a way to convince him. "Fine," I said. "Pick any object in this room, and I'll prove it to you. I'll move it with my mind."

Ray tilted his head. "Anything I want?"

"Anything."

He glanced around, contemplating something that I wouldn't be able to fabricate. Then, he looked at me with a satisfied look on his face. "All right then. Move me."

I hoped I had enough energy to make my powers work. I hadn't contemplated that when I boldly offered to showcase my talent.

Taking a deep breath, I focused on Ray. I didn't want to hurt him, but I needed the gesture to be big enough to get his attention and remove any doubt.

I set my eyes on his feet, which were in thick black boots. With my mind, I imagined giving them a tug forward. When I did, his boots promptly followed, kicking his legs straight out in front of him.

The look of shock on his face almost made me laugh, but I didn't want him to think I was making fun of him, so I held it back. However, J.T. chuckled as his brother fought to steady himself back in the chair.

"Are you convinced now?" J.T. asked with an amused grin still spread across his face.

Ray looked at me with wide eyes, quickly composed himself, and then gave me a serious nod.

"Good. Now, back to Chad Henley." J.T. turned back to me. "Is there a chance he can find you here?"

"There's always a possibility," I replied. "But I think he's preoccupied with whatever he's planning tomorrow."

I glanced toward the window, and even with the blinds tightly closed, I could tell it was evening. We were running out of time.

Ray leaned forward, resting his hands on his knees. "Talk me through what you know."

I described Natalie's dream, told him about Josie, and relayed what Shirley had told us about Henley's resentment toward her doctor. I held back the part about how Natalie and I'd broken into Dr. Rees's house but mentioned that Dr. Rees was an infectious disease specialist who'd been working with Henley.

"Could it be a virus?" J.T. asked.

I looked at him, puzzled.

"The attack," he clarified. "It doesn't sound like food poisoning. What you described sounds more like a respiratory virus. That would explain his need for an infectiologist."

A chill ran down my spine. "He experimented with a bunch of illnesses on Natalie, trying to perfect his miracle cure. But why would he want to kill a bunch of people if he wants to market his cure?"

Ray rubbed his hands roughly over his face. "Because he wants it to be memorable."

A pang of guilt stabbed at me, reminding me of how I'd already let him orchestrate killing both of my parents. I peeled back the covers, still dressed in the same clothes as earlier. The blood had dried, but it'd stained through both my pants and shirt. "We have to stop him."

J.T. placed his hands on my shoulders, gently urging me to stay put. "You can't just go hunt him down."

"Watch me." Without a doubt, I'd kill Henley on sight. I'd take out Becca and the tetrad, too, while I was at it.

"I won't let you go on a suicide mission." J.T. looked me square in the eye. "I just got you back. I'm not losing you."

"We need to know his game plan, what we're dealing with," Ray said. "There has to be someone who knows … someone close enough to him to have the details of his plan."

I brought my bare feet to the floor as a plot formed in my head. "I know who. And I have her address."

Eighteen

Natalie

"They should be back by now," I said, perched in a beige armchair in the living room.

Seth glanced down at his watch. "It's only been an hour."

"I'm not sure about this plan ..." Not only did it seem extreme, but it was also illegal.

Then again, we were running out of options and needed to do anything possible to stop Henley from murdering a roomful of innocent people.

"Find anything?" I asked Jen, who was curled up on the couch with her laptop. Seth was sitting at the far end, rubbing her feet.

Jen looked up at me and frowned. "Very little, but I'm working on it." Her eyes were still red from processing Alexander's death.

"Keep searching, babe," Seth encouraged her.

"I'm going to check on Michael again," I said, standing up, needing to do *something*. I needed a distraction from the grief that weighed heavily on my heart and the impending sense of doom that we might not be able to stop Henley in time.

I'd been bouncing back and forth from the living room to Michael's room. He'd woken up before Raina, and I broke the news to him about Alexander. Understandably, he didn't take it well and asked for some time alone. When I'd checked on him twenty minutes ago, he was asleep, but I wanted to be there when he woke up again. They were close, and I knew his death was devastating to him.

The safe house had three bedrooms, each with a queen bed as hard as a rock, but it was good enough to deal with for a couple of days. We wouldn't be here longer than that anyway.

I opened the door to the room we'd put Michael in. He was asleep in the same position as I'd left him.

I sat down in the wooden kitchen chair I'd placed next to his bed, propped my feet up by his legs, and watched him take full, peaceful breaths.

He would've died if I'd left with Luke. I shuddered as I recalled how close I'd come to going with him yesterday.

Saying good-bye to Willow and Luke hadn't been easy. Every time she cooed from her car seat on the way to pick up Luke's car, I'd considered changing my mind and leaving with them. I wished I could be a part of her life and watch her grow up. Who knew what was going to happen when we confronted Henley? I'd most likely end up dead, in jail, or back on the run. The odds of us beating Henley at his own game were minuscule.

"I don't want to let her go," I said, looking down at Willow in my arms, trying to memorize every detail of her precious face.

She contentedly looked up at me without a care in the world. She was oblivious to the painful fact that we'd likely never see each other again.

"You don't have to," Luke replied, loading the last bag into the trunk of the car before shutting it. "You can still change your mind and come with us."

I shook my head. "No, I need to stay. My place is here." I kissed Willow on the forehead before putting her in the car seat installed in Luke's getaway car. As I buckled her in, I wiped a tear from my cheek. Although I'd just met her, it was agonizing to think of moving on with my life without her.

Luke watched me intently. "I'll keep her safe."

"I know."

He turned, like he was going to leave, but then abruptly stopped to face me. "Staying is a mistake. You realize that, right?"

I shrugged, not knowing anything for certain anymore. The pressure of the decision had split my heart into two pieces—between Willow and Michael, between taking care of my niece and stopping Henley. My instinct told me to remain behind and fight.

"You're staying for a guy who wants you to leave." Each word he said wounded me.

"It's not that simple."

He reached out and firmly grasped the sides of my arms. "I don't want you to die. Just change your mind and come with us. You, me, and Willow—we can be a family,"

I glanced at Willow, a spitting image of Becca as a baby. If I held up their picture side by side, there'd be no telling who was who.

"She needs a mother."

His words ripped into my already-shredded heart. It was unlikely that Becca would ever fully regain her memory of who she had been. Even if she did, we had no way of knowing the long-term trauma all of this would cause her and if she'd be stable enough to help take care of her daughter.

For a moment, I could see myself being that person for Willow, fiercely loving and protecting her as she grew up. I'd hold her hand as she learned to walk. Cry as I dropped her off for her first day of school. Celebrate every one of her birthdays. I could care for her like a mother while telling her all the wonderful memories of her real one. If I just got in the car with Luke, I could make all of that happen.

I opened my mouth, unsure of my response.

Luke saw my hesitation and lifted his hands, cupping the sides of my face. I didn't stop him, unsure if I even wanted to. A part of me wanted him to convince me to go. Some aspects of my life would be easier if I did.

"We could be great together if you just gave us a chance. Leave with me, and I swear I'll never make you regret it."

Another tear sprang from my eye and rolled down my cheek into his hand. I'd thought I'd made my decision, but saying good-bye was heartbreaking.

"I love you," he said, his eyes pleading with me. "I think, deep down, you've suspected that for a while. But it's been easier to paint me as the villain, so you don't have to face the fact that you feel something for me too."

"I ... I don't know what to do."

"Do you love me?" he asked.

I struggled to find the words. Did I love him the way I loved Michael? No. Did I love him as a friend? I wasn't sure. Things with him had always been so complicated, so up and down that I'd never been able to fully process my feelings for him.

Growing impatient, he leaned forward and kissed me. I didn't kiss him back, but I didn't push him away either. Instead, my mind swirled with questions as I second-guessed my decision to stay.

Could I ever love Luke a fraction of the way I love Michael? Is this my one and only chance to have a somewhat-normal life and a family of my own?

I felt his lips guide mine apart, his hot breath against my mouth, and I instinctively tensed. My body gave me the answer that my mind struggled with.

My heart belonged to Michael even if he didn't want me anymore.

Luke's wounded eyes searched mine as he felt me pull away. He released me without protest and lowered his hands to his sides.

"I'm sorry," I whispered. "I care about you but ..."

"But not enough to choose me."

I winced, hating the fact that I was hurting him. But it wouldn't be fair to either of us if I tried to force myself into feeling something for him I didn't. Luke was my friend and nothing more.

"Good-bye, Luke." I stepped back, putting more distance between us. "Please take care of Willow ... and yourself."

Luke eyed me for a moment, as if hoping I'd come to my senses and change my mind. When he realized I wasn't going to, he walked around the car and climbed into the driver's seat. I approached the back window and stole one last look at Willow. I placed my hand on the glass and left it there until Luke started the car. Then, I watched them drive away.

Michael shifted slightly, but it was enough to bring me back to the present. I held my breath, wondering if he was waking up. I wanted to reach out and touch him, but I kept my hands clasped in my lap instead.

Slowly, his eyes opened. I leaned forward.

"Hi," I said softly and calmly, not wanting to startle him.

He blinked his eyes a few times. "Where are we?"

"We're still at the safe house."

He furrowed his brow. "Then, it wasn't just a dream, was it?"

"No, I'm sorry." The heartache stung my throat.

He closed his eyes and let out a broken sigh. A moment later, when he reopened them, he looked at me. "Has Raina woken up yet?"

"Yes. A little over an hour ago." I hoped he didn't ask me right off the bat where she was. He wouldn't like the answer.

He sat up, leaning his back against the walnut headboard. When he noticed I was about to stop him, he reached out a hand and assured me he was fine.

"Are you in any pain?" I asked, trying to remember if Alexander had kept pain medicine in his medical bag that we'd found in the trunk. A bullet had pierced through the backseat, barely missing it.

"No, I'm good. Better than I would've expected."

Someone knocked lightly on the bedroom door, and a moment later, Jen poked her head inside. She smiled when she saw Michael.

"Oh good! You're awake. I have news," she said. "I located Milford Crouse. He's a retired pediatric oncologist, but he does a lot of charitable work for families of children battling cancer. He lives in Miami now, but he's still on the board of a children's hospital in Chicago."

"Did you find out about his award?" Michael asked.

Jen tucked her hair behind her ear. "Yes, although it was very difficult to find information about it. I had to creep on social media, but according to Dr. Crouse's daughter, it's going to be at The Marquant, a hotel about forty minutes from here."

"Good work," Michael said.

"That's not all." She paused, giving us a warning look, as if telling us to brace ourselves. "They originally booked the event at a hotel across the street from the hospital, but about two months ago, they moved it to the newly renovated Marquant. I did some digging and found out G.G. Armand Designs had purchased it within the last year."

I turned to Michael. "It's true then. That's where he's going to attack." The memory of all the people falling to the floor in his dream, taking their last breaths, sent a shiver down my spine. "The only question left is, *how?*"

Raina's plan had to work. It was our last shot.

As if reading my mind, Jen said, "I'll let you know when Raina gets back," before slipping out of the room.

"Where did Raina go?" Michael asked me. "It isn't safe for her to be out there alone."

"She isn't alone. J.T. and Ray are with her." Just as I was about to go into the details of where they had gone, I heard the front door to the house open and close.

"Let me go!" a woman's angry voice rang out.

Michael jerked his head toward the door to the room, confused, likely because he recognized the voice but couldn't place it.

He flipped off the covers, and before I could stop him and explain what was going on, he charged out of the room.

I followed behind him, knowing he'd be furious with Raina for coming up with this plan and also with me for going along with it.

As soon as he entered the living room, he stopped short, surprised to see Tonya standing in the foyer with her hands cuffed behind her back. Raina stood, blocking the front door with her arms crossed against her chest.

Aware of our presence, Tonya turned around to face us. She scrunched her face in revulsion.

Seth and Jen sat on the couch, watching the situation unfold, as Ray latched on to Tonya's arm. He pulled her past me and Michael and down the hall. He stopped at the room Raina had been resting in and pushed Tonya inside.

"Have you officially lost your mind?" Michael asked Raina. "You *kidnapped* her?"

"Do you have a better idea?" she replied, raising her voice. "Henley is about to go on a killing spree, and she's probably one of the few people who knows exactly what he's planning to do."

Michael raked his hands through his hair. "What if they followed you? Or what if someone saw you?"

"It's fine." Raina calmed her tone, attempting to rationalize with Michael. "We were careful."

Michael pointed his finger at her. "If this backfires, it's on you."

He stormed out of the room and toward the other side of the house, where the kitchen was.

Raina moved like she was going to go after him, but I held up my hand to stop her.

"Let me talk to him," I said.

She pursed her lips but nodded in agreement.

I went after Michael and found him pacing back and forth in the kitchen.

"You knew about this?" he asked when he noticed me standing in the doorway.

"Yes."

"And you did nothing to stop her?"

I shrugged. "What did you want me to do? She's right, and if we don't do something and soon, Henley's going to murder innocent people. Our best chance of beating him is to find out exactly what he's planning. There's no telling what we'll be walking into if we just blindly bust in there."

He paused, considering my point of view. I waited patiently for him to respond, but he turned his back to me, pressing his palms into the top of the counter and bowing his head in defeat.

I wanted to wrap my arms around him and try to provide him with some sort of comfort. This was a lot for him to process after being ambushed, almost dying, and finding out his father hadn't survived. Unsure if he'd want me to touch him, I decided to just stand next to him with my back against the counter.

He swung his head to look at me. "I can't do this." His voice was low, like he was afraid someone else would hear him. "I feel like everything is hanging together by a thread that's about to snap. I'm not Alexander. I don't know what I'm doing."

"No one expects you to have all the answers."

"*I* expect me to." He jabbed his finger into his chest. "I should've known that healing Becca would give her powers. I never should've left Lorena and Jen alone with her." He shifted his hands back to the edge of the counter, tightening his grip. "I should've stopped Alexander from getting out of the car."

He thinks it's his fault.

There was no way he would've been able to predict any of that would happen.

I thought about the night on the beach right after we'd become friends when I confessed to him the guilt I'd been holding on to about Becca's kidnapping. Recalling what he'd said to me, I placed my hand on top of his and repeated it back to him. "You can't blame yourself. You did nothing wrong."

He held my eyes for a moment, and I knew he remembered telling me the same thing. Then, he looked down at our hands, and I pulled mine away.

That night, he'd also told me that the only person responsible for taking my sister was the person who took her. That applied to this scenario as well. The only people to blame for Alexander's death were Henley, Becca, and the tetrad.

Alexander had told me he was dreaming of Lorena. I wouldn't be surprised if it had really been Becca all along, invading his dreams and getting him to lower his guard so she could lure him into a trap.

Seth poked his head into the kitchen and cleared his throat. "Sorry to interrupt, but I think they are about to interrogate Tonya."

"I'll be right there," I replied. Seth ducked out, and I looked up at Michael. "They want me to read her mind and try to get answers while they ask her questions. It's the only way to confirm if she's telling the truth or holding back something."

Michael took a deep breath and nodded.

Seth, Jen, and J.T. kept watch in the living room while the rest of us gathered in the tiny bedroom to interview Tonya. Raina said they were careful when they took Tonya, but if Henley noticed she was missing, he'd easily trace it back to us. Even though we were at a safe house, it wouldn't be impossible for Henley to figure out where it was.

Inside Raina's bedroom, Tonya sat in a chair with her hands still handcuffed behind her back. She defiantly stared down Ray. Based on his body language, he was planning to lead the interrogation.

"What do you know about the attack Henley is planning?" Ray asked, crossing his arms across his chest so that his biceps flexed.

I focused on Tonya, ready to read her mind, but her eyes immediately flicked to me.

"Hydrogen. Lithium. Beryllium. Boron. Carbon."

"Ask her again," I said.

Ray repeated the question, but Tonya's thoughts continued, unwavering. *"Nitrogen. Oxygen. Fluorine. Neon."*

"What is it?" Raina asked.

I threw my hands up in the air. "She's reciting the periodic table in her head."

Raina stepped forward, agitated, and got in Tonya's face. "He's planning to kill people, which means you'll be an accomplice to *murder.*"

Ray held out his hand, creating a barrier between Raina and Tonya. His demeanor was calm, calculated, like he'd done this a thousand times. Then again, he probably had.

"Tonya," he said. His voice was kind, almost friendly. "I don't think you're a bad person."

Raina huffed.

"I think you're probably a loyal employee, and you falsely think you're doing the right thing by withholding information." Ray was clearly assuming the position of good cop. "But if you don't help us, innocent people are going to die. I know you don't want that."

Tonya narrowed her eyes. *"Sodium. Magnesium. Aluminum."*

"This isn't working," I said. "I can't get anything. Henley must've trained her to block me out."

She smiled smugly as she mentally continued her recitation.

Several hours later, we still hadn't cracked Tonya.

At around two a.m., we regrouped in the living room and decided it was time to call it a night. Raina protested at first, but Ray insisted we take a break and get some sleep.

"We're all exhausted," he told her. "Right now, Tonya's determined to fight us, and we need to wear her down. Trust me, she won't get any rest, sitting in that uncomfortable chair. Let's give her time to sit alone with her thoughts and question the extent of her loyalty to Henley."

"Not to mention the fact that we need to be rested and on top of our game. Even if she doesn't tell us anything, we have to try to stop the attack anyway," Michael said.

We spread out between the living room and the two other bedrooms in the house to get some rest. I tossed and turned but dozed off for at least a few hours. Seth had gotten some sleep while we interrogated Tonya and had volunteered to sit by the front window in the living room to keep watch again.

By eight a.m., we were awake and resumed questioning Tonya while Seth took another nap. As Ray had predicted, Tonya appeared exhausted. She struggled to recite the elements, but we still hadn't gotten her to give up any actual information yet.

Two hours later, Ray pulled us back into the hallway.

"We only have a few hours left to get this figured out, and she's not budging," he whispered. "Normally, by this point, we would've sent in another officer, someone she'd potentially relate to, to try to get her to open up."

"What are our options?" Michael asked.

Ray looked at me. "I think you should go in alone."

"Me?" Surely, I hadn't heard him correctly. I was probably the last person Tonya would talk to. She hated me. It had been clear in the way she treated me so inhumanely when I was a prisoner at Henley's facility.

"Yes," Ray replied. "If we were at the station, I'd send a female officer in there—someone who could find some common ground with her."

"Why not me?" Raina asked. "I'll go in there and just beat it out of her."

Ray frowned. "That's exactly the reason I can't send you." He looked back at me. "We've been intentionally holding back the details of what we already know. But now, I think we've got to lay our cards out on the table and try to find something that strikes a chord with her."

Michael eyed me but offered no opinion.

I nodded. "Okay, I can try it."

As I reached for the doorknob, Michael placed his hand over mine. "I'll be right here if you need me."

I pulled away first but attempted a smile. It was sweet that he still wanted to watch over me even though he didn't need to.

Tonya scowled when I entered the room.

"I don't want to be here any more than you do," I said, realizing this was the first time since she'd arrived that I addressed her directly.

She fixed her eyes straight ahead, but I didn't attempt to read her mind. I knew exactly what was running through it.

Instead, I kept the conversation going, hoping that she'd let her guard down once she felt like I wasn't actively trying to invade her mind. "It's not fun, being a hostage. Not that long ago, the roles were reversed, so I understand exactly how you feel. You just want to go home, back to your normal life and the people you care about. Do you have someone at home who's worried about where you are?"

Tonya's expression remained unchanged as she tuned me out.

"You could make this so much easier on yourself if you just told us what you know about Henley's plan. We'll let you go as soon as we stop him." I paused, waiting for her to respond but she didn't.

I paced around the room, trying to figure out the right angle to get her talking.

"How about this?" I asked, making it up as I went along. "I'll tell you what I've learned about his plan. Then, all you have to do is help us fill in the blanks."

Once again, she didn't answer, but I pressed on anyway. "We know about Josie and how much her death impacted Henley. Even though I don't agree with him on, well, really anything, I have empathy for him regarding Josie because of my sister." I sat down on the edge of the bed, facing Tonya. "We're aware that he's planning this attack as an act of revenge on her doctor, Milford Crouse. Henley blames him for Josie's death, doesn't he?"

Tonya blinked but gave me no sign that she'd heard what I said.

"I get that he's angry. I mean, Henley saw a potential opportunity to save his sister, and Dr. Crouse wouldn't help him." I kept talking, looking for the right trigger to get her to open up. "If you don't help us, there's no telling who at that event you'll impact. You might not know them personally, but they are people's parents, siblings, children ... and soon, they'll all die because they made the single mistake of attending a party tonight at The Marquant Hotel."

Tonya's eyes flashed to mine. Something had caught her attention. "What?"

I sat up a little straighter. *Finally, a response.* "These people are innocent—"

"Not that," she snapped. "Where? What hotel?"

"The Marquant," I replied, not understanding the significance. Surely, she had known it was taking place there. *Right?*

Her mouth gaped open, and she looked away, trying to process what I'd told her.

With her distracted, I seized the moment and tried to read her mind again.

"She's lying. Mr. Henley wouldn't attack The Marquant. Not tonight. This has to be a mistake."

I listened intently to her racing thoughts.

"Frank said he was heading straight there and he'd call me after."

"Who's Frank?"

She grimaced. "Get out of my head, you freak."

"I have to warn him, but his phone will be off until he lands."

I tried to pull the pieces of the puzzle together, to get her to say more. We were so close to a breakthrough. I could feel it.

Then, like a light switch being turned on, my intuition kicked in, and I realized what had her worried.

"Henley didn't share the full plan with you, did he?" I leaned in closer to her.

She didn't respond but shot me a look that made me confident I was right.

"You know someone who's attending the fundraiser." *Come on, Tonya. Give it up.*

"My brother," she said, her voice cracking. I'd never seen her show any genuine emotion before, but as Steven had always told me, everyone had a weakness. "His name is Frank, and he's a pediatrician. He's flying in from Connecticut today and heading straight to a fundraiser at The Marquant. I didn't know Dr. Crouse would be there. I didn't even know Mr. Henley was going. If I'd been aware, I would've warned Frank not to attend."

My intuition told me she was being honest. "I think Henley lured Dr. Crouse there under the pretense of giving him a lifetime achievement award." I looked her in the eyes. "Tonya, help me save your brother's life."

Tonya sniffled and tilted her chin upward. "Why should I trust you? You don't want to help me. You *hate* me."

"I don't like you. That's not a secret," I admitted. "But you should know better than anyone that I want Henley to pay for everything he's done. I value getting my life back more than I want to make you suffer for what you did to me."

She eyed me, considering it. Just as I was about to go back into her mind and try to find the right lever to make her comply, she nodded. "Fine."

I nodded back, confirming our agreement to foil Henley's plan. Then, I stood up and opened the door. Ray, Michael, and Raina were outside, waiting. They looked at me expectantly.

"She's going to help," I said. "Her brother, Frank, will be at the event, and she wants to prevent the attack."

They hurried into the room. Time was passing quickly, and we still needed to collect the details from Tonya, come up with a plan, prepare, and get to The Marquant.

Ray stood in front of Tonya. "If I remove your cuffs, can I trust you won't try anything?"

"Yes. Just save Frank."

Ray uncuffed her, and Tonya rubbed her wrists, which were red with indentations from where the metal had pressed awkwardly into her skin.

"Spill it," Raina said, getting straight to the point.

Tonya defensively held out her hands. "Mr. Henley never gave me the details about when or where he'd move forward with Project Josie."

"You expect us to believe that you didn't know Henley had purchased The Marquant and was having it renovated?" Raina asked, raising her eyebrow. "He never told you that he was hosting this fundraising event?"

"No," she replied. "Dr. Crouse retired to Florida. Mr. Henley led me to believe that when the time came, he was going to do it there."

"Do what exactly?" Ray pressed.

Tonya took a deep breath before responding. "Like I said, I don't have all the details, but Project Josie is a virus—or I should say, a cure to a virus Henley created."

My chin dropped as I recalled all the people Henley had killed at his facility.

"I don't understand," Raina said. "I thought Henley was working on some miracle cure."

"He was. That was the original plan." Tonya sighed. "He wanted to create it as a tribute to his sister, but the cure never worked correctly. As time went on, he got more and more impatient, and Project Josie morphed into something completely different." She looked at Ray with pleading eyes. "I believed in what he was trying to do."

She paused, getting lost in her thoughts. *"I've played a part in murdering my brother."*

I stepped around Ray and crouched down in front of her, taking her shaking hands in mine. "Frank isn't dead yet. We can save him, but you have to focus and tell us everything."

I wasn't sure that I'd ever forgive Tonya for what she had done to me at Henley or for the way she'd treated Michael, Raina, and Luke, but I was willing to at least put it aside for the chance to defeat Henley once and for all.

It was unrealistic to think that Tonya had suddenly changed her opinion of us. I knew what she thought of me. She believed I was a freak of nature and that Michael and Raina were less than human. But now, we'd bonded together over a common enemy with no choice but to work together.

"This virus is very dangerous," she said, her voice low. "It spreads and kills fast. Once infected, a person will experience severe symptoms within the hour and die within two."

Raina put her hand over her mouth. I wasn't sure if it was out of shock, to stop herself from saying something she shouldn't, or if it was nausea. If I had to guess, it was probably a combination of all three.

"How many people have survived after being infected?" Michael asked, looking pale himself.

Tonya shuddered. "Without the cure being administered, none of them." She looked me in the eyes. "Except you. He developed the cure based on the study of how your body had healed itself from the virus."

He'd injected me with the virus? When? I thought back to all the experiments Henley had conducted on me while I was there, but it was all a blur.

Michael anchored his fingers around the back of his neck and looked over at me. He was thinking the same thing I was.

It's a miracle I'm still alive.

"Is Henley trying to start a pandemic?" Ray asked.

"No, he doesn't want that," Tonya replied. "This virus is highly contagious but only for a short period of time. It can't survive more than an hour without a host, so if you can contain the infected in one place for three hours, the virus will die."

"So, let me get this straight. The infected person dies within two hours, and then the virus dies an hour after?" I asked, trying to make sense of it all.

"Exactly." Tonya's shoulders relaxed from having the weight of Henley's deadly secret lifted off them.

"So, what's his endgame then?" Ray asked. "Release this virus, kill Dr. Crouse and the people at the fundraiser, but then what? It seems like a lot of trouble for a three-hour event, especially when he really only has one target in mind. Why not just take out Dr. Crouse directly?"

Michael lowered his arms and then crossed them over his chest. "Henley's a narcissist. If he creates a panic over some new, mysterious virus, then he positions himself to swoop in with his cure and save the day. Not to mention, he'll make a fortune off it. I bet he's got a stockpile of cures stashed somewhere, ready to go."

I stood up and checked the copper-bell alarm clock sitting on top of the nightstand. Every second that passed became more precious. "How's Henley going to distribute the virus?"

Tonya glanced around nervously. "Honestly, he didn't share that with me. But he could disperse it as airborne or through injection. He can do either, although I doubt Mr. Henley plans to do it himself. He's too smart to risk being caught."

Ray furrowed his brow. "Any idea who he'd get to do it?"

Michael nodded. "My money's on his tetrad. Henley doesn't have much regard for them, but he groomed them to be loyal. Plus, their identity is practically untraceable."

"And they can fend off anyone trying to stop them," Raina added.

Henley's reasoning for naming his tetrad and treating them differently suddenly made sense. He'd earned their trust, so it would be easy to manipulate them into doing his dirty work while he kept Michael, Raina, and Luke as his guinea pigs for experiments.

"Are you suggesting that Henley won't attend the event himself?" Ray asked Tonya.

That scenario didn't sit right with me. In his dream, Henley had been there in person, and I knew he'd want to witness the destruction he'd caused. Not only would Henley want to see his revenge unfold on Dr. Crouse, but he was also a control freak. He'd be there to make sure everything went according to plan.

"There might be a special room, I think, at The Marquant," Tonya said. "I was waiting outside Mr. Henley's office one day while he was wrapping up a meeting with an architect. I assumed they were discussing renovations on the Charlotte facility. I heard them talking about some kind of panic room, one to use in case of an emergency. Mr. Henley wanted the ability to barricade it from the inside. I thought it made sense in case there was another incident there, but one thing stood out as strange to me at the time. Mr. Henley insisted that it have its own ventilation system, separate from the rest of the building."

I recalled the clear walls surrounding Henley after he'd unleashed the virus in his dream. He planned to go somewhere safe while everyone else perished.

I could envision how he expected it all to unfold. He'd hide in his panic room, like a coward, while one of his tetrads released the virus. Once everyone was dead, he'd emerge, telling the police and media how he'd narrowly escaped the attack. Then, claiming to be a traumatized victim, he'd volunteer to lead the charge into investigating this new virus and how to combat it. The world would be in a panic, terrified of such an incident happening again, that they'd gratefully accept his help.

Henley would become everyone's hero when he quickly produced and distributed a cure. They'd hail him a genius, unaware of the fact that he'd planned it out all along.

Without a doubt, Henley would pay off or kill anyone who threatened to expose him for the fraud he really was. He was both charming and deceiving, and he would likely get away with it unless we stopped him once and for all—*tonight*.

Nineteen

Natalie

"I've got it!" Jen announced, angling her laptop toward the center of the dining table. She'd obtained updated floor plans for The Marquant Hotel.

"I'm impressed," Ray said. "Even if I had access to my contacts right now, it would've taken me twice as long to get my hands on this."

"My babe's a genius," Seth said as he planted a fat kiss on Jen's cheek.

Jen beamed as we gathered around her laptop. She opened the document to the first page. "Okay, so this looks like the lobby." She clicked through several more pages before stopping on one with a large room big enough to host an event. "This must be the ballroom."

The room was massive, compared to the other we'd seen, with two sets of double doors leading in, another door leading to the kitchen, plus an emergency exit leading outside. The ballroom appeared to be multilevel with a balcony that ran partially across the top.

"Go to the next page," I requested.

Jen moved to the next, which showed the top floor. The balcony circled half the ballroom and led to a row of smaller rooms. They were likely meeting rooms of some sort for when the hotel hosted conference events.

"Where does this exit go?" I asked, pointing to what appeared to be one on the second floor.

Jen moved to the next page, and we got our answer. It wasn't actually an emergency exit; it was a door leading to another section of the building.

"There." I pointed to a small room within the mysterious section. "I bet that's his panic room."

The section had no other way in or out, except for the door leading back to the ballroom balcony.

We viewed the rest of the pages as well, but they were of the actual hotel—the guest rooms, luxury suites, a lounge, restaurant, and spa.

"Can you go back to the ballroom?" Michael asked, and Jen navigated to the first-floor ballroom floor plan.

Michael pointed to the emergency exit leading outside. "Henley will probably have this exit completely blocked to prevent anyone from escaping, but that still leaves the main double doors leading into the ballroom and his secret area upstairs. I guarantee he'll have people guarding each of those spots."

"Plus the kitchen," Ray said, gesturing first to the door leading from the ballroom to the kitchen and then pointing at another one that led from the kitchen down to a hallway near the restaurant, closer to the lobby.

Michael nodded in acknowledgment. "My guess is, he'll have his tetrad, plus Becca, stationed at each of those locations right before the virus gets dispersed. But he'll want to have a clear path to escape to his panic room in time, so that door will probably remain guarded throughout the event as well."

"We need to get there early enough to try picking his minions off one by one before they can get into place. We've got to figure out which one of them is carrying the virus before they find an opportunity to distribute it," Raina said.

Seth stood up straight, resting his hands on Jen's shoulders. "What happens to them if Henley gets his way? They'll be standing right in the middle of it all. Do you think they have the cure on them or ..."

"I think Henley plans to let them die," I replied. "He wouldn't allow them to use the cure because he wouldn't want anyone to know it already exists. I think he's going to pin the whole attack on the tetrad because their identities are untraceable. The only one he might plan to spare is Becca, if he's not done testing her powers."

Tonya bowed her head. "He's going to kill his children." She said it as if she hadn't thought it was possible until now.

Raina stiffened and looked back at the laptop.

Michael contemplated it for a second, walking to the other end of the table. When he stopped, he addressed Ray instead of responding to Tonya. "Any advice on the best way for us to get in there, undetected?"

"I think you should take advantage of Natalie's ability to disguise you." Ray turned to me. "Would you be able to do that for three people at once?"

"I don't know. I've only used that power one time, and I had a hard time keeping it going for only myself. And if we split up, I'm not sure how that would work."

"I don't think it has to be all or nothing," Michael said, pacing back and forth. "We can dress in the right attire for the occasion, and as long as Natalie can get us through the main doors and into the ballroom, we can do our best to blend in from there."

"You seriously want me to fight in a ballgown?" Raina asked, a look of repulsion on her face.

Jen picked up her phone and started typing. "Don't worry. I've got you."

Raina rolled her eyes. "Great ..."

"Where do you want me?" J.T. asked.

"You're staying outside," Raina replied firmly. "But we'll need you nearby with the ambulance. Once people realize something's wrong, they're going to panic, and I think we can expect some injuries. Good news is, you should have plenty of doctors there to help you tend to them all."

"I'll help too," Tonya said.

I debated declining her offer, but her thoughts told me she was being sincere.

Michael leaned on the table and looked at Seth and Jen. "Can you wait outside the front entrance to the hotel and guide people as far away as possible when they come out? Even if the virus doesn't take us out, both Becca and Lovisa can blow the building up if they want to."

They nodded, and I was grateful that he'd come up with something valuable for them to do outside the building. It wouldn't guarantee their safety, but anything was better than being inside when the chaos started.

"So, it'll be the four of us going in," Ray concluded. He seemed ready and not afraid at all even though he'd be the only one of us without a supernatural power to defend himself.

Michael pushed up from the table to stand up straight. "Yes, but you should stay away from the ballroom."

"I need to help protect those people," Ray said.

"You can by properly evacuating the hotel," Michael replied. "Who knows how many people who aren't attending the event will be in there?"

"No one is staying at the hotel yet," Jen said, her eyes glued to her phone. "I checked already, and it's been closed to guests because of the renovations."

That made things a little less complicated.

"I can still do a full sweep to make sure we get everyone out," Ray said. "At a minimum, I'd expect there to be workers in the lobby and cleaning staff."

"Are you sure we can't call for backup?" Seth asked. "Wouldn't it be better to have, like, a SWAT team or something surrounding the place?"

"We can't do that," Michael replied. "We'd be putting them in too much danger. They have no experience in dealing with Becca or the tetrad. We'd be sending them to their deaths … if they even believed us at all, that is."

"And we don't know who we can trust," I reminded Seth. "Henley already has some of the higher-ups at the police in his back pocket. If we tell them what we suspect, they'll tip Henley off, and we'll miss our opportunity to stop him for good."

Ray rubbed his chin as he thought it through. "I agree. There are a few corrupt leaders, but most of the officers on the force are good people. But you're right; they aren't trained for this. We'd never expect to meet someone with the ability to read our minds, remove our weapons with just a thought, or make us believe they were someone else. It would be disastrous."

Seth looked up at the ceiling and then back at me. The muscles in his face were tense, and I sensed he was afraid. "It's going to be three of you against four of them, plus Becca and Henley."

I wished there were a way that I could reassure him we'd be fine, but the numbers weren't in our favor. "Regardless, we have to try." The alternative was to allow Henley to move forward with his evil plan, and I wouldn't be able to live with myself, knowing I'd taken the cowardly route.

Seth opened his mouth, probably to argue with me, but then closed it. He knew it was the right thing to do.

"If we don't come out, we're counting on the rest of you to make sure Henley doesn't get away with this." As much as I didn't want to add insult to injury, it needed to be said.

Someone had to make sure Henley never benefited from the attack. Also, if he survived and we didn't, he'd shift his focus to finding Willow. She needed our protection.

Seth gritted his teeth. "He'll pay for it. I promise you that."

Jen looked up from her phone. "I'll expose him through the media. He'll never see a dime of profit off that cure."

Ray nodded and looked around the room at each of us. "If everyone is clear on their assignments, can we be ready to leave in two hours?"

"I'll text Stan and give him a list of what we need. He's never let us down before," Michael replied, and the rest of us bobbed our heads in response.

Jen put her phone down on the table. "I sent you the information about the outfits we need delivered. Each of the stores is local, so worst-case scenario, I could just go pick them up."

Michael shook his head. "I don't want anyone venturing out until it's time to leave. I'll see if Stan can have them delivered." He pulled his phone out of his pocket and left the room.

Jen glanced between me and Raina. "I can do your hair and makeup for you." She set her eyes on Raina. "Can we take out your nose ring?"

Raina glared at her. "*No*."

As everyone began diving in to side conversations, I bowed out to check on Michael. We hadn't finished our discussion from earlier, and I felt like he had a lot he needed to get off his chest. I wanted him to have a clear head before the fight.

He wasn't in the living room, and I assumed he wouldn't be outside, so I went down the hall to the bedroom we'd put him in to recover. I found him inside, sitting on the bed, staring down at the phone in his hand.

As I entered the room, I closed the door to give us some privacy. I wanted him to speak freely about all the things that were bothering him without worrying that someone would overhear. "Did you get ahold of Stan?"

He looked up at me, dejected. "Yeah. Everything will be here. He always comes through."

"What's wrong?" I stepped closer until I was standing directly in front of him.

"When I texted him, I realized he hadn't heard about Alexander, so I had to tell him." His voice was flat and tired.

"I know that wasn't easy. For either of you."

"I just can't believe he's gone." He shook his head in disbelief. "I owe that man everything, and I didn't get the chance to tell him … to say good-bye."

I reached out and placed my hands on his shoulders, lightly massaging them. "He knew how much you loved and appreciated him. Never doubt that."

"I just wish that I could've saved him."

"I'm so sorry for what my sister has done to your family." I couldn't take away his pain, but it only seemed right that I apologize for Becca's actions. Someone had to.

"That's not what I meant. I don't blame you for what she did. In fact, I'm the one who should apologize to you, to everyone."

"What are you talking about?" I gave his shoulders an encouraging squeeze, hoping it would urge him to get whatever was bothering him out in the open.

"She slipped past me again and got to Alexander. Don't you see now?" He paused, and when I didn't respond, he stood up. "You're in this mess because of me, and what if I can't protect you?"

Is that what he thinks? Does he really believe that if I hadn't met him, I would just be going about my life, living carefree?

"I was already in it, even before I met you," I said, dropping my hands so that my palms rested against his chest. His proximity reminded me of how things used to be, and for a moment, I contemplated parting from him. But he didn't try to put distance between us, so I stayed. "I became a part of this the night they took Becca from our home. As far as protecting me? You saved me, Michael, and not just from the car accident, but also from myself. I was a broken shell of my former self when I first met you. In fact, I hated myself." He flinched as the words came out of my mouth, but I continued on. "I believed I was to blame for not stopping Becca's abduction. I felt guilty, afraid, and helpless. And I lost all hope for my life. *Until you.*"

He pressed his forehead to mine and reached up, intertwining his fingers in my hair. "The way I handled things was wrong, and I'm sorry. I never wanted you to leave with Luke. I'm just scared of something happening to you because of me."

"I don't need you to protect me. I can protect myself now. You've made sure of that."

He lifted his head back slightly, contemplating what I'd said.

"I just need you to love me," I whispered, the ache in my heart returning.

"You don't get it." His hand lightly squeezed the base of my neck as he brought his forehead back to mine. "I'm completely consumed by my love for you."

He kissed me, sending a wave of warmth and want throughout my entire body.

This is what it's supposed to feel like.

Michael was and always would be the one I desired, the one I craved. Every inch of me belonged solely to him.

We took three separate cars to The Marquant Hotel. I rode with Michael and Raina while Seth and Jen followed closely behind. J.T., Ray, and Tonya were ahead of us in the ambulance.

I glanced back at Raina in the backseat and saw her fidgeting in her dress.

"Careful," I said. "You don't want it to come apart yet. I have no clue how to put it back together if it does."

Jen had found us dresses that were used mainly for stage productions. They looked like real formal dresses, but the long skirts easily tore away to reveal pants underneath. Seth was right; Jen was a genius.

For Raina, Jen had chosen a black gown with gold embroidered flowers on it. For me, she'd selected a navy-blue one with just enough sparkle to dress it up, but not so much that I would stand out in a crowd. Both dresses were sleeveless to give us some mobility but thick enough to where they should stay intact during a fight.

Raina pursed her lips together, which were heavily coated in red lipstick, thanks to Jen. Instead of Raina sporting her usual edgy look with magenta lip gloss and heavy black eyeliner, Jen had made her up differently to look glamorous, like a movie star.

I didn't look like myself either, but I was becoming used to that when Jen got her hands on me. I pulled down the mirror in the passenger seat visor to make sure I hadn't accidentally smudged my makeup. Thankfully, Jen had sprayed my face down with something she called setting spray, and it still looked flawless.

Michael wore a tux, but Jen had somehow found one that had some stretch in the fabric to help him maneuver during a fight. If things got bad, he could always remove the jacket, but for now, he had to keep it on in order to conceal his gun holster.

He was the only one of the three of us that was armed. I still wasn't great at shooting a gun, and Raina couldn't figure out a way to carry hers with her outfit. Any way she'd tried it, it was either concealed or easy to access, but never both at once.

Michael looked over at me from the driver's seat. "Are you sure you're ready? This could get complicated quick, especially if Becca is there."

I nodded but didn't reply. Deep down, I hoped she would come to her senses, see that Henley was wrong, and join our side. I mean, if Tonya could turn on him, anything was possible. But I also knew that wasn't realistic, and a fight with her was likely to happen.

The Marquant came into view, and we watched J.T. pull the ambulance into the parking lot across the street. There were valet attendants positioned at the entrance of the hotel, so we'd told him to stay back until people started coming out. I watched in the side mirror as Seth followed him into the lot.

As Michael pulled us up to the front of the hotel, I focused, imagining in my head that the three of us looked like different people. I'd studied pictures online from another fundraiser and picked out who each of us would be. In order for this to work, I had to have a clear vision of what I wanted everyone else to see.

"Showtime," Michael mumbled as he stopped the car in front of the valet stand.

We got out, and I remained silent as I concentrated on keeping the guise. I didn't see any traces of Henley, Becca, or the tetrad, but there was no telling if they were around somewhere, watching.

Michael handed the valet his keys, shoved the receipt in his pants pocket, and held the door open for me and Raina.

Once inside, we stopped briefly at the entrance to get our bearings. A woman in a professional burgundy dress and friendly smile approached us.

"Good evening," she greeted us. "The grand ballroom is just down that hall and to the right." She gestured toward the hallway.

Michael dipped his head. "Thank you."

I tried to appear confident as we made our way toward the ballroom, but my hands were trembling. We didn't know what we were walking into, but we had to figure it out fast. There was no way of predicting exactly when Henley would execute his attack, and we had to stop him before he got the chance.

As the two sets of double doors came into view on the right, I forced myself to stay focused on our disguises. This was the actual test to see if we could make it through. Without a doubt, our enemies were on the other side of the wall.

They'd propped the doors open to welcome guests, and I could hear Prelude in E Minor playing inside. As we stepped through the doorway, the familiarity of the room was overwhelming. It felt like I was back in Henley's dream, and for a moment, I forgot how to breathe. I looked up at the ceiling, which had to be at least thirty-five feet tall, and saw the balcony high above.

"Are you okay?" Michael whispered close to my ear.

As I lowered my eyes, I saw the stage at the far end of the room, the microphone placed front and center. The sight of it made me nauseous.

I need to get it together.

TWENTY

MICHAEL

Natalie's lack of response was alarming. If she lost focus of our disguises, it could all be over before it ever began.

I gently nudged her with my elbow, trying to remain discreet.

She nodded. "Yeah, I'm all right."

I stole a quick glance at her, and she was pale, but I could tell she was still centered enough to provide us cover. As we stepped farther into the ballroom, we blended into the crowd. There were about a hundred people inside. We'd timed it just right. There were plenty of guests, so we didn't stand out, but we'd arrived early enough to give us some time to stop Henley's attack. We couldn't know for sure when that would be, but if I had to guess, he'd wait until he was sure most of the attendees had arrived.

Although many partygoers had gathered downstairs in the main ballroom area, I noticed a few upstairs as I scanned the balcony above us. There was no trace of Henley, Becca, or the tetrad.

I turned to face Natalie and Raina. "If we don't spot them soon, we might need to split up." A dozen more guests entered the room. "You guys remember what to do, right?"

"Isolate them," Raina said.

Our plan was to herd them into the smaller rooms on the second floor, if possible, to minimize the likelihood of innocent people getting hurt during the fight.

Raina looked above me, checking the balcony once more. I watched as her eyes trailed from left to right. When they widened, I knew she'd located someone.

I casually stepped to Raina's side, following her gaze.

Lovisa stood, facing the ballroom, looking out over the crowd with her arms resting on the railing. She had her blonde hair tucked behind her ears, and she wore a black pantsuit. She appeared to be alone, but I sensed the others were there, somewhere.

I checked to make sure the double doors were still clear, and they were. More guests continued to file in.

"Come on," I said.

If we were lucky, Becca and the rest of the tetrad were upstairs as well. That would make it easier to corral them into the separate rooms.

We ascended the massive staircase, and I kept Lovisa in my line of sight but was conscientious not to stare at her. I didn't want to tip her off. When we finally reached the top, I spotted Viktor across the room. He stood against the wall with his hands folded in front of himself. He wore a suit similar to Lovisa's.

There was still no sign of the others.

"You two get Lovisa, and I'll take care of Viktor," I whispered. "*Be careful.*"

I stepped away from them and moved in the direction where Viktor was standing. To the left was a series of doors, the ones that led to the conference rooms, according to the floor plan. Viktor stood close to one of them, and I hoped it was unlocked, so I could take him by surprise and get him in there quickly.

Viktor glanced in my direction, but I was still under Natalie's protective guise. He quickly dismissed me and continued scanning the room.

As I grew closer, I felt my adrenaline spike, preparing me to fight. I was about to lunge at him when I heard Henley's voice echo throughout the room.

"Ladies and gentlemen, may I have your attention, please?"

Out of the corner of my eye, I saw Natalie halt. Raina paused, noticing that something was wrong.

I turned to look at Natalie to see if she needed my help. She was staring down at the ground, her eyes wide with panic. Then, she lifted her eyes and blinked, no longer focused.

Now exposed, I spun back to face Viktor. He spotted me and immediately pushed off the wall, rushing toward me.

Here we go.

I kicked off my right foot and charged.

There were a few gasps as I whipped past people standing nearby, but I quickened my pace anyway. I locked eyes with Viktor a moment before we collided. I hit him with enough force to send him tumbling to the ground toward the meeting room door, right where I wanted him.

To my right, I heard a commotion, which I assumed was a combination of Natalie and Raina confronting Lovisa and party guests fleeing to get out of the way. Henley was no longer speaking, so the sound of me crashing into Viktor must have made its way down to the main floor.

Viktor scrambled to get back up, and just as I reached him, he caught me with his shoulder. Digging it into my rib cage as he stood, he lifted me off the ground. He turned, and I lost my footing before he slammed me down. I looked up to see his foot about to collide with my face and rolled away just in time. His shoe stomped into the ground where I'd been. As he repositioned himself, I hopped back to my feet.

We circled each other, each waiting to see if the other would make the first move. When his back was to the conference room door, I sprang at him, pushing him backward. His back hit the door, and it gave under the force. It flew open, and he fell inside.

Behind me, I heard glass shatter. I turned to see Raina on top of Lovisa, pinning her to the ground. Her tear-away skirt had been removed, and beside them was a cocktail table overturned on its side. Shards of what had likely been champagne bottles and glasses shimmered all around them.

I didn't see Natalie at first. Then, I heard a woman scream as she ran down the staircase. That was when I noticed her near the top of the stairs, fighting with Becca. Natalie pushed her up against the wall, but Becca grabbed a fistful of Natalie's hair and pulled her down to the ground.

I wanted to help her, but I needed to take care of Viktor first. I wouldn't be able to fight both of them at once.

Viktor shook his head, and I noticed a gash above his eye. Inside the conference room, there was a rectangular eight-seater table.

Judging from the blood dripping from the corner, he'd smacked his head, trying to catch himself after I shoved him into the room.

I stormed over to him, grabbing him by his shirt collar. His head bobbed as he tried to comprehend what was happening.

"Which one of you has the virus?" I demanded. "Who's doing Henley's dirty work for him?" He laughed, and I punched him in the face. "Tell me!"

With one hand still wrapped around his collar, I used the other to search his jacket pockets but found nothing.

"You're all going to die." Viktor looked up at me and laughed, exposing a layer of blood stuck to his teeth. "Except your girlfriend. Father said I can have her once you're dead."

I punched him again, harder this time. A tooth flew from his mouth and hit the wall.

"The things I plan to do to her …" He laughed again as a stream of blood gushed from his mouth.

I twisted the neck of his shirt in my fist and pulled him until he was standing. He wobbled, weak and disoriented, but I held him still as I searched his pants pockets for something containing the virus.

"I don't have it," he said, mocking me. "Looks like you picked the wrong guy."

"Who has it?" Losing what little patience I had left, I tightened my grip on him but was mindful not to touch his skin and heal him from the pain I'd inflicted.

"What are you going to do? You don't have it in you to kill me." He cackled.

Although it went against every natural instinct I had, I knew I couldn't let him live. He'd always be a threat to us, and if something happened to me and I died, there was no way in hell I was leaving him alive to hurt Natalie.

I growled and gritted my teeth as I lifted him off the ground and back toward the window.

He attempted to fight back, but he was weak from his injuries. Realizing he was about to lose, he looked over my shoulder and shouted, "Hemming!"

Without hesitation, I jerked to the side and then spun back toward the window, releasing Viktor with all the force I could muster. He bellowed before hitting the window and smashing through it. The glass crumbled all over the floor as his roar came to an abrupt stop outside.

I looked out the window and down at him, sprawled out in a bloody heap on the ground.

He'd called out for Hemming, which meant he was nearby. I raced out of the meeting room just in time to see Lovisa stab Raina in the arm. Raina cried out, and Lovisa dropped the dart she'd used. Lovisa seized the opportunity to catch Raina off guard and flip her over onto her back. I ran toward them as Lovisa's hands clasped around Raina's neck. Raina flailed her arm out to the side, reaching until she found a half-broken champagne bottle. She wrapped her hand around the neck of it and slammed it up and into the side of Lovisa's throat.

Raina watched in horror as Lovisa bled out before collapsing on top of her. I yanked Lovisa's body off of her and helped her to her feet.

"Are you okay?" I pressed one hand on the side of her arm and the other to her palm, healing her wounds.

She trembled. "She stabbed me with something."

I reached down and picked up the dart. It was identical to the one Lovisa had used on me and Natalie at the warehouse. "You don't have your powers."

"I don't care," she said, her jaw set with determination. "We've come too far. I'm not giving up now."

I looked around, alarmed. "Where's Natalie?" I saw her skirt, tossed off to the side, but no trace of her or Becca.

"I think she and Becca tumbled down the stairs, but I'm not sure. I lost track of them," she replied.

"Hemming is nearby," I said, eyeing the emergency exit door that led to Henley's panic room. "I need you to go find Natalie and help her. Can you do that?" As much as I wanted to go save Natalie myself, I had this overwhelming feeling that Hemming was the one charged with distributing the virus, and it was critical that we got our hands on it before that happened.

"I'll protect her. I promise."

I pulled my sister to me, hugging her and praying it wouldn't be the last time. We'd already lost our parents, and I couldn't take it if I lost her too.

I reluctantly released her and backed toward the exit door. "Keep an eye out for Rolf. I haven't seen him yet."

I watched as she pivoted around and sprinted toward the staircase before I ran to the door that led to Henley's secret space. I ripped off my jacket and tie and tossed them on the ground before pushing open the door.

To my surprise, it was quiet on the other side. The area was dimly lit with no windows. Several fluorescent light fixtures lined the ceiling, but only one was on.

This section didn't match the luxurious ambiance of the rest of the hotel. It was clear that Henley had rushed to get it built in time for the event. The area was minimal with no furniture, decor, or even paint on the walls. There were a few stacks of wood piled on the floor and some leftover tools, showing the area was still a work in progress. Henley likely planned to transition it into something else later, when this entire ordeal was over. But for now, it was here to serve only one purpose— to keep Henley alive while everyone else perished.

I stepped forward, cautious and quiet. As I moved around a sawhorse, I hoped Hemming hadn't slipped past Raina and gone downstairs. If so, she and Natalie could be in grave danger. I wasn't sure they could take on both Hemming and Becca, especially since Raina didn't have her powers. And if Rolf was there too, they'd likely perish.

A part of me wanted to run down there and check on them, but another piece of me felt oddly confident that someone was in the room with me. I couldn't see or hear them yet, but I sensed a presence.

As I reached the opposite end of the room, I noticed an oversize steel door with a square glass window. The door was open, but there was a gap between the door and the inside of the room. I was certain that I'd find Hemming hiding behind it until I heard a noise come from the shadows to my right.

I twisted around, prepared to fight.

"It's just me," Natalie said, holding her hands out as she came into view.

I sighed with relief, grateful she was safe. "Where's Becca?"

"In the ballroom. I kicked her down the stairs and then ran in here to hide."

I paused, surprised that Raina hadn't seen her flee but then realized she'd been busy, trying to fend off Lovisa.

"Have you already scoped this area out? I'm trying to find Hemming. I think he might have the virus on him."

"He's not here. I'm sure of it," she replied.

I started toward her, planning to reach for her hand and take her out with me so we could find Raina. But I hesitated as I realized something didn't quite seem right. I looked her over.

The last time I'd seen Natalie, Becca had had a fistful of her hair. They'd been tangled up, fighting. The Natalie standing in front of me looked flawless. Every single hair was perfectly in place, and her skirt was still attached to her outfit.

"What is it?"

I forced a calm smile despite the pounding in my chest. "Nothing. You look beautiful. It reminds me of the night of the *masquerade*."

"Thank you." She smiled at me.

"What about me? Do I remind you of anything?" I asked.

There was no way she'd forget to say *fireworks*. The code words had been her idea to begin with.

She stared at me, her puzzled expression confirming my suspicions.

It's Hemming.

As the revelation sank in, I watched as her image faded out until Hemming was there, standing in her place. He wore the same black suit as Viktor and Lovisa.

Careful not to react, I shook my head and smiled again. "It's not important. Let's go find Raina." I reached my hand out as I'd originally planned to do when I thought he was Natalie.

Hemming stepped closer, thinking he had the advantage of a disguise, but I knew he was about to make his move. As I predicted, he acted like he was about to take my hand, but then, at the last minute, he swung at me. Expecting his attack, I ducked, and his fist flew past my face. The momentum took him off-balance, and I gripped the back of his head before slamming him into the wall.

His body flailed like a rag doll as I grabbed him and hurled him into the panic room. He skidded across the floor until he hit the far back wall and bounced off. I stood at the entrance to the room, debating on trapping him in there. If he had the virus on him, that would be a good way to ensure it stayed contained. But I had no way to know for sure that he did.

What if I'm wrong and someone else has it?

Hemming scrambled to his feet and reached a hand into the inside pocket of his jacket, and instinctively, I drew my gun from its holster.

"Don't move," I warned, pointing it at him and closing the distance between us.

He paused, as if debating his next move.

As far as I knew, mind reading and manipulation were the only powers he possessed. My mind was unreadable, and I'd already figured out his manipulation tactic, so there was nothing left for him, except physical combat. There was a strong possibility that he'd armed himself and he was going for his gun. I was confident he was the one who'd shot us during the ambush.

His arm moved further into his jacket as my finger hovered by the trigger.

"I mean it," I said, giving him one last chance.

My hair stood on end as his lips curled into a smile, and he pulled his hand from his jacket. Certain it was a gun, I fired three consecutive shots, each one hitting him in the chest. His body jolted as each bullet struck him.

He collapsed to his knees, his eyes still set on me with a malicious grin on his face. And that was when I saw a solid black ball in his hand, the size of a grapefruit.

As his eyes rolled into the back of his head, I noticed a small, blinking red light on the ball.

Realizing what was about to happen, I dived back toward the door. The moment I heard a beep and the light stopped flashing was the same second my hand hit the door, slamming it shut and sealing us in.

TWENTY-ONE

NATALIE

Lovisa hit me with a blast of energy that sent me flying backward. I hit the ground and rolled across the floor.

Raina tackled Lovisa, and they crashed into a nearby table. The legs of the table gave way, sending it toppling onto its side. As Raina wrestled with Lovisa, the champagne bottles hit the floor and burst while the flutes took turns popping apart.

I stood up and tore off my skirt. I prepared to jump back in and help Raina when someone grabbed me from behind. They yanked the back of my hair, winding it into their fist. I cried out in pain as they hurled me backward, forcing me back down to the ground. I twisted my head and saw that it was Becca.

The hatred in her eyes reminded me of the time she'd tried to choke me after being rescued from Henley. She'd almost killed me then, and she would've succeeded if Michael hadn't been there to save me. With Michael fighting his own battle with Viktor, I had no choice but to fight back and try to save myself this time.

Remembering my lessons with Steven, I maneuvered one leg in front of her while the other kicked her in the back of the knee, making her buckle. She let go of my hair as she tumbled to the floor. I jumped on top of her, pinning her arms down.

"Becca," I said, pleading. "Look at me. I don't want to do this with you."

She snarled, brought her head back, and slammed her forehead into my face. I heard my nose crack and immediately felt the mind-numbing pain from the impact. My eyes watered uncontrollably.

While I was stunned and unable to see, she kicked me in the chest before I felt her squirm away. I scooted backward, digging my hands and heels into the floor, trying to gain traction to retreat before she struck again.

The pain subsided, and I quickly regained my vision. I rolled out of the way just in time as she lunged at me again. I forced myself back up, got into my fighting stance, and tried to predict her next move.

I watched her feet. When she stepped off her right, I realized she was about to throw another punch. I caught her arm and mustered up enough strength to send a burst of energy at her point-blank. It poured out of my hand and into hers, sending a blast big enough to catapult her across the room. She bounced off the wall next to the stairs.

Just as she was about to stand up, I charged toward her and pushed her back up against the wall. I heard her head bump and thought maybe I'd hurt her enough to where she'd give up, but she didn't. Instead, the pain seemed to have the opposite effect on her, and it just fueled her rage. She glared at me as she reached up and grabbed another fistful of my hair. Releasing an energy burst of her own, she slammed me down on the floor.

A sharp pain radiated from my tailbone, and I tried to keep my wits about me. I knew whatever injury I had sustained would heal. I just needed a minute or two to recover, but Becca had other plans.

She clutched something in her hand, and for a brief second, I feared it was the virus. I reached down and caught her as she tried to jab me with it. She crawled until she was directly on top of me again. I used all of my strength to hold her back as she pushed her body weight down, trying to stick me with whatever she was holding.

I peered down and realized it wasn't the virus or a knife. It was a dart—the same kind Lovisa had used to disable my powers at the warehouse. If Becca managed to prick me with it, I'd lose the fight. Without my abilities, she'd easily defeat and kill me.

Unable to get her off of me, I desperately looked for an alternative solution to free myself. I tilted my head to the right, but we were at the top landing leading all the way back down to the main floor of the ballroom. Another inch or two, and we'd fall off. I looked to the left, but there was nothing, except tiled flooring.

Becca grunted and gained momentum and was within an inch of being able to pierce my skin.

I made the split-second decision to rock myself toward the right. She toppled off of me and fell over the top of the stairs. I followed, tumbling after her.

As I flipped over and over, I felt different bones crush and break. Halfway down the staircase, I pushed my leg to the wall to stop myself.

At first, I wasn't sure if I'd be able to move. The pain was everywhere, but I was still alive, and as long as I was breathing, I was going to continue to fight.

With a groan, I forced myself up, holding on to the railing for support. I could almost feel my body frantically trying to repair all the trauma. Looking down the staircase, I saw Becca hadn't been able to stop herself, and she lay motionless at the very bottom.

I hobbled down, one step at a time, unsure of what I'd do once I reached her.

I can't kill her.

And then a terrifying thought crossed my mind. *Maybe I already did.*

"No," I said aloud as I continued my descent. I was three steps from the bottom when I noticed the dart was sticking out of her leg. It must've fallen out of her hand as she fell.

I glanced around, taking in my surroundings. The ballroom had completely cleared out, and we were the only two in the room. All that remained were items people had lost or dropped as they fled—a few broken flutes, a tray of smashed hors d'oeuvres, and a stiletto. For a brief second, I wondered where Henley had gone. I doubted he'd left with the partygoers. My intuition told me he was still somewhere inside the hotel. He wouldn't give up that easily.

When I reached the bottom, Becca stirred. I hurried to her side and rolled her over, grateful she'd survived the fall.

"Let me help you." I reached for her cheek to heal her.

She popped up and recoiled, scooting away until her back was to the wall. "Get away from me."

"I'm your sister." *How can I make her understand that?* "Becca, we don't have to do this to each other."

She didn't respond, and I opened my mouth, ready to talk sense into her when we heard footsteps above. Becca looked up, and I followed her gaze to see Raina running down the stairs. She looked banged up, and there was blood smeared on her chest and down her dress. She narrowed her eyes on Becca, eager for revenge.

I held a hand up to stop Raina. "Wait! *Please*. She doesn't have her powers. Give me a second."

Confusion swept over Raina's face, but she stopped, as I'd asked her to do.

I turned back to Becca. "There has to be a part of you that remembers who you are. When I showed you that memory of you and Seth, you freaked out because, deep down, you knew it'd really happened."

She eyed me like a cornered animal, scared and desperate. It hurt to see how much my presence terrified her.

I don't want to harm her.

"You know Luke was telling the truth about how Henley forced him to brainwash you. You recalled that moment and showed it to me for a reason. I'm sure it all feels scary and confusing, but I'll help you figure it out."

Slowly, Becca stood to her feet with her hands behind her back for support. She shifted her eyes toward Raina and mustered up all the strength and power she had left and unleashed it on her. It wasn't the magnitude that Becca could normally do, but it was enough to knock Raina off-balance. Raina slipped, bouncing off the remaining steps until she landed at Becca's feet.

Becca grabbed Raina by the throat and pulled her up, using her as a shield. From the waistband at the back of her pants, she produced a knife. She positioned its five-inch blade at Raina's neck.

"Get back," Becca warned me.

I put my arms up, showing compliance. "Please don't do this."

"I'll slash her throat. Come an inch closer, and I swear I'll open her up."

Raina looked at me, her eyes wide with horror. We both knew that this version of Becca wouldn't hesitate to follow through with it.

If Becca were to cut Raina, I might not be able to heal her. It would depend on the severity of the injury and how long it'd take me to wrestle her away from Becca's grasp.

Becca parted from the wall, and at first, I thought she was going to try to escape. But instead of heading toward the double doors, she dragged Raina away with her as she moved in the opposite direction, toward the stage.

I realized there was only one of two places Becca could be going. The first option was the emergency exit, but that was likely already barricaded. So, that only left the kitchen, which was to the left of the stage.

"Where's my daughter?" Becca demanded.

"She's somewhere safe, I promise," I replied.

"Tell me where she is." She pressed the blade against Raina's throat. If she applied any more pressure, she'd break the skin.

I met Raina's eyes, trying to figure out what to do to get her out of this mess.

Raina mouthed, *No*, and I understood she was telling me she'd rather die than give up information on Willow's whereabouts.

"You want her to grow up in Henley's facility?" I tried to keep the conversation going while I came up with a plan. "You want her to be tortured and mistreated her entire life? Because that's what you'd be signing her up for."

Becca shook her head. "No, you're wrong. Henley is going to change the world. He'll save everyone from any injury or illness imaginable, and her powers are the key to making it happen."

She inched closer toward the kitchen, and my stomach clenched, warning me I was almost out of time. I glanced around, desperate to find a solution.

"He's the one who's going to save us all." Becca tilted her lips toward Raina's ear. "Well, everyone, except you."

The second she said it, I was certain she was going to slit Raina's throat.

Out of options, I reacted purely on instinct. From the corner of my eye, I saw the microphone stand still in place at the center of the stage. Using my mind, I shot a burst of energy in its direction. It flew backward, crashing into the wall behind the stage with such force that it pierced the drywall.

The sound startled Becca, and she dropped the knife. Raina used the opportunity to twist out of Becca's grip. Before Becca could comprehend what was going on, I set my sights on the knife, picked it up with my mind, and plunged it straight into her abdomen.

The realization of what I'd done hit me and Becca at the same time. She looked down at the knife handle sticking out of her stomach and then up at me in complete and total shock. As she did, I felt my whole body turn to ice.

What have I done?

Becca pulled the knife out and dropped it to the floor. Her red-stained hand pressed against the wound, but it was useless. The blood seeped between her fingertips, dripping to the floor.

She stumbled once and then collapsed to the ground.

Raina threw her hands over her mouth as I ran to Becca. When I reached her, I used the lapel of her jacket to lift her slightly so that her head rested in my lap. It was everything I'd feared since the night of her kidnapping.

My sister is going to die.

A hot tear slid down my cheek as I looked down at her. Just a second ago, she'd been the enemy, a killer, brainwashed by a madman. But as I watched her in the last moments of her life, I saw my big sister—the one who had always looked out for me and had my back, no matter what. The one who used to braid my hair and help me with my homework. She was my best friend, my favorite person in the world, the person I'd once aspired to be.

I could choose to heal her. All I had to do was reach out and stroke her cheek. With the simple act of touching my skin to hers, I could take away her pain, and she would recover. I could spare myself the anguish of losing her forever.

But despite the overwhelming sorrow and aching in my heart, I couldn't bring myself to do it.

I'd wanted so badly to get her back that I hadn't been willing to see the truth. The Becca I loved was long gone. No matter what memories I showed her or how much I tried to reason with her, she wasn't coming back. If I healed her, I wouldn't be saving the real Becca. I'd be reviving a monster, one who wanted to kill me and everyone I loved, and I couldn't let that happen.

Becca looked up at me, and I wasn't sure if she could hear me or not, but I talked to her anyway. "I never wanted it to come to this." My vision blurred. "Despite everything that's happened between us, I love you so much, and I promise that I'll never forget the memories we had together before they took you away. And someday, when I see your daughter, Willow, again, I'll tell her all about you—the *real* you. She'll know what an amazing person you were."

Her eyes widened slightly, a flash of hope sweeping across them. "Willow ..." she murmured.

228

I nodded as one of my tears fell and landed in her soft mahogany hair. "We'll keep her safe. I'll love her as my own."

Her eyes slowly drifted away from my face, and she drew her final breath. As I witnessed the life leave my sister's body, I crumbled forward, pulling her to me. She was dead, and the grief was so much worse than I'd ever imagined. My face pressed into her hair as I sobbed.

I killed her.

Willow would never get a chance to see her mother again. I'd just robbed her of that opportunity. I wasn't sure if Willow would ever be able to understand why I'd done it or if I'd even be able to forgive myself.

Someone tentatively touched my shoulder, and I looked up to find Raina sitting on her knees beside me. Her eyes were soft and full of concern as she searched my face. Having just lost both her parents, she knew better than anyone the agony I felt in that moment.

My head fell toward her, and she wrapped her arm around me, letting me cry on her.

As Raina held me, I reflected on my last words to Becca and vowed to keep my promise. I'd make sure that Henley never got his hands on Willow. I could never make up for the fact that I'd chosen to end her life, but it was a start. It was the least I could do.

When my breathing felt more under control, I pulled away from Raina and wiped the tears from my face. I'd have to wait to process my loss. Our mission wasn't finished yet.

"We need to find Henley and end this once and for all." I slid my legs out from underneath Becca and gently rested her head on the floor.

Raina stood up. "He was onstage when the fight started, but I haven't seen him since."

I looked over at the kitchen, where Becca had planned to escape, but my intuition told me he was no longer in there. He'd likely fled when he heard the commotion in the ballroom or when he realized we'd defeated Becca.

"Where's Michael?" I asked. I hadn't seen him since the fight had first broken out.

"He's fine," Raina replied. "He went to the hidden section to chase down Hemming after he took out Viktor."

That meant Rolf was the only one unaccounted for besides Henley. If Hemming had been guarding the panic room, then Rolf was likely guarding Henley. Henley wouldn't leave himself defenseless against us.

"I don't have my powers," Raina said. "Lovisa stuck me with one of those darts."

I was about to suggest that we head to the new wing to find Michael first when a knot formed in my stomach.

Raina noticed me clutching my abdomen. "What is it?"

The warning became more urgent, and I knew there wouldn't be time to get Michael. The danger was imminent.

"Henley. He's about to do something, and we need to stop him. I don't think we have much time."

Raina helped me to my feet. My stomach tightened until I doubled over.

We need to hurry.

According to the floor plan, the only way Henley could've made it to the panic room was up the ballroom stairs. He couldn't have slipped past both me and Raina to get up there, so that meant he was hiding somewhere else in the hotel.

"He could be anywhere," Raina said. "There are over three hundred guest rooms in this hotel."

I stared at the floor, keeping Becca out of my line of sight, as I tried to focus on where he could be.

I doubted he would pick a normal guest room to execute whatever evil trick he had up his sleeve. No, Henley would want an audience. He'd come all this way, and he wanted all the attention on himself as he sought his revenge. In his deranged mind, he'd want the moment to be special. If he thought he was going to lose, he'd want to go out with a big production.

My mind drifted back to the floor plans and the different spaces within the hotel, trying to decipher which one might have an impact now. There were no guests in the hotel, and everyone who'd been in the ballroom was now outside.

And that was when it hit me. He was planning to hurt the people outside. That not only included the guests who'd attended the charity event, but also our friends, who were outside to help them as they fled.

I looked at Raina in shock as my intuition confirmed I was right. As the knot loosened and the pain subsided into a dull ache, I stood upright and gained clarity.

"He's in the penthouse suite," I said, pulling her arm toward the double doors.

She hesitated, confused. "Why would he be there?"

I released her and rushed toward the exit. "Because of the balcony. It's directly over the front entrance of the hotel."

Raina was at my heels as I ran out of the ballroom and into the lobby. I spotted the sign for the elevator and sprinted toward it. As I slowed down to hit the button to call it, Raina shot past me.

"We need to take the stairs." She shoved open the door leading to the stairwell, and I hurried after her. "If Henley suspects we're coming, he could stall the elevator and trap us."

We sprinted up four flights, and as we approached the last few steps, Raina came to a stop, so we could catch our breath.

"Rolf is probably with Henley," I whispered. "Are you sure you're up for this? I could go alone."

We had no way of knowing how long it would take Raina to get her abilities back, and I hated the fact that she was going in there, defenseless.

She shook her head. "No way. You and I are in this together."

I nodded, mirroring her resolution to defeat Henley, avenge our loved ones, and remove this constant, looming fear that his presence created in our lives every single day. Raina and I didn't agree on much, but I knew that we'd fight to the death for a chance to reclaim our future.

I pressed my ear up against the door, listening for any noise on the other side. Rolf could be there, waiting to ambush us. When I heard nothing suspicious, I chanced it and took a peek.

As quietly as possible, I pressed on the handle and pulled the door open a crack. On the other side was a hallway, and I poked my head out to get a better view. It was empty.

I stepped forward and motioned for Raina to follow. As we crept down the hall, I tried to get my bearings to figure out which room was the penthouse suite overlooking the front of the building. The hotel room doors all looked the same, and I could feel myself getting overwhelmed. If we broke into the wrong one, Henley might hear us and realize we were coming for him. It could make him decide to execute his plan early.

I stopped walking and closed my eyes, trying to get in tune with my intuition, begging it to guide me. The knot pulled more gently than before, urging me forward. I took one step after another, following where it wanted to steer me.

After about twenty paces, the knot gave a final tug. I opened my eyes and shot Raina a knowing look before turning to face the door.

He's in there.

We had no choice but to go into the suite. And I suspected that with Rolf's sense of extraordinary hearing, if he didn't already know we were there, he would the second we touched the door. As much as I wanted to just blast the door open and take the offensive approach, we had to be more methodical than that. We needed to at least attempt to take them by surprise.

I placed one hand on the door handle and the other over the room key scanner, and I focused on the dead bolt connected to it. I imagined the dead bolt slowly sliding open until I heard a soft click, unlocking the door.

Raina and I looked at each other one last time, confirming we were both ready for whatever was waiting for us inside. Then, as I pushed the door open, it jerked forward suddenly as someone stronger than me yanked it from the other side. I fell off-balance, spilling into the foyer of the suite. As I looked up from the floor, I saw Rolf towering over me.

He brought his foot back, positioned to kick me in the head, but abruptly tipped over and fell sideways. I scrambled to my feet and realized that Raina had tackled him to the ground. Without her being able to tap into her adrenaline, Rolf quickly overpowered her, flipping her off of him and onto her back. He had her pinned to the ground.

I jumped onto his back, squeezing my arms as tightly as I could around his thick neck. I felt my adrenaline spike as I adjusted my arms to get a better position to deliver a fatal squeeze. He stood up, wearing me like a human backpack, and charged backward into the wall, crushing me between him and it.

I let out a yelp, feeling my ribs crack upon impact. As he pulled away from the wall, my arms gave out, and I slid off of him. Before I could get my bearings, his fist slammed into my stomach, and I doubled over, heaving.

Raina lunged at him again, forcing him into the living room area. I managed to straighten upright and then heard a crash. I rushed into the living room to find the coffee table in pieces as Raina and Rolf circled around it. Raina kept her stance low but agile while Rolf towered over her like a crazed giant.

Behind Raina was a plush couch that probably cost more than my first car. The living room was extravagant but lived in. A photograph of Josie sat next to a lamp on an end table across the room.

When I'd tried to hunt Henley down, the private investigator had told me that Henley hadn't been home. I realized this was where he'd been hiding out.

A sparkle of light caught my eye, and I looked up to see a giant chandelier. It wasn't just any chandelier; it was the one from Henley's dream. The one from his childhood home.

I felt eyes on me and looked toward the balcony to find Henley staring at me. He stood outside, still wearing his tuxedo from the party, his square jaw tight. In his hand, he held a strange black ball.

My stomach twisted as the reality of Henley's unrelenting evil sank in, and I realized what was inside the ball.

The virus.

TWENTY-TWO

NATALIE

We hadn't expected Henley to have the virus on him. We'd been so sure that he'd leave that deadly task to someone in his tetrad. It shouldn't have come as a surprise though that Henley would have a backup plan in case things fell apart. He'd been planning this massacre for quite some time, and it wasn't in his nature to give up.

I wasn't exactly sure how the ball worked to release the virus inside it, but I was certain that all Henley had to do was drop it off the balcony and let it break against the concrete below to accomplish his mission. If that happened, he'd quickly infect anyone around, and the magnitude of his impact would be far greater than he'd originally planned. There was no telling how quickly or how far it would spread if it got outdoors. And if he did it, I wouldn't be able to kill him because he'd be the only one with the cure to stop it.

I thought about our friends below, working to help the people who'd fled the building, and I realized Michael might be down there as well, looking for me and Raina. If it hadn't been for my intuition, we never would've found Henley in his suite, so I doubted Michael was on his way up to help us.

As if Henley could read my mind, he smiled smugly at me, confident he'd won.

Rolf shoved Raina into me. Distracted, I hadn't seen her coming. She landed on top of me and quickly rolled off. Rolf was right behind her, and as he dived for me, I shot a blast of energy at him. It delivered a punch big enough to spin him in the opposite direction.

"Henley's holding the virus," I told Raina as we climbed back to our feet.

Rolf, refusing to relent, charged at us again. Raina let out a yell and mustered up enough energy to pick up the lamp with her mind and smash it against the back of his head. Her powers were coming back.

"Go," she said. "Stop him."

Rolf groaned as I hurried around him and toward the balcony. When I reached the door leading outside, I realized the balcony stretched across the front of the living room and farther down to where I assumed the bedroom was. I didn't see Henley.

My sweet Josie, it's almost time.

I heard it clear as day, and I realized I was picking up on Henley's thoughts.

I've waited so long to avenge you. In a few short minutes, it will be the exact time of your passing, and they will pay for failing you.

My stomach twisted with a sense of urgency.

We'll make them all see that I could've been the one to save you, if they'd just given me the chance.

I rushed toward the door, but an image of Michael flashed in my head. It was the memory of him lifting my hand to his mouth and kissing it after I told him I'd decided not to risk my life at the warehouse. Even though I believed I could take out Lovisa at the time, I also remembered that moment of clarity where I had known that failure meant certain death. Instead of recklessly taking my shot, I'd listened to Michael's plea and fled with him.

Acting impulsively was a weakness of mine. One that I'd been working on for some time. I'd realized that I could be thoughtless about my personal safety, especially when other people's lives were at stake. In the past, I hadn't worried about what could happen to me. No amount of physical pain could ever compare to the emotional suffering I'd experienced when I lost Becca as a teenager. I would've died to avoid it happening again.

But what Henley failed to realize was that I valued my life so much more now. I no longer carried the guilt of failing to stop her kidnapping that night so many years ago. It hadn't been my fault. I had just been a kid at the time, one who possessed powers far greater than she could comprehend.

The only person responsible for taking my sister is the one who took her.

I'd since come to terms with my unique abilities, and I actually embraced them now. These powers that I'd once considered a curse had turned into a blessing, as they provided me with the means to protect myself and the people I loved.

Everyone has a weakness. Even Henley.

The difference was that I understood what mine was, and I'd learned to deal with it, to work through it. The temptation would always be there to revert to my old ways since they had been my preferred method of coping with the trauma I'd experienced. But I could recognize it most of the time now and choose a different path.

Henley, however, hadn't identified his weakness. He mistook his thirst for revenge for his strength. He believed it to be a noble character trait. It was there, plain as day, but he was so blinded by his own ego that he didn't recognize it. Luckily for me, I knew exactly what it was *and* how to use it against him.

I confidently opened the back door leading out to the balcony, stood in the threshold, and called out to him, "Chaddy?"

There was no response, but his mind told me he'd recognized my voice. *Her* voice.

"Chaddy, where are you?" I asked, placing one foot on the balcony. To me, it was my foot in a navy ballet flat, but to Henley, it would be a tiny pink Mary Jane over white tights.

I heard a commotion in the room behind me and did my best to tune it out. I couldn't allow myself to get distracted. We were running out of time, and my impersonation needed to be impeccable.

To my right, I heard Henley let out a breath. "Josie …"

I stepped fully onto the balcony and found him standing off to the side. He'd been waiting for just the right moment to execute his plan and toss the ball over the railing. But as Henley stood there, blinking at me in awe, his plan was the last thing on his mind. He was trying to reconcile how Josie was standing right there in front of him when he'd just been talking to her in his head.

Surely, Henley could figure it out if he really tried. He was dangerously intelligent, and he already knew mind manipulation was an ability I possessed because I'd used it to steal Willow from under his nose. But because Josie was his weakness and he never recovered from the grief of her death, he wouldn't allow himself to rationalize that she wasn't in fact standing there with him.

From where I stood, I couldn't see anyone on the ground below. Even if I looked over the side, there would be an awning blocking my view. Henley stood to the side of it, but I doubted anyone would look upward, expecting him to be there. I contemplated screaming to them, telling them to run, but I worried if I did, the ruse would be over, and Henley would drop the virus before I could stop him.

"What are you doing here?" Henley asked.

I'd purposely chosen to show him Josie in the same fluffy pink dress she'd worn in his dream right before the virus killed her. His thoughts told me he remembered it vividly.

"It's not safe for you to be here."

I recalled Josie's wide, scared blue eyes and projected that into my impersonation. "What are you doing with that?" I pointed to the device in his hand. "Are you going to hurt me?"

He looked down at the ball and shook his head. "No." His eyes lifted, pleading with me. "No, you don't understand. I would never hurt you. I want to hurt *them*." He leaned against the railing and gestured outward, and for a moment, I felt like my heart had stopped, worried that he would either purposely or accidentally drop the virus. "They need to pay."

Panic was creeping in, and I tried to take steady breaths.

Beads of sweat formed on his forehead. "I'm doing all of this for you, don't you see? You didn't have to die. I found something out there to help you get better, but they wouldn't listen. They thought I was stupid and incompetent."

I wanted to argue with Henley and tell him he hadn't done it for Josie. Yes, she'd given him the motivation, and I believed that he truly loved her, but when it really came down to it, he'd done it all for himself, to prove a point. I wasn't sure if it had been to show his dad, the doctors, himself, or a combination of all three, but that was the real reason for his madness. Josie was his convenient justification for all the terrible things he did.

Trying my best not to tremble, I extended a hand toward him. "Come with me. I've missed you."

He looked curiously down at my hand and then back up to my face. As he did, I focused on all the features I could remember about Josie, trying to make it as real for him as possible. His hesitation concerned me, and as much as I wanted to read his mind, I was afraid that if I tried again, it would break my concentration and ruin the illusion. I was going to have to trust my intuition instead.

I was close to the door leading back inside. A part of me wanted to get closer to him, grab his hand, and lead him into the suite. But I worried that if he realized who I really was, he'd snatch me up and throw me over the side.

Know your enemy. Anticipate their next move.

I stretched my fingers out farther toward him but kept my feet planted where they were.

The suite behind me was quiet, and I wasn't sure if it was because the fight had left the room, or if it was over, or if I'd just gotten that good at blocking out the noise. Without knowing for sure, I'd have to be prudent. If Henley went into the suite, he could easily detect the guise the moment he realized Raina was battling with Rolf.

Henley gave one last look over the railing, as if deciding whether the death of those down below was worth more to him than a conversation with his dead sister.

Just as I thought he'd figured me out and he was going to drop the virus over the edge, he turned away from the railing and reached out for my hand.

His clammy hand engulfed mine as I guided him back into the suite, toward the center of the living room, beneath the chandelier. He balanced the small globe on the palm of his other hand. I stopped when he was at a safe enough distance that I could prevent him from running back onto the balcony if he discovered who I really was. I didn't want to die, and I would do everything in my power to stay alive. But if it came down to it, I'd sacrifice myself to ensure the virus never left the hotel.

Raina and Rolf were nowhere to be found, but I heard a noise coming from farther down the hall. Henley didn't seem to notice; he only cared about Josie.

I gracefully pulled my hand away and stepped back. I needed to get the virus away from him—and soon. The intensity of his gaze made me nervous. If he looked hard enough, he'd eventually see a flaw and realize I wasn't Josie. It was just a matter of time.

My heart raced in anticipation. I'd have to be fast and precise. If I messed up, he could get away, or I could unintentionally release the virus myself.

I gave my hands a quick flex at my sides as I felt the energy building within me. The slight change in me was enough to tip him off, and the second I saw the lightbulb go off in his head, I took action. I raised my left hand, using my mind to yank the double doors closed behind him, and then shifted my attention toward holding Henley in place.

He pushed against the invisible barrier that I'd placed around him, trying to turn around and go back outside. I wasn't sure how long I could restrain him, but for now, I had him trapped.

His nostrils flared as he glared at me with pure hatred. I struggled to hold him still with my mind, and he took a small step forward. As I readjusted my concentration to his feet, I noticed a movement in his hand. He was trying to reposition the ball in his palm, not to get a better handle on it, but to get a different grip.

My energy was depleting, and my grasp on him broke. I attempted to grab him again with my mind but couldn't hold on.

Henley smirked at my failed attempt. "I didn't want to kill you, Natalie. You have so much potential, and I had big plans on how to use your talents."

Behind me, I heard footsteps run into the suite and then come to a sudden stop. I turned my head to see Raina standing behind me, her hair a matted mess.

She lifted her hand, ready to strike Henley down.

Did she regain her powers?

I cringed, waiting for her to send a blast that would not only kill Henley, but also make the ball explode. Just as I was certain she was going to do it, she noticed the device in his hand. She lowered her arm to her side and looked at me.

I willed her to turn around and run, to get out of there as fast as she could before he could infect her, too, but she looked into my pleading eyes and pressed her lips tightly together as she came to my side. She looked at Henley with confident defiance.

The smile wiped from his face. *He doesn't like that at all.*

"You, on the other hand," he said, pointing to Raina, "I'm going to enjoy watching you die."

She narrowed her eyes. "Word has it, I'll have two hours before I do, so you'd better have a good backup plan for yourself after you hit that button."

I looked at the ball and noticed a tiny button flush against the surface of it, near his thumb. All he had to do was reach another inch and press it.

"You were a failed experiment," he said. "The only reason I didn't terminate you was because the other one had grown attached to you and I could use you against him."

I thought about the video Michael had shown me right after we met to help me understand who he really was. The footage was of him as a child at Henley's facility. The doctors tried to force him to heal himself and then used Raina as a tool to try to coax the ability out of him. They threatened to mutilate her if Michael refused to cooperate. In that instance, Alexander had intervened, but Henley would've followed through with it if he hadn't.

A fresh flame ignited within my chest.

Michael might have been able to heal Raina from the physical wounds Henley had inflicted on her, but the emotional ones that they'd both suffered would remain forever. Despite what Henley believed, Michael never had the ability to heal himself. His thick scars were proof of that.

Henley was relentless in his mission, and I'd experienced it firsthand while held captive at his facility, but my short duration there could never compare to the amount of suffering that Michael, Raina, Luke, and Becca had endured over many *years*.

The fire within me spread as I recalled how Henley had not only hurt the people I cared about, but he'd also killed several of them. It was because of him that Lorena and Alexander were dead. Two of the kindest people I'd ever known had been killed, and even though he hadn't executed them himself, their blood was on his hands.

It was also Henley's fault that I'd lost my sister. Because of him, I'd lost her three times in fact. The first was when he'd orchestrated having her kidnapped from our home, the second when he'd brainwashed her against me, and finally tonight, when he'd left me no other choice but to kill her in order to save Raina's life.

My heart ached at the thought of her still lying on the ballroom floor, lifeless and alone. My face flushed, and the tips of my ears burned.

Even though Henley had killed three of the people that mattered most to me, I knew he wouldn't stop until he murdered us all. I recalled Henley's dream and the four dead bodies on the gurney. If he hit that button on the orb, he'd be one step closer to making that nightmare a reality.

And then there was Michael. He was likely outside and safe from the virus, but if Henley somehow escaped, unscathed, he'd continue to hunt Michael down for the rest of his life.

The heat pulsated throughout my entire body, wanting out.

Raina clenched her fists at her sides as she stared Henley down. "You're going to rot in hell for everything you've done."

"There isn't a cure within a hundred miles of here, but it doesn't matter. I'm already immune," Henley thought as his eyes lit up in amusement. "Maybe someday perhaps, but not today."

He infected himself with the virus, and he used the cure to build up immunity. He didn't even need the panic room to survive. It was a secondary safeguard, a way to explain how he survived when everyone else at the hotel perished.

Raina gritted her teeth. "We'll see about that."

I stood silent as I tried to suppress the rage threatening to pour out of me.

"Once I hit this button, you'll be writhing on the floor, struggling to breathe, and I'll just stroll out of here and go about my life." He looked pointedly at me. "I'm disappointed to lose your talent since I've already lost your sister, but I'll have something even better once I find your niece—*my new raven.*"

The image of Willow, tiny and helpless in my arms, flashed before my eyes. The thought of her having to live her life on the run, in fear of Henley, was unimaginable.

What if Luke isn't able to stop Henley from finding them?

Henley would harm her just as he'd hurt all of us.

"I always get what I want, one way or another." Henley's words from his dream echoed in my mind as I realized that if he caught Willow, he'd brutalize her, brainwash her, and then use her to hunt down and kill Michael.

I trembled from the lava coursing through my veins. Henley watched me attentively, noticing the change in my demeanor. His finger hovered over the button, ready to strike first, but I refused to contain my rage anymore.

If he was going to release the virus on us, I was going to take my shot.

I have nothing to lose.

A scream escaped my lungs as I lifted my hands in the air, but instead of sending a blast, I pulled downward on the chandelier. The crystals clanked together as it shook.

As Henley realized what I was trying to do, the ball rotated in his hand, and he lost the precise placement he'd had on it. He looked down at the object, grasped it between both palms, and frantically tried to locate the button. He pressed his fingers into it, hoping to find it by chance.

I grunted and continued pulling with my mind. Raina thrust her hands up and layered her powers on top of mine.

The chandelier rocked as pieces of Sheetrock fell down around us.

I'd made the mistake once of sparing Henley's life. At the time, I'd worried that if I killed him, it would mean that I was malevolent, like him. I'd been so unsure of who I was back then, so terrified of who I'd become because of what I could do with my powers.

When Michael had healed me from my car accident, it'd activated these dormant abilities within me. We didn't understand it at the time because it had never happened to anyone else. Alexander theorized it was the product of evolution. He thought nature was using me to course-correct something unnatural and bigger than any of us. Michael had assumed my abilities existed to counterbalance the ones he and Raina possessed, but that wasn't true.

Their births hadn't been a mistake, and I hadn't been born to offset some imbalance that they'd set off in the universe by existing.

I was born for this moment, right here and now—to stop Henley. He is the unnatural force that needs to be eliminated. Killing him is my purpose, my destiny.

I expelled the rest of the breath from my lungs as I allowed one last wave of adrenaline and energy to gush out of me and toward the ceiling. The lights on the chandelier short-circuited, and hardware that supported the massive fixture shifted and popped apart. Henley looked up at it but froze as it rained sparks down on top of him.

The chandelier fell, and as it did, Raina thrust her arms out. Henley let go of the device as he attempted to shield himself from the impact. His effort was useless though as the chandelier, which had to weigh several hundred pounds, crashed on top of him.

The moment I saw it hit his head, I shut my eyes and turned my face away. When it finally hit the ground with a loud crash, I felt pieces of crystal and shards of glass splash up, cutting into my arms and legs.

Then, just as quickly as it had happened, it was silent again. I turned back toward the wreckage and opened my eyes.

The chandelier had engulfed Henley, pinning him underneath. I could barely make out his clothes under the pile of metal, crystal, and broken glass, but a large red pool crept across the slick marble floor. I didn't see the ball among the wreckage, but there was zero chance it would've withstood that kind of impact.

Out of the corner of my eye, I saw Raina take a small step forward. I looked over at her, wanting to make sure she was okay, and my eyes immediately landed on the round device cradled in her hands.

She used her powers to grab it when Henley let go.

She turned to me, her eyes wide with shock as they began to well. "It's finally over?"

I nodded. "He's gone."

Her face crumpled, and I recognized it was out of sheer relief that this nightmare she'd endured throughout her life had finally ended.

I reached out and cautiously took the ball from her, giving her the full freedom to enjoy this deserved moment.

As we stood there, I felt traces of blood trickling down my legs and arms. My wounds were minimal, and I knew I'd heal, but I had used so much energy that it would take longer than usual.

Raina had a nasty gash on her arm and a purple bruise on her cheek as well as several smaller nicks on her legs.

"Come on. Let's get this thing somewhere safe." I nodded to the globe between my palms.

I couldn't wait to see Michael and give him the news that we'd done it. We'd defeated Henley. Although it would never undo all the evil Henley had committed in his life or bring back Lorena, Alexander, or Becca, we'd at least stopped him from continuing to inflict pain and destruction on the world.

Raina followed me out of the suite. As we got onto the elevator to head downstairs, we passed Rolf's body, facedown. The glass on the emergency fire box mounted to the wall had been shattered, and a bloody extinguisher lay on the floor beside him.

When the elevator stopped on the first floor, I was instantly flooded with relief. The lobby doors were just straight ahead, and soon, this ordeal would officially be over. We'd reunite with Michael and our friends and start rebuilding our lives, free of Henley.

Raina walked ahead of me, pushing the main door open while I delicately carried the deadly virus in my hands.

As we stepped outside, I quickly noted our surroundings, making sure that there was no one left who could pose a threat. My eyes trailed across several police cars and officers, ambulances on standby, scared partygoers, but not any of the members of the tetrad. We must have killed them all.

"Raina!" J.T. yelled when he saw us. He rushed over and snatched her into his arms, hugging her close.

I glanced around for Michael, who was most likely close by, healing the wounded.

Seth and Jen ran up to me, and I took a step back, aware of the threat I carried between my palms.

"Careful. The virus is in this thing."

Ray walked up behind them and reached out his hands. "I can take that from you. The Center for Disease Control is sending a team, and they're almost here."

"There's a button that I think will release the virus, so keep it flat against the palms of your hands." I gradually transferred the ball from my hands to his.

Four white vans pulled up with the blue CDC logo on the sides, and Ray took the device over to them.

Seth and Jen simultaneously pulled me into a group hug, and I let out an audible sigh of relief. It felt so good to be there, safe with my friends.

When they pulled away, I noticed that some of the blood from my open cuts had gotten on their shirts. "Sorry," I said, pointing to Jen's pink T-shirt.

She dismissively waved her hand. "I don't care. I'm just glad you're okay. We were so worried about you."

"Henley ... is he ..." Seth raised his eyebrows.

"Dead. It's over."

Seth sighed. "And Becca?"

I shook my head. "There was no other way. I tried, but I couldn't get through to her, and ..." My throat ached with emotion as I willed myself to hold it together.

He reached out and gave my shoulder a reassuring squeeze.

"She did it to save me," Raina said, looking at me with heartfelt sincerity in her eyes. "Thank you."

I nodded at her, knowing that even though I hadn't done the painless thing, I'd done the right thing. Raina and I had our differences, for sure, but we were family too. She might not be my blood, but Raina would be my sister for the rest of our lives.

J.T. pulled away from Raina and inspected her arm. "This cut is pretty deep. I need to get you patched up." He took her hand and led her toward the ambulance.

"Where's Michael?" I asked, finding it strange that he hadn't seen the reunion by now and come over. He could heal her arm in seconds.

Seth and Jen exchanged a look.

"What?" My stomach dropped to my feet.

"We assumed he was with you," Jen replied.

I looked at them in disbelief, waiting for one of them to crack a smile and say they were playing a joke on me. "He never came out?" I asked when they didn't.

Seth creased his brows and shook his head.

I turned around and looked back at the hotel.

He's still somewhere inside.

TWENTY-THREE

NATALIE

It was possible that Michael was fine. Perhaps he'd stayed behind, searching for me and Raina. Or maybe he'd been on his way out when he heard the commotion coming from the suite. If he'd taken the stairs, it was possible that we'd missed him when we came down on the elevator.

Despite all the logical answers, I sensed something was off. My intuition didn't lead me to believe it was an impending danger but filled me with an overwhelming sense of dread.

What if he didn't defeat Hemming? What if he's …

Without hesitation, I left Seth and Jen and charged back into the hotel. I heard Seth call out to me, but I didn't stop. I needed to find Michael.

The lobby was as quiet as we'd left it. I turned to the left and down the hallway, running back toward the ballroom. The last time Raina had seen Michael, he had gone to Henley's secret area to locate Hemming. That was where I'd start.

I turned right and hurried through the doors leading into the ballroom. Becca's body remained on the floor, where we'd left her. The knife lay on the ground, crusted in her blood. Fearful that my powers hadn't fully returned after using all my energy to dislodge the chandelier, I picked it up. Just in case.

I quietly ascended the stairs, running through the possibilities of what I might find once I reached the top.

Hemming was a mind manipulator, but Michael was smart and always vigilant. And he was strong. He could easily overpower Hemming.

Straight ahead, I saw a body lying on the floor, but it wasn't Michael's. The figure was much smaller, and the long blonde hair that fanned over her face told me it was Lovisa.

I spotted the closed door leading to the renovated section and walked toward it. A black jacket and tie lay on the ground, and I knew they belonged to Michael. All I could hear was the sound of my breath as I took steady, determined steps.

If they are still fighting, shouldn't I hear something?

The row of small rooms was to my left. The door to the last one was open, and as I peeked inside, I saw it was in disarray. There was blood on the table and floor, and something had completely busted the window out, but there was no trace of Michael or Hemming.

There was one body unaccounted for, and my heart sank as I realized it was Viktor. Hemming might not be powerful enough to defeat Michael, but Viktor had superior strength too. Raina had said that Michael had taken Viktor out, but what if he hadn't actually killed him? What if Viktor had somehow survived? If Hemming and Viktor both teamed up against Michael, it was possible that they could win.

I tightened my grip on the knife as I pushed the fake exit door open. I stood there for a moment, waiting and listening to see if I heard anyone inside but it was silent.

I crossed the threshold and gently guided the door until it shut quietly behind me. Then, I turned and looked around for any sign of Michael or of trouble. The room was dim and unfinished.

To the left, I noticed a door. It was closed, but I recognized its placement as the panic room that Henley had planned to hide in. A red light beamed above it.

Maybe Michael got attacked by Hemming and Viktor and barricaded himself inside?

As I hurried toward the door, I knew that scenario was unlikely. Michael would never give up and hide.

The door had a glass window, which I assumed was for Henley to keep watch after he secured himself inside. I walked up to it, gripped the door handle, and froze.

My eyes first landed on Hemming, who was on the ground with his torso propped up against the wall. Beneath his jacket, his white button-up shirt dripped with blood. His eyes were open but devoid of life.

Then, I noticed Michael on the right side of the room. He was on the floor as well but sitting with his arm propped up on his knee. His face was pale, and he had blood on him, but I could tell he was alive. He hadn't seen me yet.

Did he get trapped inside?

I tried to turn the door handle, but it didn't budge, so I pounded on the window.

Michael looked up, and that was when I realized his eyes were red and swollen, and the bags below them were a deep shade of purple.

He doesn't look right.

Directly above his head was a row of monitors, presenting different views of the ballroom, balcony, and lobby. I cringed, thinking of how Henley had planned to hide in there and watch everyone die.

Michael pushed himself off the floor and staggered toward the door. His legs seemed heavy and uncoordinated, and I worried maybe Hemming had hurt him. I yanked on the handle again, eager to get inside and try to heal him.

And that was when I saw the remnants of the black device that had shattered on the floor, in the space between Hemming and Michael. It was identical to the one Henley had planned to activate.

No.

Michael made it to the door and pressed himself against it for balance as he looked out at me. His expression was apologetic.

I shook my head violently. "No. You're going to be fine. Open the door. I can heal you." I recalled how Tonya had told us Henley designed the panic room so that he could lock himself inside. That meant Michael should be able to get out.

He pressed his hand against the glass, as if trying to feel me through it. "We can't risk it."

I could barely hear him through the thick barrier that separated us.

Tears stung at my eyes. "If Henley tested it on me, maybe I'm immune. Let me at least try." I continued to shake the handle, determined to get it open.

"Even if that's true, we can't let this virus get loose."

I knew he was right, but I still pressed my body to the door, wondering if I could muster up enough energy to force it open.

He leaned into the door on the other side for support. "I saw what happened with Becca. I'm so sorry, Natalie."

I looked up at the monitor, her body clearly in view.

I can't lose them both.

"Did you find Henley?" he asked.

I nodded as tears escaped my eyes. "He's gone. It's over. We're safe. We can restart our lives once you get out of here." I hoped my optimism would convince him to open the door and let me in.

He managed a smile. "That's all I've ever wanted for you, and you're going to get that chance now."

Why is he giving up? It isn't over. Not yet.

"I don't want any of it without you."

He coughed and gagged with such force that I worried he might vomit. Saliva dripped from his mouth, and he wiped it away with his sleeve before turning back to me. "You should go. I don't want you to see what's going to happen to me." He stood upright. "Please tell Raina that I love her and that I'm sorry for everything."

I slammed my hand against the door, trying to get through to him. "Stop it! Don't you dare give up."

I heard footsteps behind me, but I couldn't bring myself to turn around to see who it was. I didn't care if it was Viktor—I couldn't take my eyes off Michael.

Michael looked over my shoulder, and from the regret on his face, I could tell it wasn't Viktor. He was about to say another good-bye.

An arm wrapped around my shoulders and pulled me close. As he squeezed me protectively under his arm, I realized it was Seth. I peeked up at him and noticed how he stared at Michael with a horrified expression on his face as he assessed the situation.

"The CDC is outside. Do you want me to get them?" Seth asked.

Michael coughed again. "Not unless they know where to find the cure."

Seth loosened his grip on me, ready to go run if we needed him to. "I'll search the hotel and see if Henley stashed it somewhere."

I shook my head, defeated. "No. I heard Henley's thoughts. He made himself immune to the virus, just in case. The cure isn't here, and there's no telling where he stored it."

"There has to be something we can do," Seth insisted.

Michael heaved and doubled over, struggling to breathe. I flattened my palm against the glass, desperately wanting to help him.

When Michael finished, he forced himself to stand up straight again. "I think this room can detect that the virus is present. There's a red light above the door that lit up after Hemming activated it. But don't let them remove me for a few hours after I die, just to be safe."

Hearing the words come out of his mouth crushed me. I tried to stifle my tears, but they resurfaced anyway.

Michael lifted his hand back to the glass, directly on the other side of mine. "Hey. It's going to be okay." His voice was gentle, wanting to comfort me.

Nothing is ever going to be okay again.

I shook my head as my mind raced to find a way to save him.

"You're going to walk out of here and finally be able to live the life you deserve to have." As he said the words, his breathing became more labored. "I love you, Natalie. From the moment you began to appear in my dreams, I've loved you."

I wanted to tell him I loved him, too, that I couldn't fathom going on with my life without him, but my throat was so tight that I couldn't speak.

Michael shifted his wet, bloodshot eyes to Seth. "Take care of her."

"Of course I will."

"You're a good friend, the best one I could've asked for," Michael said. "Can I ask you for one more favor?"

"Anything."

Michael gasped for a breath and then winced, clearly in pain. "Can you take her out of here before it happens? I don't think it's going to be much longer."

Seth nodded, and I felt him gently attempt to pull me from the door.

I defiantly shook away from him as Michael's eyes settled back on me. He was so calm, so resolved to the fact that he was about to die, but I hadn't accepted it yet.

I won't accept it.

Seth tried again to get me to go with him, and I pulled away, more aggressively this time. As long as Michael was still breathing, I was going to spend every moment I could with him.

Michael's eyes pleaded with me to cooperate, to *go*.

Seth looped his arm around my waist, forcing me to part with the door.

"No!" I shouted, fighting him. My adrenaline spiked, but not enough for me to break free. I still didn't have my powers fully back.

I screamed as I uselessly pushed against Seth's arms, which were still firmly around my waist. He propped open the door and carried me through. Once we passed the other side and it closed behind us, I stopped fighting. I collapsed into him, sobbing uncontrollably into his chest.

The reality that it had all been for nothing consumed me. Sure, we'd defeated Henley, but I'd killed my sister to do it, and now, the love of my life was going to die. Freedom from Henley meant absolutely nothing to me if I didn't have Michael to share it with.

After everything we'd been through, it was going to end *like this*.

Seth held me tight, but nothing could fill the hollow aching in my chest.

"Come on," he whispered, tucking me under his arm and guiding me back down the stairs.

I couldn't bring myself to look at Becca when we got to the bottom. He swallowed hard at the sight of her. I turned my face into his chest as he led me out of the ballroom.

The walk to the lobby was a blur. I clung to Seth as I closed my eyes. I felt disconnected from my body, as if I were floating aimlessly in a horrible nightmare, just waiting to wake up.

Please let me wake up.

Fresh air hit my lungs as Seth opened the door and brought me outside. I coaxed my eyes open, and through the haziness, I saw Jen. Her face fell when she saw us. She looked at Seth in disbelief as she realized something had happened to Michael.

Raina sat on the back of the ambulance with J.T. He'd wrapped gauze around her bicep to stop her arm from bleeding. They hopped up when they saw me and Seth, and I watched as Raina searched the doors, expecting Michael to come out behind us.

She looked at me, and I saw her flip through a series of emotions, starting with confusion, then anger, and ending in denial. Seth guided me toward her, and she retreated, as if she could delay the inevitable if she didn't actually talk to us.

When we reached her, I could tell that she was barely holding it together. She cringed, waiting for me to confirm what she already suspected to be true.

I cleared my throat, which was dry and hoarse. I wasn't even sure if I could get actual words out. But for her, I tried. "He wanted you to know that he loves you and that he's sorry."

She stared at me for a moment, processing what I'd told her before her legs gave out and she fell apart. J.T. caught her and lowered to the ground, pulling her into his lap, as she cried out in devastating pain.

My tears had stopped, but I felt the hole in my heart that Michael had once filled. I knew there would be no mending it. It had always belonged to him, and even though he was gone, he'd forever possess it.

I let Seth lead me over to the sidewalk to sit down next to him. Jen sat on the other side of me, rubbing circles on my back with her palm.

We sat in silence as more police showed up. Ray intervened to fill them in on the situation. Then, he directed them to the event attendees who'd fled, so they could give their statements first. We'd have to talk to the police eventually, but I appreciated how Ray was trying to buy us a little time before we had to. Raina and I needed to pull ourselves together first. I'd be useless right now.

The police secured the perimeter around the hotel, and as they did, one of them discovered Viktor's body on the side of the building. Several officers disappeared around the corner, likely to document the scene before removing him.

Although we couldn't hear what they were saying, we saw several CDC workers and police officers speaking with Tonya. I assumed they were trying to gather as many details as they could about the virus, the cure, and Henley's involvement.

When they finished, two CDC workers put on hazmat suits before loading the round device into a box that looked like a deep freezer in the back of the van. They took off while the other workers remained behind. They suited up as well, and I realized they were likely gearing up to go in and retrieve Michael's body.

My mind flashed back to Henley's dream, and all I could picture was Michael, purple and cold, while his eyes stared blankly into nowhere.

"I can't be here when they bring him out," I whispered.

Seth leaned in close to me. "We can go, if you want. The police want to interview us, but maybe they can just follow us back to the house."

"Yeah …" The house sounded better than staying, but the pain wouldn't magically go away once we got there.

It will never go away.

Seth helped me to my feet, and Jen took my arm in hers.

"Raina should come with us," I said.

Even though I was stable enough to walk on my own, I let Seth and Jen lead me. It was comforting, having them close by.

Raina was still on the ground, curled up in J.T.'s arms. They looked up at us as we approached. Her eyes were puffy and dazed, but she wasn't crying anymore.

"We're going to leave before they bring him out." The words hurt, coming out of my mouth.

J.T. smoothed back Raina's hair. "I need to stay for a little longer, but you should go with them."

She shifted her head to look at him, and he gave her a reassuring peck on the lips.

I removed my arm from Jen's and took a step closer toward them.

Her cheek.

I squatted down to be eye-level with her. She turned and eyed me, wondering why I was studying her so intently.

With shaking hands and a pounding heart, I reached out to the bandage on her arm. Careful not to touch her skin, I removed the tape from the gauze and started unwinding.

Raina relaxed a little, assuming that I was just going to heal her. I didn't stop to correct her though. I couldn't speak as I focused on unwrapping the never-ending stream of fabric.

Everyone was silent around me. Or I had tuned them out. I wasn't sure which.

Finally, as I saw the first trace of skin underneath it, I held my breath, realizing I was at the end.

The air in my lungs escaped in broken bits as I trembled. I placed my hand on the ground to keep myself from falling over.

Raina and J.T. watched me with concern.

"What is it?" Raina asked, twisting her head, trying to get a better look at her arm to understand what I was seeing.

But it wasn't what I saw that had me so stunned. It was what I *didn't see.*

Her wound healed.

I could only stare at her in awe as I pushed myself back up to standing.

How can it be? I never touched her. I'm certain of it.

Raina didn't have the ability to heal others or herself. I knew that for a fact. If she had, she would've healed Lorena when she found her unconscious. Or she would've healed Alexander or Michael after the shooting. She couldn't heal herself because her gunshot wound had still been open when she fainted. I watched it mend with my own two eyes but only after I placed my hand on the skin next to it. After healing her, her vitals were still unsteady. Without Alexander there to provide guidance, I turned to J.T. for his medical advice. That was when he'd suggested we do the blood transfusions.

"What do you want from me?" I recalled asking Henley in his dream.

He'd looked at me with a snarl on his lips and replied, *"Your blood, of course."* That was right before he'd dreamed of slashing my throat open.

I took a few clumsy steps backward.

Raina looked at J.T., worried, and then turned back to me. "Natalie? Are you okay?"

Her question didn't register as I played the dream scene with Henley in my head over and over.

My blood.

It was the only explanation that I could think of for Raina being able to heal herself now.

My blood, of course.

It was how Henley had come up with a cure to his virus. Tonya had said so herself. He'd run blood tests on me after I healed myself from the unnatural illness he'd created.

Henley had believed he was immune to the virus, which was why he hadn't been worried about setting it off inside the hotel. Assuming Henley was right about his own immunity, then perhaps that meant I was immune as well.

Not only can I heal myself, but I also have the antibodies to fight the virus in my blood.

Raina hadn't been the only one to receive a blood transfusion from me the day of the ambush. Michael had received one as well.

I spun around to face the hotel.

If Raina healed herself, then—

I didn't even finish the thought. Instead, I sprinted for the hotel doors. A cop noticed and tried to stop me, but Ray reached out and pulled him back, letting me pass.

I flew through the lobby and down the hall, running as fast as my legs would carry me. When I reached the doors to the ballroom, my feet skidded against the floor as I turned. It didn't slow me down though. I dashed through the double doors, into the ballroom, and to the stairs.

My lungs burned as I raced up the staircase. And when I reached the top, everything appeared the same as before. Lovisa was still on the floor, and the door to the secret space was closed. I tried to catch my breath as I opened it and walked through.

There would be no one on the other side to hurt me—I was certain of that. But what lay ahead had significantly greater power to destroy me.

If I'm wrong about this, I will never recover.

I stopped and waited, but all I heard was deafening silence. Feeling the early sting of disappointment, I had to force myself to continue walking toward the panic room. The last thing I wanted to do was see Michael—*my Michael*—dead on the floor inside. But now that I had this glimmer of hope that he'd somehow pull through, I knew I needed to see him for myself.

As the door to the panic room came into view, I saw it was still closed, and my heart immediately sank. I wasn't sure how long ago Michael had been infected, but I was pretty sure it'd been close to three hours. According to Tonya, people didn't survive past two. The red light was off, making me believe that the virus had died after taking Michael out first.

I faced the door to the panic room, trying to get up the courage to look through the window. Unable to do it, I turned around, not wanting to even risk an accidental glance. As the disappointment washed over me, I felt the hollowness grow even deeper.

Lowering my head in defeat, I decided to leave.

It had been foolish of me to think I could somehow change his fate. Perhaps there was another explanation for why Raina's wound had healed. I was so distraught that I wasn't thinking clearly, and there was likely a perfectly rational explanation for it all.

Then, I heard metal gliding across metal, and I paused. There was a click, followed by the sound of a hinge creaking.

I was afraid to look, worried that I'd mentally snapped and no one would be there. As traumatic as the day had been, it was possible that I was hearing the door open because I wanted it so badly.

I'd give anything for that door to open.

"Natalie?" It was his voice, but I didn't trust that it was real. It could very well just be a figment of my imagination.

As terrified as I was to turn around and see no one there, I forced myself to do it anyway. I had to know.

I found him standing just outside the panic room, facing me. He looked fine, just as healthy as when we'd first arrived at the hotel.

He took a step closer and then paused, confused himself. "Am I dead? I collapsed after you left, and now, I feel *fine*." His eyes traced my body until they landed on my eyes. "I can't be dead though if you're here, right?"

Either I had officially lost my mind or my instinct had been correct and he'd been able to heal himself from the virus. Although I hadn't ruled out the possibility of a complete mental breakdown, I allowed myself to explore the truth as I rushed to close the distance between us.

I threw myself into his arms, hitting him with such force that he had to take a step back to keep us from toppling over. I didn't care though. I just clung to his neck as he held me tightly. He lifted me off the ground, and I closed my eyes, breathing in his scent as I nuzzled my nose into the crook of his neck.

His body was warm, alive, and strong. The realization took my breath away.

He set me down and pulled back to look at me. "I don't understand how this is even possible." His blue eyes searched mine.

I smiled as I laced my fingers behind his neck, refusing to let go for even a second. "The beauty of it is, we have plenty of time for me to fill you in."

He reached up and gently pushed a wild strand of hair out of my face. "We have all the time in the world."

EPILOGUE

NATALIE

I rolled over and pulled the covers up to my chin. I was happy and content and not ready to move just yet.

Michael reached out and pulled me to him, and I felt my bare back press into his warm chest.

"We need to get up," he whispered in my ear.

I didn't open my eyes. "Mmhmm ..."

"Come on, Mrs. Nolan. They'll be here soon."

The sound of my name brought a smile to my lips. It had been six months since we'd tied the knot, and I still felt giddy anytime I heard it. Out of all the last names Michael had had throughout his life, I was glad that he'd settled on Nolan when it came time for him to choose a real legal name. Nolan was his last name when we'd first met.

I opened my eyes and drank in the sunlight pouring into our bedroom. It was going to be another beautiful day in St. Augustine. Maybe after brunch, we could pile into a couple of cars and drive over to the beach for a stroll. Willow loved to watch the waves.

Michael propped himself up on his elbow, checking to see if I was awake.

"All right, Mr. Nolan, I'm getting up." I laughed as I rolled onto my back.

He smiled at me as he pecked me on the lips. Then, he pulled the covers down and planted a kiss on my belly before hopping out of bed. "I'll go get the eggs started." He pulled on his boxers, a pair of jeans, and a T-shirt before heading into the kitchen.

The brunch might have been my idea, but he wasn't fooling anyone. He was just as excited as I was to share our news.

He was right though; everyone would arrive in less than thirty minutes, and I didn't want to keep them waiting. Jen was five months pregnant, but Seth had claimed he was the one eating for two. Without a doubt, we needed to have some food ready.

I got up, got dressed, and brushed my teeth. By the time I made it into the kitchen, Michael had the eggs ready, and I could smell the bacon in the oven.

"That smells so good," I said. "I think I'm craving bacon dipped in both syrup *and* chocolate sauce."

He turned to beam at me. "What can I say? Our kid's got good taste."

The doorbell rang, and I went to answer it while Michael put a pot of coffee on. There would be hell to pay if we didn't have that ready to go when Raina arrived.

It was nice to answer the door again without fear of who might be on the other side. Although, since I'd gotten pregnant, my intuition had been in high gear, and I already predicted it would be Luke and Willow before I opened the door.

Sure enough, Luke stood on our stoop. He expertly held Willow in one arm, the three baby dolls she refused to leave the house without in the other, and had a diaper bag slung over his shoulder. He looked frazzled and exhausted as I held the door open for them to come inside. It'd been a rough year for him, adjusting to being a dad, but I had to admit, he was doing a great job. Michael and I always offered to babysit for him if he needed a break, but he rarely ever took us up on it. He'd said he was too afraid of missing something important and wanted to spend as much time with Willow as possible.

Willow reached her tiny arms out to me, and Luke smiled gratefully as I took her from him.

"Well, hello there," I greeted her.

Her short red pigtails sat lopsided on the top of her head in pink ribbons.

"I attempted to put together an outfit for her since Jen would be here," Luke said.

Willow had on a pink shirt covered in white daisies with a pair of denim overalls.

"She looks cute as a button." I lightly tapped the tip of her nose, making her giggle.

"I have orange juice and about two dozen doughnuts in the car," he said, dropping the diaper bag on the floor and heading back out.

As he approached the door, he practically ran into Raina and J.T.

"Hey, sis," he said to her and then bumped fists with J.T.

Raina looked as if she'd just rolled out of bed. She attempted a smile though, which I appreciated.

"Coffee should be ready shortly," I told her.

She perked up and then promptly headed for the kitchen.

J.T. shook his head and playfully rolled his eyes. "It's a miracle we made it on time. You know how she is in the morning."

"I heard that," Raina yelled from the kitchen.

"Good morning!" Jen called cheerfully as she and Seth walked into the house. "We brought a casserole, but there is a portion missing." She gave Seth a pointed look.

Seth threw his hands up. "Hey, I just needed to test it out to make sure it was edible before we served it."

Jen placed the casserole on the dining room table as Luke returned with the doughnuts and orange juice.

Looking around, I felt grateful that everyone could make it. Even though we all lived within a one-hour drive from each other, it was rare that we were all in the same place at the same time. Everyone had settled into their new lives, and those came with additional responsibilities.

J.T. had taken a job as a paramedic in St. Augustine. When Raina had told him she wanted to live near us, he hadn't hesitated to follow her. It took her some time to figure out what she wanted to do with her life, but after some lengthy conversations with Ray, she'd decided she wanted to join the police academy. She only had two weeks left to go before graduation.

Luke had his hands full with Willow but had gotten a security job, working for Jen's dad at Casa de la Belleza during the day while she went to day care.

When Willow had been less than two months old, we'd noticed that she started developing abilities, similar to both her mother and her father. At first, Luke had debated about sending her to day care but then decided it would be best to let her be around other kids. He wanted her to be comfortable with who she was even if she was different. I fully supported his decision, knowing that was what her mother would've wanted for her as well.

Luke and Michael were getting along better now. Their mutual love for Willow and the fact that Luke had stopped trying to pursue me had helped. After we'd reunited with Luke and Willow, Luke had made peace with the fact that I loved Michael, and he understood that my feelings for Michael would never change.

I wouldn't say Michael and Luke considered themselves to be brothers or even close friends, but as Raina and I'd found out, sometimes, relationships took a while to evolve.

Jen was back at the Jacksonville news station full-time. Within three months of being back, they'd offered her an anchor spot in the morning weekday segment, and she was quickly becoming a viewer favorite. I loved turning on the news in the morning and seeing her bubbly personality before I got my day started.

After we'd returned to Florida, Seth's dad had sold his share in Clark and Weber back to my father. Of course, he never offered an explanation as to why he wanted to leave their business, but I assumed it was a combination of guilt and also a way to bail out of the debt he'd created for himself. Shortly after, my father reached out to Seth, asking him if he was interested in coming back to learn the business. Seth had agreed to try it out and now ran Clark and Weber's Jacksonville branch and was potentially going to gain another by the end of the year.

As for Michael and me, we'd reopened The Treasure Chest in downtown St. Augustine in memory of Lorena and Alexander. Business was booming, but more than anything, we enjoyed being able to spend our days together. Over the course of the last two months, we'd hired some really outstanding employees, and we got to enjoy an occasional day off together too.

As everyone found a seat at the table, I passed Willow back to Luke and slipped out of the room. I went into the bedroom, opened the top drawer of my dresser, and pulled out a small stack of envelopes. Inside were the first sonogram pictures of our son. We planned to hand them out to everyone as a surprise before brunch.

It was too early for the doctor to confirm our baby was a boy, but I already knew he was. If I closed my eyes and concentrated hard enough, I could see what he was going to look like after he was born. He'd have my auburn hair and Michael's perfect blue eyes. We planned to name him Alexander.

THE AWAKENING

As I stepped back from the dresser, I noticed the lotus necklace around my neck in the mirror. I wore it every day as a reminder of the good times Becca and I'd shared. Dealing with her death hadn't been easy, but I'd made peace with it. And now, I consistently kept my promise by sharing her memory with Willow.

Regardless of everything Becca had done wrong, I had to acknowledge the good. Because of her, we had Willow, who brought so much joy into our lives. Without Becca, I wouldn't have met Michael. If she hadn't steered him into my life, I would've perished in that car accident.

If it wasn't for Becca, I never would've experienced true love or learned to accept who I really was. I'd forever be grateful to her for that.

As I clutched the envelopes in my hand and made my way back into the dining room, my heart swelled. I had so much more than I'd ever dreamed possible.

I gazed across the table, full of the people I loved the most.

We'd survived everything, against the direst of circumstances. Even when it'd felt like all hope was lost at times, we'd emerged from the ashes, seeking freedom and fighting for our future.

And together, we had persevered.

THE END

ACKNOWLEDGMENTS

First, I want to thank all of the readers who've passionately embraced this series. When I began writing *The Unveiling*, I wasn't sure I'd publish it. Ultimately, I decided to by convincing myself that if I found one reader who enjoyed it, it would be worth it. And then I found all of you, who have come to love these characters as much as I do. You gave me the motivation to continue writing this trilogy and pursue my dream. I am so grateful for each and every one of you.

Dran, thank you for supporting this writing obsession of mine and for always being ready with a fresh pot of coffee when I need it. You are my rock. I love you.

Brian, I would never have gotten the opportunity to finish this series without you. You are a real-life hero, and I can never repay you for all that you've done for us.

Jovana, I truly couldn't ask for a better editor. I've learned so much from you over the past few years to improve my craft, and I am elated that I get to work with you.

Mom, Melissa, and Pam—Thank you for not only being the first to read *The Awakening* and giving me your honest, valuable feedback, but also for your endless encouragement throughout this journey.

Brande, I couldn't have done this without you. Thanks for always lending an ear and offering solid advice. Your friendship means everything.

Michelle, I always look forward to our road trips and appreciate how you're always game to spend countless hours browsing through bookstores with me.

Tim, thank you for designing the beautiful covers for this series. It has been an absolute pleasure to work with you.

My friends and family—I could write pages and pages about all of the ways you've enriched my life and contributed to the success of this series. I love and appreciate you.

About the Author

Laurie Harrison is a romantic suspense novelist who graduated from the University of Central Florida. When she's not writing, Laurie enjoys spending time with her husband, traveling, and getting lost in a good book.

Connect Online

laurieharrisonauthor.com

facebook.com/laurieharrisonauthor

instagram.com/laurieharrisonauthor

goodreads.com/laurieharrison

BOOKS BY
LAURIE HARRISON

The Unveiling

The Deceiving

The Awakening

Visit laurieharrisonauthor.com and subscribe to Laurie's newsletter to receive exclusive content and updates on new releases.

9 781733 285957

I stepped back to create distance between us. The gesture was for his safety as much as it was my own. He'd helped Henley brainwash Becca, and now, thanks to him, she didn't know who she was anymore.

Not only was I angry with Luke, but I was also hurt because he'd deliberately hidden the truth from me. He stood by and watched as we tried to get through to Becca and to the bottom of why she hated me so much. He'd played dumb, all the while knowing he'd reshaped her memories to make her believe I was the enemy.

Sure, Luke hadn't met me when he reconditioned her, but that didn't excuse his actions or the fact that he'd lied about it. He hadn't admitted to it until I discovered the truth while visiting Becca's dreams.

"What are you doing here? You know I don't want to see you." My words came out sharp, and I didn't care how deeply they cut him.

"I need your help."

My intuition believed he was sincere, but Luke was a master manipulator, and I didn't know if I could truly sense if he was being dishonest. He'd fooled me more than once in the past.

"Of course." My tone was sarcastic as I threw my hands up in frustration. "You come out of the woodwork the second you need help to fulfill whatever agenda you have." I resented Luke's games and contemplated just knocking him out in order to end the conversation.

He frowned. "This isn't for me. Well, not exactly anyway."

My dress drooped to one side, but luckily, the other strap was intact to hold it up. I examined the dangling piece, which was frayed at the end from being ripped at the seam. There'd be no fixing it without a needle and thread.

"Fine. What do you want?"

"First, promise that you won't hurt me."

Oh, this is going to be good.

"I'm not promising anything. Start talking."

A hint of a smile crept across his lips as he assessed me.

I raised my eyebrows, mentally giving him two seconds to speak before I left him standing there.

His expression grew serious again, and I sensed a heavy wave of worry roll over him. My anger quickly evaporated into a cloud of angst that mirrored his.

"What?" I asked again, close to losing my patience.

He sighed. "There's no easy way to say this."

"Just say it."